Dying over Spilled Milk

The Heathervale Mysteries, Volume 2

Matilda Swift

Published by Matilda Swift, 2019.

This is a work of fiction. Similarities to real people, places, or events are entirely coincidental.

DYING OVER SPILLED MILK

First edition. November 13, 2019.

Copyright © 2019 Matilda Swift.

Written by Matilda Swift.

By Matilda Swift

The Heathervale Mysteries
Rotten to the Marrow
The Slay of the Land
Dying over Spilled Milk
Fresh out of Cluck
Wreathed in Mystery

Dedication and Notes

For Rachel Evans, the best shower buddy a person could ever have.

***

I think there were not in all the city four merrier people than the hungry little girls who gave away their breakfasts and contented themselves with bread and milk that Christmas morning.
Louisa May Alcott

***

Note: This book is written in British English. In Heathervale, people eat biscuits not cookies, wear trousers not pants, say got instead of gotten, and use all manner of charming spellings which should help you feel more at home in this book's cosy English setting.

1

Arrina Fenn searched the large, busy hall for the student she'd left in charge of signs that morning. The girl's name was Patience, which had sounded old-fashioned and quaint when Arrina first heard it but had quickly turned into a plea. *Patience,* Arrina muttered under her breath whenever she dealt with the well-meaning student.

Once again, Arrina strained for a little more of that virtue as she looked at the girl's efforts. Patience had worked quickly and efficiently, hanging thirty signs around the large main hall in a matter of minutes and marking out key areas of Heathervale College's first annual Careers Fair. However, each and every sign was in the wrong place. Surely, random chance should have landed one or two in the right spot. But Patience had defied the odds. *Patience,* Arrina muttered once again as she surveyed the girl's handiwork.

The sign for refreshments was above the first aid station. The emergency exit was labelled as an information point, and the arrow to the toilets pointed at a blank brick wall. The wild halo of dark-blonde curls that made Patience easy to find in a crowd was nowhere to be seen, so Arrina looked for a ladder to fix the problem herself.

Instead, she spotted Julie Wen, who was staring in apparent confusion at a sign saying University Prospectuses. Julie ran the popular *Sound of Music*-themed café in the centre of Heathervale Village, and, more importantly, she was Arrina's best friend. Five minutes with her would brighten up Arrina's morning and give her the energy she needed to get through the rest of the long and busy day. Arrina waved across the hall at one of the dozen teachers assisting her that morning. She pointed at the signs, and the teacher gave her a thumbs up in return. Arrina jogged over to Julie's table on the far side of the hall and wrapped her generous curves in a tight hug.

'Am I missing something?' Julie asked, nodding at the sign above her stall. 'Are you pushing me out in favour of brochures full of teens with impossibly perfect skin?'

'Not at all,' Arrina said. 'That's just a mix-up. And in fact, we don't *have* any prospectuses at the moment, so I couldn't replace you even if I wanted to.'

The loss of ten boxes of prospectuses was just one of the many problems Arrina was dealing with that day. As the head of Heathervale College, she was responsible for any difficulty there. The worst issue she'd faced so far that day was the heating system, which had chosen to break down overnight, just as the forecast promised another cold snap would descend over the Peak District.

'Thanks again for lending Phil to me this morning,' Arrina said. Julie's dairy farmer husband, Phil, could fix pretty much anything. When Arrina had called Julie in a panic over hissing pipes and icy air at six am, Phil had been dispatched to take care of it.

'That's what I keep him around for. I'm only sorry he couldn't sort out the heating in here. I'm freezing, and *I've* come prepared with ample insulation!' Julie hugged a fluffy coat around her plump, cake-fuelled frame. 'How are you surviving?'

DYING OVER SPILLED MILK

Arrina pulled at the lapels of her suit jacket, trying to cover the expanse of bare neck left by her pixie cut. 'I did have a coat earlier...' She looked around the busy hall, which had over forty different tables set up in it. All bore displays, piles of leaflets, sign-up forms, and no sign of her coat anywhere.

'You must have had one when Phil came by,' Julie said, 'or he'd have forced you into that ugly waxed jacket he wears. He's always worrying you don't take good care of yourself.' Julie eyed Arrina suspiciously and looked ready to press her own pillar box-red coat on Arrina. The large, furry garment suited Julie, but it would swamp Arrina's smaller frame, and it didn't entirely match her outfit or professional image. Arrina tried to look warm and absolutely *not* in need of another layer.

'Well, he wasn't worrying today,' she said. 'At least, not about me. I made a comment about his enormous toolbelt, and I think he took it as a come-on.'

Julie's surprised expression quickly broke into a grin. 'He thought you were flirting?' Her smile grew into a laugh that echoed off the high walls of the hall and bounced back at her and Arrina like a peal of bells. 'Oh my goodness! Oh my days!'

'It's not funny,' Arrina said, as a blush warmed her cheeks. She glanced around at the many helpers who'd come to the hall to get the Careers Fair ready. Nobody was close enough to overhear them. 'He really *does* have a big toolbelt.'

Julie grabbed the edge of the table to stay upright. 'That's my husband you're talking about.' She struggled to get her laughter under control. 'Don't make me fight you for him.'

Several heads turned their way, and Arrina's first impulse was to drop the conversation and resume it later. She'd spent most of her teaching career in the nearby city of Manchester, where a head teacher was expected to be stiff and authoritative. But it wasn't like that in Heathervale, so she continued, 'I was mortified. I tried to explain, though I think I actually made it worse. I really did just mean his toolbelt. It's very big.'

'I know,' Julie said, still giggling. 'And it's ridiculous, because he fixes pretty much everything with that never-ending length of twine he keeps in there.'

Arrina couldn't smile about the toolbelt mix-up quite yet, but Julie's laughter lightened her worries about it. 'He used the twine this morning.'

'See! And yet he still carries fourteen different wrenches and a hundred types of screw whenever he sets out to mend something.'

'It did help, though. He couldn't really fix the heating, but he got it to stop its horrible clanking by tying some of the pipes together. He said that would hold it till the maintenance crew comes on Monday.'

'That's good. And maybe one of the maintenance crew will catch your eye so you keep your mitts off my husband.' Julie started giggling again.

Arrina ignored Julie's comment. A painful break-up at the end of last year had left scars that were yet to fully heal. The experience had also inspired the pixie cut that currently left her neck freezing in the hall's icy air. She wondered if she'd ever get used to the short style of her russet-coloured hair.

Shuffling from foot to foot to keep warm, Arrina looked around the busy hall. People were sorting out the signs, and milling helpers were neatening displays, pushing empty boxes beneath tables, and giving the floor a final sweep. For once that morning, nobody waved her over to enlist her help with a problem.

Arrina looked down at the table in front of her. She was not entirely surprised to find it covered in boxes of cakes rather than the information on catering careers she'd suggested Julie bring. Julie's café, Do-Re-Mi, served a delicious variety of baked goods, including crumpets, teacakes, and the best scones Arrina had ever tasted. But it seemed that Julie had only brought her stickiest, most sugar-laden offerings that day.

'There's a new sign coming your way, which—when it gets here—will say Have You Considered a Career in Catering? Perhaps we should change it to Have You Considered a Career as a Professional Diabetic?'

'I don't know what you mean.'

'Really?' Arrina asked as she peered into boxes of fondant fancies, iced cinnamon rolls, and millionaire's shortbread. Beneath these sat a host of other heart-stopping treats.

'No, well, yes,' Julie started. 'I can *maybe* see what you're getting at, but the thing is, it's going to be a very long day, and lots of the teenagers will be here with their parents, and they'll be talking about serious issues like work and university, and that can cause a bit of tension, can't it? And what eases tension better than a sugary treat?'

Arrina raised an eyebrow in response to her best friend's mile-a-minute explanation.

'Plus,' Julie said, tapping a Tupperware container of miniature pecan pies, 'everybody knows you catch more flies with honey.'

'And are you *trying* to catch flies?' Arrina struggled to keep a serious face.

'No. That would be crazy. It's a whatsit... a metaphor.' Julie ran a hand through her jet-black bob, raking it into its usual disarray. 'Or is it an idiom?'

'It's a proverb,' Arrina said, smiling.

'Right,' Julie said. 'That's why *you're* the teacher and I'm just the mixer of flour and eggs.'

Arrina picked up a mini Bakewell tart. She'd missed breakfast that morning, so she polished the small treat off in a single bite. 'No, this is why you're the best baker in the entire Hope Valley.'

'Just the Hope Valley?'

'Maybe the Peak District. I'd have to sample a few more items to be certain.'

'That's more like it.' Julie pressed a sticky piece of flapjack on Arrina and unpacked the rest of the box onto a waiting cake stand.

'Perhaps I should consider a career change myself. Cakes are a lot nicer than broken heating systems and lost prospectuses.'

Julie looked at her friend from the corner of one black eye. 'I've tasted your baking.' She winked. 'Don't give up the day job.'

Arrina laughed and shoved her friend playfully.

'Look at that,' Julie added. 'The fair's not even started and I'm already dispensing expert careers advice.'

'You're a natural,' Arrina said, rolling her eyes, which earned her a shove in return.

The two women chatted for a few minutes more while the Careers Fair slowly but surely came together around them. The fair was the result of two solid months of hard work, including more late nights than Arrina cared to think of. But it had all been worth it.

A wide variety of stalls was spread around the room, each one brightly adorned with posters, leaflets, and a range of other information for her students to take away. The sixth form college was—contrary to the belief of the Americans who emailed to apply—not a university. The college was for students aged 16 to 18, and it prepared them to head into the world of work or the ivory towers of higher education. A Careers Fair was a great step in those directions, and Arrina was glad to have finally set one up. The college was only five years old, but it was now well on the way to becoming a top-level establishment.

Given the college's location in the heart of the Peak District, several agricultural options were represented that day, including William Brown's display about pig-farming. The man had been dozing since his arrival earlier that morning, but his sister, Zena, had just joined him. The lavender-haired woman never ceased to surprise Arrina, and indeed, right then, the tech-savvy septuagenarian was setting up a VR headset in front of a screen that displayed different types of pig-unit.

Arrina had also invited representatives from various local businesses. Among them were the staff from Wolferton Manor, an old country house that had been converted into a fancy hotel; Maggie Lee, whose new natural pesticide company was based at the farm behind the college; and Sylvie Morgan, who sold detailed wood carvings in Present and Correct, the gift and stationery shop on the village's simply named High Street.

Arrina had even, reluctantly, allotted a table to the local police force. Her history with the man standing beside the table made her regret this decision already. The man was Tony Mellor, and *he* was the reason behind the pixie cut that left her neck exposed and freezing that morning. He had suddenly ended their relationship a year earlier, and a drastic chop had felt like the only way to get through the break-up. Tony's familiar broad chest and dark eyes tried to draw Arrina to his corner of the room, but she knew nothing good would come of that.

She looked away and focused on Julie's flapjack, which was hard and chewy in the hall's frigid air. Arrina worked on the last bite of the flapjack, enjoying the syrupy oats better than any breakfast she might have rustled up in her underused kitchen at home. Her sleek, silver cat, Tinsel, ate more meals in there than Arrina did by a long way.

As she licked her fingers clean, her phone buzzed in her pocket. The mobile signal at the college was virtually non-existent, and it only ever seemed to reach Arrina to bring her bad news. She ignored the phone until it buzzed several more times. Finally, Arrina looked at her screen and found her fears confirmed.

'It's a message from Gillian DeViers,' Arrina said. 'A long one.'

Julie grimaced and fumbled through her stacks of Tupperware. She held out a box to Arrina.

'Are those what I think they are?'

Julie nodded, and Arrina popped one of her friend's famous ganache-and-dash tartlets into her mouth. The creamy dark chocolate was laced with a powerful kick of espresso, making the desserts just what Arrina needed right then.

Julie claimed the tartlets were a pain to make, so she almost never baked them, but Arrina suspected she liked to create a little excitement through their scarcity. She chewed the delicious treat slowly as she read.

'How bad is it?' Julie asked when Arrina looked up from her phone.

'At least another ganache-and-dash worth.' Arrina took a second chocolatey treat. 'It's the Lantern Parade fundraiser tomorrow, and apparently I promised to contribute something for the bake sale.'

Julie held the box of tartlets out towards Arrina. 'Problem solved. You can take these.' She nabbed a sample of the treats for herself before handing over the box. 'I've left a few at the café, but they'll be long gone by tomorrow. These will go like hotcakes at the fundraiser, and Gillian will be over the moon—or whatever her version of that is—mildly pleased, I suppose.' She bit into the tartlet and smiled. 'I'm really firing on all cylinders today. Next stop, world peace!'

'That seems like the logical move.' Arrina peered at the neat, dark circles inside the box. Julie was famous for her coffee and chocolate tartlets. Arrina wondered about shaking them around a bit. Otherwise, nobody would believe for a second that she'd made them herself. Her phone buzzed once more. She already knew who it would be. 'Gillian would also like to remind me that the deadline for donations was nine this morning.'

Arrina could have kicked herself for forgetting about her bake sale commitment. Not only did she *love* the Lantern Parade—the first official event of the Christmas season—but she also knew better than to get on Gillian's bad side.

'It's quarter past already,' Julie said. She rummaged through her boxes again and shook her head. 'It looks like I've left my time machine at home. Gillian will just have to wait. I'm seeing her later to finalise the announcement of the internship, though I'm not sure how much there is to finalise about me standing on stage and reading a bit of paper. But anyway, I'll drop the tartlets off for you then.'

'You're a lifesaver.' Arrina handed back the box with a grateful smile. 'That's four hundred and twenty-nine favours I owe you now.' Arrina made a mental note to get Julie some flowers to celebrate the official launch of her internship programme. That programme was the culmination of a lot of hard work, and it was every bit as important to Julie as the Careers Fair was to Arrina.

'Four hundred and twenty-three at most,' replied Julie with a wink. 'And I'm sure you'll pay me back soon.'

Arrina gave her friend a grateful hug. She wished she could stay beside her all morning, chatting and eating sugary treats. But the Careers Fair officially opened in only fifteen minutes, and Arrina could see yet another problem on the far side of the room.

The man who'd been sent to run the Environment Agency stall was not at his table. And now that Arrina thought about it, she realised she hadn't seen him since early that morning.

Arrina thanked Julie once again for her help and dashed off. She paused in her path to the Environment Agency booth to give instructions to a couple of stall holders, check the progress with the signs, and take on a few fresh problems. Then she headed over to see if the missing man had left any clue about where he'd disappeared to.

2

Arrina had reserved a large space at the Careers Fair for the Environment Agency, and she dashed over to it then. The Agency wasn't popular locally. The environmental-protection arm of the government had the power to hand out large fines and take people to court. According to talk in the Horse and Hound, they did so *far* more often than was necessary.

Indeed, just a couple of months earlier, they'd investigated Julie and her husband, Phil, over a simple milk spillage caused by a broken machine.

Arrina had been shocked to learn that spreading milk on your own land required a permit. And since their milk spillage had been accidental, Julie and Phil hadn't got one. Even if the person *had* a permit, milk needed to be diluted with water, could only be spread in specific amounts on certain types of fields, and couldn't be allowed to get into the sewage system or nearby waterways. Arrina had been astounded by how complex the matter was. The situation made the regulations around working with kids seem relatively relaxed for once.

Phil's dairy business was struggling enough in the face of low milk prices, and the investigation into the spillage on his land was the last thing he and Julie needed. Arrina had checked that Julie was OK with having the Environment Agency at the Careers Fair. Arrina wanted more locals to work at the agency—they'd protect the interests of farming communities in ways that outsiders didn't always seem to do.

Julie had agreed immediately. But still, Arrina had put her friend's stall a good distance away from the agency's.

As Arrina reached the empty stall now, she thought she might have wasted her efforts entirely. At half past eight that morning, Kingsley Peters, the representative from the Environment Agency, had shown up with all manner of brochures and forms. He'd put them on display and then promptly disappeared.

The rest of the hall was a hive of activity. Arrina had made it clear that all stallholders were to be at their tables from 9.15, ready for the doors to open at half past. If Kingsley wasn't at his stall to promote the Environment Agency, people would probably not give it a second glance.

Could Kingsley really have abandoned his commitment so easily? Arrina sighed in disappointment. Then she gazed around at the random arrangement of signs around the large hall. In the distance, Patience's wild curls flew behind her as she raced to help the teacher who was putting the posters in their right places. But Kingsley could easily have been misled by a sign earlier. Arrina imagined him searching for the bathroom in the warren of the arts wing, or somehow wandering outside, shaking the many locked entrances, and being unable to find his way back in.

Arrina was just about to go and look for him when the hall doors opened and in walked Kingsley Peters himself—smiling widely and carrying two take-out coffees in a cardboard tray.

She ran a hand through her short hair and forced her toes to unclench. Kingsley had simply set up and gone to get coffee from Julie's part-timers in the village. Perhaps Phil was right to worry about her, Arrina thought. She was clearly too stressed if something as simple as a coffee run could put her on edge. She looked forward to finally relaxing that evening and doing nothing more demanding than stroking her cat and drinking a huge pot of tea.

As Kingsley walked past Julie's table, Arrina expected her friend to ask about the service he'd received in Do-Re-Mi—Julie never quite trusted that the café could survive without her. But she kept her focus on her cake display and didn't interrupt Kingsley's path back to his booth.

He didn't turn his head towards Julie either, or even seem to notice her tempting array of treats. He kept his attention squarely focused on Arrina. He raised the pair of Do-Re-Mi coffee cups and smiled again.

Before she'd met Kingsley, Arrina had expected him to look like a stooped old farmer, with round, sun-pinked cheeks and hair that was combed only by the wind. She'd been surprised to see a tall, well-groomed man who was around her age. Kingsley's face had a narrow elegance that Arrina didn't usually find attractive. But his smile tucked crookedly up into one dimpled cheek in a way that made it impossible to resist smiling back at him.

He held Arrina's gaze as he walked across the large hall towards her. After a few moments, she turned away, neatened a pot of pens, and flicked through various leaflets. She deliberately did *not* let her eyes stray to the table in the far corner where her ex-boyfriend Tony Mellor stood.

Arrina focused on the display stuck to the wall nearby. The display was an enlarged copy of a newspaper article about a local environmental-protection case, and a picture beside it showed a field piled high with rubbish. When Kingsley put a warm coffee cup in her hand, she nodded her thanks and pointed at the image.

'Did you work on that case?' Her voice came out far louder than she'd intended.

'The Drabbles,' he said. 'Good eye. Yes, you can just about spot me in there collecting evidence.'

Arrina followed his finger and squinted at the blurry background of the image. She couldn't pick Kingsley out from the crowd of high-vis jacket-wearers there. The only distinctive people in the photo were the group at the front who all shared the same bright red hair.

'I'd like to have got more of the family,' Kingsley continued, 'but we only had concrete evidence on the father. He was the worst of them, though. I'd never have heard the end of it if he'd got off scot-free as well.'

'What did they do?' Arrina tried to recall the snippets she'd heard about the Drabbles since she'd moved to Heathervale. The family lived a couple of villages away, and though Arrina had never seen them in the flesh, she was familiar with them. Their name was part of the background texture of the area, just like the greying fleece fibres snagged on barbed wire fences and the sound of the River Derwent in the depths of the valley below.

'You're not from around here, then?' Kingsley asked.

Arrina shook her head.

'It's more a question of what *didn't* they do. Every local family's got a story about the Drabbles.' Then he looked Arrina up and down, as though to say he'd known at a glance that she wasn't from the area. Neither was he, and she could tell. He had a slight hint of the North in his vowels but not enough to make him local. Further clues lay in his stiff brown brogues and neatly pressed chinos. Those were the clothes that city people wore in the country, thinking they would fit in.

'They've committed all sorts of crimes over the years,' Kingsley continued. 'But the fires are what we got them for in the end. The old man was setting fire to construction waste in his fields, even old fridges and freezers. Then he spread the ashes on his land—cadmium, arsenic, lead... you name it. All the sorts of deadly toxins you don't want getting into the groundwater—he put them right on the soil and didn't care about the consequences. And the rest of his family knew what he was doing, no matter how much they claimed to be innocent.'

'On his own farm?' Arrina asked. 'Why would he damage it like that?'

'That's farmers for you.' Kingsley took a long swig of his coffee and then swallowed. 'Thick as the you-know-what they shovel.'

'I don't think—'

'You wouldn't believe the things they do. It's a wonder they can tie their own shoes in the morning.'

'I'm sure you don't mean *all* farmers,' Arrina said. 'In your line of work, you must run into some terrible cases, but—'

'Oh, you really wouldn't believe—'

'But I'm *certain* the Environment Agency doesn't tar all rural workers with the same brush.'

Kingsley paused and looked at Arrina. Clearly, he'd thought she would side with him against the locals. He shot her another dimpled grin. 'Not at all. And certainly not the ones studying here. I really admire the work your college does. It gives me a lot of hope for the future.'

'Right,' Arrina said, glancing down at her watch and taking a small step away. Her eyes longed to turn in Tony's direction, just to see if he was looking her way too. But she forced her gaze back from her watch to Kingsley. 'I'm sure you'll be very impressed when you meet them.'

The front doors were due to open any minute, and her students would come in to learn about the wealth of employment opportunities available to them. The Environment Agency was an important part of that. Arrina smiled tightly at Kingsley and looked at her watch again.

'It's time I—'

'I'm sorry,' Kingsley said, lowering his voice and stepping closer to Arrina. 'I think I've offended you. I didn't mean to speak so harshly. It's just that... what I see in my line of work... well, sometimes it can affect my outlook. The Drabble case has been particularly difficult.'

Arrina looked again at the posters and leaflets in Kingsley's booth. They depicted images of poisoned fish, starving animals and mountains of rubbish piled high in ruined fields.

'I can understand that.' She took another sip of her coffee.

'This here is the least of it.' Kingsley shook his head. 'The things some people do to their land and animals...'

'I'm lucky, I suppose. In my job, the worst I see is teenage moodiness, and even that's pretty rare in the hardworking kids who come here. For the most part, they're bright, engaged and optimistic.'

'Your job sounds wonderful, and I know it must require a lot of commitment as well. I really admire those in the teaching profession,' Kingsley said in a deep, warm voice.

'It's demanding work,' Arrina said, 'but very much worth it.'

'I can imagine.' Kingsley stepped even closer to Arrina, and she could smell his clean shirt and spiced vanilla aftershave. Arrina felt a warm awareness of being watched, and only half her mind wondered if Tony was the one looking her way.

She realised that it had been several months since she'd last stood alone with a man and talked in a tone that sparkled with promise.

He touched her arm lightly. 'I want to say how much I appreciate being invited here today. I'm sure being around these fantastic kids of yours is just what I need. I meant to thank you before, but my manners seem to have got a bit rusty.'

'You're welcome. It's a real pleasure to have you here. The Agency, I mean... well, you, as a representative of it.' Arrina fiddled with the coffee cup in her hands. 'I really think the students will appreciate it.'

Kingsley smiled at her again. 'I'm more than happy to be here. Let me know if you want me to come back for any other events. And if there are any follow-up questions, perhaps we should swap numbers, so you can get in touch.'

'I... well...' Arrina cleared her throat. 'That sounds like a good plan.'

Kingsley pulled out his phone and took Arrina's details. 'Nine twenty-seven on a Saturday morning and I've already got the number of an accomplished, beautiful woman. This must be my lucky day.'

Heat rose in Arrina's cold-numbed cheeks. She focused on typing with her icy fingers as he gave his number in return. She felt a tingle of excitement at the thought of calling him and wondered whether she could now bring herself to delete Tony's number from her contact list.

Then she glanced over at Kingsley's screen. Up flashed an image of him and a tall blonde woman with an easy, beaming smile, standing on a sunny beach and laughing. He quickly locked his phone and put it back in his pocket.

'A for Arrina,' he said. 'That puts you right up near the top of my contacts. Easy to find if I need you.'

The woman in the picture could be his sister or a friend, she told herself. She was still getting over a heartbreak and was determined not to let it ruin her faith in men.

Then Arrina flicked her gaze over to Kingsley's left hand. A pale band of skin ran around his ring finger. Very pale. Arrina's smile froze.

She stepped away from Kingsley and glanced around the hall, where students were already starting to flow into the fair. They blocked her view of Tony, and, she was glad, his view of her in return.

'Well,' Arrina said, taking another step away, 'I must be getting on. Thank you for the coffee.'

'You're very welcome. Perhaps next time, I can get you one in a real cup, and we can sit down and enjoy it properly.'

She smiled politely but said nothing. Then she looked around the hall again and saw several students pointing eagerly at the Environment Agency sign above the stall. When they spotted Arrina, they grinned widely. *This* was what she wanted—her students learning about careers with the Environment Agency. She waved them over and introduced them to Kingsley then slipped away as soon as they were engrossed in conversation with the man.

Arrina headed back in the direction of Julie's table. She needed a best-friend analysis of what had just happened. And another espresso-laced dark chocolate tartlet or maybe five. At this rate, there'd be none left to donate to the Lantern Parade fundraiser, and she could never persuade Julie to make any more, but she'd have to deal with that later.

Before she could get to Julie's table, though, a loud crash near the front of the hall dragged her away.

Arrina raced off towards the source of the noise and discovered a panicked young boy—too young, surely, to be one of her students—strapped into a VR unit. The boy was running, dragging cables behind him, and knocking into tables and piles of leaflets.

A glance at the display screen behind him showed what he was afraid of—a giant, long-tusked boar had him cornered in a pig pen and was preparing to charge.

Zena Brown had her arms around the boy's waist, trying to tackle him to the ground, but the shrunken old woman wasn't having much effect. Arrina dashed over to Zena's computer and pulled the plug. The image of the angry boar faded away in an instant. The frightened boy tore off his VR headset and dove into the arms of a student Arrina recognised—an older brother, she assumed—who'd been standing nearby on the verge of both panic and laughter. Arrina led the pair of them to comfy seats in the first aid station, where they caught their breath. Then she fetched them two cups of hot, sweet tea.

Arrina kept busy all morning troubleshooting an ever-expanding list of problems, including lost parents, a temperamental tea urn, a flare of tensions between two local families, and someone making themselves sick by gobbling down a whole box of cupcakes.

Every time Arrina dashed past the Environment Agency's booth, Kingsley Peters smiled widely, and she averted her gaze. When Kingsley didn't return after a lunch break, she was annoyed but not surprised. She knew she couldn't trust him.

At least he'd stocked his booth with a range of useful leaflets and had left a sign-up form for students who were interested in learning about the agency.

Julie had also disappeared at some point. She'd said earlier that she had to arrange her internship announcement with Gillian. The task shouldn't have taken any time at all, since Julie was reading from a pre-approved script. But Gillian was involved in the arrangements, so it didn't surprise Arrina that it wound up taking all day.

By the tail end of the afternoon, when the last of the students left, there was only a slightly squashed cinnamon roll and half a miniature meringue remaining on Julie's previously well-stocked stall. Arrina polished these off and nodded in satisfaction as she looked around the almost-empty hall.

Each teenager who'd attended the Careers Fair had been filled with the vibrant, sparkling enthusiasm that came from having a whole life ahead of them. For a few hours, Arrina had felt that same energy run through her own veins. She'd felt young again.

Now, as she watched people pack away their stalls, take down signs, and fold up tables, her body remembered that she was a little over twice the average student's age.

Her joints were stiff from a whole day of tensing against the cold, and her feet felt worn down to stumps.

Arrina was looking forward to a long soak in her tub. She imagined herself stretched out in the soothing water, up to her neck in bubbles, with a marshmallow-topped hot chocolate close by. Perhaps first, she'd watch *Holiday Inn* while curled up on the sofa with Tinsel.

Then she remembered the many broken hearts and unfaithful lovers in the movie, which made her think of the pale band on Kingsley Peters' finger. She switched her viewing plans to *The Muppet Christmas Carol* instead.

Images of singing mice and lettuces were disrupted by a nearby whisper of 'Kingsley Peters.' Had he come back? She looked around but saw no sign of him. Perhaps her tired mind was imagining things. But then she heard the name again, skittering across the icy air in the hall.

When she saw people staring at her—colleagues, lingering stallholders and student volunteers alike—she started to get an idea of what they might be saying. Arrina's five-minute conversation with a handsome man would be a topic of village gossip for weeks. Rumours could spring up very easily in Heathervale, especially during the dull winter months when people had precious little else of interest to pass the time with.

She ignored them and focused on packing up Julie's things instead. People would grow bored of the gossip eventually, especially when nothing came of it—and nothing would, Arrina was certain. She wouldn't see the slippery man again. She wouldn't even think of him. Arrina returned to planning out the evening ahead of her. Her rumbling stomach reminded her that she hadn't eaten anything substantial at all that day, just too many of Julie's sugary treats and nothing even resembling nutrition.

She would swing by Do-Re-Mi on her way home and return Julie's Tupperware boxes, over which the woman was very protective. She could pick up a sandwich and a scone while she was there—perhaps even persuade her friend to join the movie-watching, even though, in Julie's words, it was *far too early for Christmas*.

Arrina looked up from the table to see Julie dashing through the hall doors right then. Pleasantly surprised, Arrina smiled and headed towards her friend on tired legs.

Then Arrina registered the look of anguish on Julie's face and sprinted to meet her in the middle of the icy room.

Julie ran straight into Arrina's awaiting hug and clung to her.

'What's wrong?' Arrina asked. 'What's happened? Are you OK?'

'It's Phil,' Julie said, her voice high and shaking with tears. Arrina's heart leapt into her throat as she imagined an accident at the farm—some sharp machine taking Julie's loving husband away. She tried to push this worry from her mind. That couldn't be. Phil was a safe and steady man who never put himself in danger.

'Phil's been arrested,' Julie continued. 'They've locked him up, and I can't even see him till tomorrow.' A choked sob swallowed her next words, and Arrina had to strain to understand them. 'Phil's been arrested for the murder of Kingsley Peters.'

3

Arrina rushed Julie out of the back of the college, leaving behind the two dozen helpers in the hall. The orange lights in the car park pooled limply around a few remaining vehicles. Beyond those lights lay only the deep black of a rural night, stretching out into farmland, woods, and rolling hills.

Arrina's temperamental XJ6 took just two turns of the key to get going. The car's loud, thrumming engine seemed to soothe Julie, whose sobs quietened to sniffles. Julie's parents lived in the village, and Arrina thought of driving straight to them. But instead, she headed to her own cottage, knowing that Julie's mother was going through a bad patch with her health and couldn't take the stress of Julie's current state.

Julie let herself be led inside the small hill-top house. Arrina unlaced her friend's shoes and eased her coat over her shoulders.

In the small cottage, silence hung thick in the air. Arrina's thoughts raced so wildly that she expected them to seep out and fill the place with their clamour. Kingsley Peters was dead. The man had been at the college just that morning, and by the evening, he was gone. It didn't make sense. Even harder to believe was that Phil had been arrested for his murder.

Phil, Julie's husband—the sweet man who had raced out to fix the college's heating system at six am—had been arrested for *murder*. The idea seemed impossible. Around and around, Arrina's thoughts raced, swirling into a giant question mark that threatened to explode in her brain.

But she couldn't let the panic and confusion overtake her. She had to focus on Julie, who was right then staring blankly down Arrina's short hallway and gently shaking her head.

Arrina led Julie to the living room. Then she dashed around, turning on every light in the cottage. The darkness outside seemed absolute, as though the sun might never return, and Arrina needed some brightness to push that feeling away.

Back in the living room, Arrina pulled her squeaking sofa bed out. Tinsel, who'd been curled up nearby, yowled loudly and glared before bounding off to the kitchen. Arrina knew that the sleek silver cat would sniff haughtily at the bowl of food she'd put down in there and then polish the whole thing off in a matter of moments. She left him to it.

'It's a bit early for bed, I know,' Arrina said as she eased Julie down into a nest of pillows and quilts. It was in fact *very* early for bed, despite the darkness outside. 'But there's nothing we can do tonight. Tomorrow, in the fresh light of day, we'll be able to work all this out, I'm sure.'

Arrina didn't feel sure of what she said at all. She didn't even understand what was happening. Was this real? Had *Phil* been arrested?

Julie sat and stared at the wall. 'Phil loves our bed,' she murmured. 'It's too soft for me really. We fell out about that when we bought it. But he loves it.'

Arrina sat down next to Julie and stroked her friend's arm, not knowing what to say. She thought of her earlier plan to watch Christmas movies and knew how good it would feel to be lost in their soothing, snow-blanketed world. But they wouldn't help Julie.

'What can I get you to eat?' This was usually Julie's question in times of crisis. 'I think I've got some of those nice oat biscuits you like. Though we might have finished them off with the Stilton last week. I'm sure I've got a box of your mince pies in the freezer. You said they'd save for three months, so they'll still be good. I can put them in the oven and—'

Julie slipped her hand into Arrina's and laced their fingers tightly together. She shook her head.

'Not even a cup of tea?' Arrina asked. 'I've just got a new box of Lady Grey. The orange peel and lavender in there are supposed to be very soothing.'

Julie tightened her fingers around Arrina's but didn't say anything. Arrina glanced at her friend's face and saw a frightening emptiness in her black eyes. Julie was so vibrant usually. She wasn't someone to curl up meekly and let tears slip down her cheeks. Arrina couldn't bear to see her like this.

She looked around the small, low-ceilinged living room, where she and Julie had spent so much time together over the years, drinking tea and eating cakes. Until recently, they'd had an unmissable appointment to watch *The Great British Bake Off* each week. When the series had ended the month before, they'd joked that their friendship was over till next year.

Arrina found a saved episode of the series on her TV. She kept the volume low and let the gentle images of sifted flour, stirred milk, and warming ovens pass across the screen.

Slowly, Julie's fingers relaxed around Arrina's hand. Julie's eyes wandered to the screen, and she breathed more easily as she watched the tiny dramas of amateur baking.

Arrina tutted as a contestant frantically whisked the contents of a pan. When Julie didn't say anything, Arrina added, 'That crème pat's never going to thicken.' She caught a small nod from the corner of her eye.

The TV judges raised sceptical eyebrows at a pie tin of pale pastry. Arrina said, 'She should have blind baked for at least fifteen minutes. Anyone can see she's going to get a soggy bottom if she carries on like this.'

Julie huffed her annoyance at the contestant's mistake, and Arrina knew watching *Bake Off* had been the right decision.

When it came to the last challenge of the show, Arrina gestured at the screen. 'What are they complaining about? All this palaver over a *croque-en-bouche*. What's the big deal? It's just a bunch of profiteroles with some sugar blobbed on. I could make that. Easy.'

'You could *not* make that,' Julie said in a thick, hoarse voice that pained Arrina to hear. 'You can barely manage a scone.'

'I absolutely could,' Arrina said. 'I think it's time I come clean and let you know that I'm actually a fantastic baker. I merely pretend to be bad in order to protect your pride.'

Julie snuffled out what might have been a laugh. 'Is that why your biscuits can chip teeth? To protect my pride?'

'Yes. Absolutely.' Arrina turned to face Julie and squared her shoulders. 'But you can never ask me to demonstrate the true extent of my abilities. I took a solemn oath against it.'

The two women stared at each other and smiled softly.

Julie let go of Arrina's hand and ran her fingers through her own messy black hair. Arrina was glad to see her friend's dark eyes glowing with life once again, even if they were still painfully red-rimmed from crying.

'I got to the farm just a few minutes before the police arrived,' Julie whispered. 'I should have gone straight there when I left the college this morning.' She swiped away a tear that crawled down her cheek. 'When I saw that man walk into the hall, I should have just gone straight to Phil. Then none of this would have happened.'

Arrina's mind raced, trying to work out what Julie was saying. She worried that if she pushed Julie, she'd sink back into blank-eyed numbness. But Arrina didn't understand what her friend was talking about.

Then suddenly she did. 'Do you mean Kingsley Peters?'

Julie nodded slowly. 'When he walked into the hall, it was such a shock.'

'I didn't know you knew him. I didn't know Phil...' Arrina trailed off as she realized what Julie meant. 'Was Kingsley the one who investigated your milk spillage?'

Julie nodded.

'I'm so sorry. I didn't even consider that. I didn't think the Environment Agency would send someone who'd actually investigated farms in Heathervale. I... I didn't think. I'm so sorry.'

'It's all right,' Julie said. 'Just for a minute, I felt like I'd be fine being in the same room with him. Then I saw him holding one of my coffees and I just... I had to get out of there.'

Fat tears trickled down Julie's pink-flushed cheeks, and this time, she didn't wipe them away.

'I should have gone straight to Phil then,' Julie continued. 'But I went to the café. I don't know why. I just wanted to... It sounds so stupid now... I wanted to make sure that man hadn't done anything to the place. Then I got sidetracked by biscuit shortages and squashed cakes and who knows what. And before I knew it, the day had disappeared. I had to speak to Gillian about the internship after that, so I didn't get home until late afternoon. I only arrived a few minutes before... before the police came and—' A choked sob cut off the rest of her words.

Julie buried her face in her hands, and Arrina felt an ache in her chest to see her friend in so much pain.

'Why would they arrest Phil?' Arrina asked, as gently as she could.

Julie's sobs grew louder. 'I don't know.' Through the muffled barrier of her hands, she repeated, 'I don't know. I don't know. I don't know.'

She uttered these words over and over again until Arrina wrapped her up in a tight embrace. It was a long time before her weeping quietened down.

When it finally did, Arrina got up to make some tea. As she left the living room, she dimmed the lights, hoping that Julie would be able to sleep soon.

Then she crept into the kitchen to put on the kettle.

She took out her phone while the water heated, and she pulled up a number that was stored as DO NOT CALL.

The number belonged to Tony Mellor, or Sergeant Mellor, to give him his official title. He was the man who'd stood by the police table at the Careers Fair earlier that day and who Arrina had not wanted even to *see*. Now she needed his help.

They'd grown closer again that summer, or at least Arrina had *thought* so. But since then, he'd kept his distance, and Arrina had done her very best not to care.

Now, she stared at his number while the kettle began to steam. Her thumb hovered above the call button. He would have information about what was going on with Phil. He could help Arrina make sense of what was happening. But he was a straitlaced rule-follower and would never reveal confidential information like that. Perhaps it would be enough just to ask. Just to talk to him about it. Just to hear his voice saying he was handling everything.

Tinsel meowed from a cushion on the window seat, and Arrina almost pressed the green button in surprise. Then her phone buzzed. Arrina fumbled it, thinking she'd called Tony and suddenly desperate to hang up. But it was just an email coming in.

Arrina was about to ignore it. Then she saw who it was from—the Board of Governors, the select group of parents and villagers who oversaw the college. Arrina hadn't even thought about them since Julie ran into the hall. She hadn't thought about anything but helping her friend.

However, Kingsley Peters had been at the college that morning, and then he was murdered. The man who'd been arrested for that killing was the husband of Julie Wen, another helper at the Careers Fair. Telling the Board of Governors about the college's mix-up in the murder should have been the first thing she did.

She winced in preparation as she opened the email now, expecting recriminations for not notifying the board about the issue.

But they didn't mention it. In fact, the email wasn't to her at all, at least not specifically. It was to all staff and students at the college. As she skimmed the first few lines, a lead ball of worry formed in her stomach. The anxiety grew bigger and heavier as she read on.

Dear all,

It is with deepest regret that we write in relation to a tragic event which took place earlier today in Heathervale. As you will no doubt have heard, a member of the Environment Agency has unfortunately perished under suspicious circumstances.

The police are pursuing every avenue and have made a surprisingly swift arrest in the case. It is our hope that this matter should not affect the college in any way. Although the man was working at the Careers Fair this morning, there is no sign of connection between that and his death. To this end, please assist us in distancing Heathervale College from the situation to the greatest possible extent.

We ask that all staff and students refrain from gossiping or speaking with any members of the press whatsoever regarding the case. It also goes without saying that you ought not to be in contact with anyone directly involved in this case. Otherwise, we shall have no option but to—

The kettle came to a furious boil and snapped Arrina out of her shock at what she was reading. She didn't want to see the rest anyway—didn't want to know what consequence the board was threatening.

Their instruction was clear—keep the college as far away as possible from the terrible crime. Don't speak to the press about it. Don't even gossip with other people in the village. And certainly, don't have any contact with people connected to the murder.

Arrina glanced over her shoulder towards the living room. In no way would the Board of Governors want her taking care of the murder suspect's wife. That could only pull the college further into the terrible situation. But this was *Julie*. For once, Arrina couldn't put the college first. She had to help her friend.

Arrina turned off her phone and put it down on the counter in the kitchen. She didn't want anything to distract her from Julie, and emails like this didn't help.

Then she made the tea and carried two cups into the living room. She hoped that the orange peel and lavender in this Lady Grey really *were* as soothing as the box claimed.

As Arrina got back under the covers of the sofa bed, Julie took her tea gratefully and gazed at the opening credits of another *Bake Off* episode. When she finished the drink, her eyelids started to droop, but she didn't shuffle down in the bed to go to sleep.

Instead, she turned to Arrina and clutched her friend's hand once again.

'You'll sort this mix-up with Phil, won't you?' Julie asked, her voice still strained and raw. 'You know he didn't do this, and you'll help me get him free. You can do that, can't you?'

The ghost of the Board of Governors' email flashed in front of Arrina's eyes, but she stared through it at her best friend's pained and pleading face.

'Of course,' Arrina said. 'I'll do everything I can.' Then, when Julie clutched more urgently, she added, 'I'll fix this. I promise. I'll help you get him free.'

Once they turned out the lights, Julie's breaths soon eased into the smooth lull of sleep. Arrina listened for a long time before she also finally drifted off into a night of uneasy dreams.

4

Arrina woke to darkness and a twitching tail tickling her cheek. She reached out a hand from under her warm covers to scratch the itch. But her fingers didn't get as far as her face. A smooth wall of fur pushed itself in the way.

Arrina opened one eye and saw her silver tomcat's silhouette turning and padding gently towards her. His cold nose pressed against her cheek, and then he aimed a sharp meow directly into her ear.

'OK,' Arrina murmured. 'OK. I get your incredibly subtle hints.'

She pulled her thick duvet down a bit and shuffled over. Tinsel leapt into the warm patch of bed she left for him. He nuzzled up against her and purred loudly. Arrina's eyes drifted closed, and the heavy blanket of sleep began to settle over her once more.

She snuggled into her mattress. Shuffled. Tried to wriggle into a comfy spot but couldn't find one. Her bed felt lumpy and unwelcoming.

Then Arrina remembered where she was—*not* in her bed but on the hard pull-out sofa in her living room.

The events of the day before came rushing back. Arrina's hand grew still on Tinsel's sleek fur. He mewled a complaint, but Arrina didn't respond.

Julie's husband, Phil, had been arrested for murder. The victim, Kingsley Peters, had flirted with Arrina just hours before his death. The Board of Governors had instructed everyone at the college to distance themselves from the case.

But Julie, her best friend in all the world, had asked for Arrina's help. And when it came to Julie, Arrina had no hesitation. Julie meant more than any job, even one Arrina loved.

When Arrina thought of the pain in her friend's eyes the night before, she pushed all thoughts of the college away.

She turned over on the sofa bed, hoping that Julie was still safely tucked in the soothing arms of sleep and not also awake in the middle of the night.

But Julie wasn't there. Arrina reached across to her side of the bed. It was cold. She turned on a lamp. Julie's bag was gone as well. There was no sign of her at all, not even a note. Perhaps she'd left a message on Arrina's phone. But she couldn't see that either. A tightness crept through Arrina's chest.

'Julie!' she called out. She could *feel* the emptiness of the house as her voice echoed around it.

Arrina's sleep-fogged brain struggled into wakefulness. She stood up into an iron-cold room, and a small gasp escaped at the slap of icy air against her skin.

She hunted around again for a note, her phone, anything. But all that caught her eye was Tinsel's satisfied shoulder wriggle. The cat settled into the wide expanse of warmth Arrina had left behind. She frowned at him.

Then Arrina remembered where she'd left her phone the night before. The phone was in the kitchen—turned off and face down by the kettle. Arrina raced into the room—surely Julie would have sent a message to say where she'd gone.

Arrina got three steps across the floor before her feet registered the sharp pain of cold stones beneath them. The kitchen floor was like ice. If the heating system hadn't kicked in yet, then it really *must* be the middle of the night. Unless the rickety old thing was broken. But the heating at the college had broken just the day before, and that seemed like too big a coincidence. Plus, it *couldn't* be broken, because then she'd have to ask someone other than Phil to fix it, and that was unthinkable. A stab of worry about Phil passed through her chest, matching the needles of ice in her feet. Arrina hopped from foot to foot on the cold stone floor as she checked that the boiler was OK.

The boiler seemed to be working: the timer was set, the display looked fine, and it was clear why it wasn't on—the clock on the front read 5.15, a full half hour before it was due to kick in. But if that was right, then why wasn't Julie still tucked up in bed? Arrina grabbed her phone from the nearby counter and turned it on. The clock on the screen confirmed it—5.15 am.

Arrina called Julie. She listened for a ringing somewhere inside her cottage. But the air was stiff with silence.

Arrina's legs shook beneath her as the call rang and rang.

There was a murderer in the village. The police had arrested Phil, but he definitely hadn't done it. So the person who'd killed Kingsley was still on the loose. Had the murderer got Julie too?

Then Julie answered. 'What are you doing up?'

Arrina couldn't speak for a moment.

'Arrina?' Julie asked. A loud mooing at Julie's end explained exactly where she was.

'You're doing the milking,' Arrina said. Her eyes prickled with tears of relief at this simple explanation. *Of course* Julie was doing the milking. If Phil was being held by the police overnight, nobody else could do it.

'Yes. Phil won't let me hear the end of it if he gets back later and finds they've not been milked. Sorry if I woke you when I left. I didn't think you'd be up for hours. Do you need anything?'

Arrina blinked and took a few seconds to process Julie's lively stream of words before she replied. 'I don't need anything, thanks.' Julie sounded so different from the night before, and Arrina was too cold and tired to work out if that was a good thing. She pushed the button to override the timer on the boiler, and a satisfying whir promised warmth would soon be soaking into her bones. 'Do you want me to come over and help?'

'Well, I've actually borrowed your car,' Julie said. 'I hope that's OK.'

'Yes, of course.' Arrina didn't know why she hadn't realised this before. She'd driven Julie to her cottage the evening before, and no local taxis were available that early on a Sunday morning. 'I hope it wasn't too temperamental.'

'No,' Julie said, speaking loudly over the background lowing of cows. 'I think it could sense I'm up to my eyeballs right now. It started first time.'

'You must have got the magic touch. It never does that for me.'

'Keep your fingers crossed my luck holds out and these cows all go through the parlour smoothly. They only really behave well for Phil. But I suppose, if there are any problems, he can sort them out later.'

The brightness in Julie's voice was a *big* change from the evening before. Arrina tried her best to be comforted by this. But it wasn't right. It wasn't Julie. Arrina was the one who pushed through problems with flinty determination. For Julie to sound so *sure* that things would be back to normal later that day...

Arrina shivered and stood closer to the rumbling boiler. Maybe a bright and cheery attitude was what Julie needed right then.

'I'll run you a bath when you get back,' she said. 'It must be freezing out there on the farm. And I'll make breakfast. How about pancakes? Even *I* can't mess up pancakes. I'll do a batch with...' Arrina flung open her cupboard doors and looked at the mostly empty shelves inside. 'With an assorted array of mystery toppings?'

She wasn't quite sure whether tinned peaches and muesli would go well on a pancake, but she'd give it a try. As she rifled through a baking cupboard that largely consisted of things Julie had left in the cottage, she turned up some miniature marshmallows, chocolate drops, and golden syrup. She could rustle a feast up from what she'd got. Just about.

'That sounds good,' Julie said. 'I'll have to be quick, though. I need to be at the café before seven.'

Arrina hesitated. 'The café? You're going in today?' She was drowned out by an impatient-sounding mooing from the other end of the phone.

'See you soon!' Julie shouted and then hung up.

Julie was going into Do-Re-Mi. She was going to open her café in the centre of the High Street just like it was any ordinary day.

Arrina got out the ingredients for pancakes and her strange selection of toppings and tried to convince herself that this was the best plan of action. Everything was going to be fine. It would all be absolutely OK.

5

By the time Julie got back from milking, Arrina's cottage was warm and cosy. But, as Julie had promised, she hurried through both her bath and pancakes and was back in Arrina's car before the sun even broke over the horizon.

Arrina was in the driver's seat this time, cursing the engine for not cooperating the way it had apparently done for Julie. She didn't care too much, though—her struggle with the car made Julie smile, and that was all Arrina wanted.

'You're twisting it,' Julie said. 'You need more of a scooping action. Imagine you're lifting an egg yolk from a bowl.'

'As I so often do.'

'*Imagine*, I said.'

'OK. I'm *imagining* I know what it feels like to pick up an egg yolk.'

'To *scoop* up an egg yolk.'

'And I'm using my imaginary scooping action to turn my freezing cold metal key, and...'

The car roared to life.

Julie gave a whoop of success. Arrina glared at her dashboard and muttered, 'Traitor.'

Then she eased her car slowly down the narrow hill road, keeping an eye out for patches of ice on the unsalted, dimly lit surface. As she emerged from the tunnel of trees that covered the first part of the road, she was glad to break through into a clear morning, with a view of a pale sky that promised the sun would soon be with them. It was the sort of startling winter morning when every leaf, pebble, and blade of grass was outlined in frost, as though the fragile world had been sewn up in glittering armour with silver seams.

But then Julie sighed, and the view turned hard and unwelcoming. Arrina had known Julie's mood was too good to be true. It was *Arrina's* habit to hide her feelings and power through the difficult times, not Julie's. And now, the baker's real emotions were seeping out. Arrina glanced over at her friend, who clenched her hands together tightly in her lap.

'Perhaps,' Arrina started gently, 'well, maybe the café could take a snow day today. I know there's not technically any snow, but the forecast says it's on the way.'

Julie said nothing.

'I heard that Wolferton Manor has got a new Sunday brunch menu.' As Arrina said this, she knew how stupid it sounded. Julie didn't want mimosas and eggs benedict while her husband was being held by the police.

'Or, we keep saying we're going to gather some sloes for gin.' Arrina's voice was brittle with brightness. 'We've had the first frosts now, so it's the perfect time. We could go into the hills and pick some today.'

'Maybe next week.' Julie squeezed her fingers together, turning her knuckles white. 'I've got to do the baking for the café.'

Arrina slowed down, preparing to pull over and give Julie a hug to calm the tears she could see welling in her friend's eyes. 'Could Rochelle maybe do that?'

'She's had another flare-up with her back. She's off her feet for a couple of weeks,' Julie said, uncharacteristically slowly.

'Or what about one of the Sunday girls? You're always saying how they're so good they'll be stealing your job soon.'

Julie unclenched her hands and laid them neatly on her thighs. She patted her fingers over her kneecaps then leaned back and sat straight in her seat. 'They both worked yesterday so I could go to the college.'

Arrina felt a stab of guilt over this, even though Julie hadn't sounded annoyed when she said it. 'Well, maybe—'

'It's for the best, though,' Julie said. 'Baking will keep my thoughts off... off everything that's going on. The police said I could come down to the station this afternoon to get Phil, so I need to keep busy this morning, and then...' Her voice quivered and climbed to a high pitch. 'I just need to keep busy.'

Arrina saw a layby here she could pull into. She fingered the indicator but didn't flick it. Instead, she increased her speed again and headed through the glowing light of the new day towards the café. Julie had made a plan, and Arrina knew how good it could feel to check items off a list, especially in times of crisis. Arrina would help her with that.

'You're absolutely right,' she said. 'You'll keep busy this morning. Then once you've picked Phil up, you'll go home and bake him an enormous pie. A Desperate Dan-sized portion that he'll barely make a dent in before he goes out to check on his cows. Then you'll bring half the pie over to my house, and Tinsel and I will eat like kings for a week.'

Julie nodded slowly along with Arrina. 'Do you think so?'

'I'm sure of it. I don't know what's got into the police, but I'm certain the delusion will have left them by now, and they'll see that there's no way Phil could have done this.' At least, Arrina *hoped* so. In a village as small as Heathervale, though, the police didn't jump to arresting residents quickly. That sort of behaviour led to lifelong grudges, or at the very least, friends of the wrongly accused knocking over pints in the Horse and Hound.

Arrina slowed down as she approached the High Street. Sunday mornings at Do-Re-Mi usually started out quietly but soon got busy. This could be her last chance to be alone with Julie.

But when she opened her mouth to ask for details of Phil's arrest, nothing came out. Arrina had promised that she'd help get the man free, but all she had right now was hope that the police would let him go. Surely, she needed more than that. But could she really cause Julie more stress and ask what she knew?

It could wait, Arrina promised herself. Right now, her focus was on Julie. She pulled up outside of Do-Re-Mi, covered her worried thoughts with a bright smile, and said, 'Let's get baking!'

6

Inside Do-Re-Mi's kitchen, Julie kept up a lecture for a full five minutes on why Arrina was *not* to do any actual baking that day. No matter how often Arrina agreed with her or insisted she'd just been joking in the car, she couldn't get Julie to drop it.

'I'm just worried that too much *Bake Off* has gone to your head.' Julie got ingredients out of her storeroom and watched Arrina with hawk-like attention to be sure she didn't touch anything.

'It hasn't, I—'

'It looks so easy when you see people doing it on TV, I know. But in fact, it takes years of training to be able to prepare food at a commercial level.'

'I'm sure it does. I've seen that *Julie and Julia* film you like so much—I'm aware of how tough it is just to get into the Cordon Bleu, let alone keep up with the level of onion chopping there.'

'I know you're joking, but—'

'I *am* joking,' Arrina said. 'I'm really just here to help in whatever way you decide. I'm excellent at washing up, and if there was a *Great British Mop Off*, I'd be a shoo-in for the top prize.'

'OK.' Julie lined up huge quantities of flour, sugar, butter, and eggs on a stainless-steel surface. Then she looked over at the picture of Julie Andrews on the wall above the counter. This was who Julie Wen was named after, and she took the connection very seriously. Julie winked at the image of the wimple-clad woman before turning back to Arrina. 'Me and my twin sister here will handle the baking. You can maybe... measure out some ingredients for us. Maybe?'

'Thanks for the vote of confidence.'

'You have to be careful.'

'Even *I* can weigh flour,' Arrina said, pulling the large sack of the stuff towards herself. 'How much do you need?' She wrestled the bag open, and a puff of fine powder filled the air. She turned away and sneezed.

When she turned back, she found Julie's jet-black bob dusted with white and her dark eyes narrowed to slits. 'Perhaps you can put the chairs out in the café instead.' Julie slid the bag of flour back to the far side of the counter.

'You're feeling nervous after I revealed the truth about my baking skills, I see. You don't want me around judging your work.'

'Hmmmm,' Julie replied. 'Something like that.'

Arrina walked through the door to the dining area and pulled tables and chairs into their usual positions. She straightened up vases of edelweiss and smiled fondly at the *Sound of Music* scenes captured in huge framed images above each table. Her favourite showed the children walking on the rim of a fountain in Salzburg—a place she and Julie had promised to visit one day.

'Didn't I make great pancakes this morning?' Arrina shouted in the direction of the kitchen. Julie didn't answer, but Arrina was sure she was smiling at the memory of Arrina's curious concoctions.

Arrina's personal favourite topping had been marmalade and marshmallows, which had turned out to be a surprisingly delicious combination. Julie had sampled a few different offerings and had eaten half of a cornflake-and-honey-topped pancake before claiming she was full. At least she'd eaten something. That was the important thing. She just needed to keep going until she could pick up Phil that afternoon.

As Arrina straightened chairs and pulled open the huge green and white curtains—just like the ones turned into play clothes in the movie—at the front of the café, she tried to push away her doubts about Phil's release. The police had promised Julie they'd let him go, so they had to do it, didn't they?

The goat marionettes hanging from the ceiling seemed to follow her with their eyes. The niggle of doubt wouldn't go away. Even if the police did let Phil go, would that be the end of it? Not in a village like Heathervale. Rumours would fly until the case was solved, and Arrina knew that for Julie and Phil, that would feel like the end of the world.

As Arrina dragged the last chair into place, she heard a loud scream. Her heart lurched in her chest. She knocked over chairs and pushed tables out of her way as she raced back to the kitchen. She could barely breathe for fear of what she'd find.

Bursting through the door, she was stopped short by Julie's glare.

'What on *earth* have you done in there?' Julie asked. She peered over Arrina's shoulder as the door swung shut behind her. One last toppling chair crashed to the ground, and Arrina winced.

But Julie was OK, which, again, was the most important thing. She seemed more than OK, in fact. Her hands were planted firmly on the broad curves of her hips, and she shook her head at Arrina.

'What have *I* done? You almost gave me a heart attack. Why did you scream?'

A figure moved in the corner. Arrina let out a scream of her own.

'See!' Julie said, turning to the figure, who now stepped forwards and revealed herself to be Maggie Lee. 'You can't go creeping up on people like that.' Then Julie turned back to Arrina. '*That's* what frightened me. This one here sneaked in and leapt out at me.'

'I didn't leap, Aunty Julie,' Maggie said.

'I'm an old woman,' Julie said, walking over to the mixing bowl on the counter and then stirring its contents. 'Even a slightly vigorous hop is too much for me.' Her tone was sharp, but Arrina could see she was smiling. Maggie had only come into her life a few months earlier, but the two women's parents went back a long way—far enough that they considered one another family.

'You're not old,' Maggie said with a smile. However, Arrina could see that this statement was the polite indulgence of a woman in her mid-twenties. To Maggie, who still tied up her swishy ponytail with a length of bright ribbon, Julie was ancient. 'But I'm sorry for scaring you. I heard what happened to...' She dropped her eyes to the floor and blinked quickly. 'I thought I'd come here and help for the day.'

'It's all a silly misunderstanding,' Julie said. 'But thank you for coming. I know you're busy cooking up those magical potions to keep insects away.'

'Natural pesticides,' Maggie corrected. She glanced over at Arrina then quickly looked away. Maggie had originally come to Heathervale to work as a chemistry teacher at Arrina's college, but she'd changed her plans before the start of the school year. Now she used her new farm to experiment with natural pesticides and was trying to turn these experiments into a business.

Arrina had still not filled Maggie's position, and it was costing a fortune in substitute teacher bills to keep the chemistry department going. Maggie looked a little more sheepish each time someone mentioned the college or her new company. However, since Maggie was letting the college use a large portion of her land for an agriculture programme, Arrina herself had no problem with Maggie's path in life. The new classes were quickly becoming the talk of the entire Peak District.

'I could certainly use a hand today,' Julie said. 'What with everything that's going on, I feel *very* old indeed.' She pantomimed a doddering shuffle and a turtle-like hunch. 'Somewhere around a hundred and forty-seven.'

'Well, you don't look it,' Arrina said. 'You look fantastic for a woman approaching fifty.'

Julie's shoulders tensed back up, and she spun around. She propped her mixing bowl on one hip and beat the contents as she walked over to Arrina. 'Fifty! I'm years away from that, and you know it. Don't go pushing your worries about your upcoming four-oh onto me.'

'Oh, Aunty Julie,' Maggie said, dashing over and wrapping her slender arm around Julie's shoulders. 'Please don't be cross. I'm sorry for starting all this.'

Arrina and Julie caught each other's eyes and smiled.

'You're right,' said Julie. 'Your old aunt shouldn't be mad at Arrina, even though she's singlehandedly trying to destroy my café this morning.' She gestured in the direction of the toppled chairs in the dining area.

'Destroy your café,' Arrina said. 'The cheek! I was rushing in here selflessly to save you.'

'A likely story.' Julie winked. 'I'm sure you'll find a way to make up for flinging my furniture around. Perhaps making us all a cup of tea.'

Arrina let out a laugh that seemed to confuse poor Maggie Lee, who frowned and left to make herself busy. Then Arrina went over to the kettle and set about making their first drinks of what she knew would be a very long day.

As the water boiled, she watched Maggie head over to the ingredients on the counter and get straight to work. She, unlike Arrina, had a natural talent for baking. Maggie was also an excellent distraction for Julie, who threw herself into teaching her how to complete a whole day's baking for the café.

Arrina did her best to be useful while they worked—fetching, carrying, washing up, and keeping out of the way. Then when it was time to open the café, she helped with the service at the front of house. From time to time, her thoughts flicked back to the email she'd received the night before—the one that had expressly forbidden contact with people connected to Kingsley's death—but she quickly pushed these thoughts away.

Besides, it was Sunday, and most of the people in the café were day-trippers. Their spotless cagouls and mud-free hiking boots marked them out clearly. Those who came into the café that early on a Sunday weren't even the sort of serious hikers who were likely to return. They were the type to stroll along the High Street, amble to a country pub for lunch, and count that as their rural exposure for the year.

But then she caught sight of a distinctive twitching moustache through the window. It belonged to Victor Stones, the chair of the college's Board of Governors, and surely the person who'd written that strongly worded email. As he turned to glance into the café, Arrina ducked behind a table and pretended to tie her shoe. She couldn't face a confrontation with the man this morning. He was certainly not beyond shouting at her in front of the crowd of customers.

As soon as he'd passed by, Arrina headed back to the kitchen. The pile of dishes to wash up had grown to mountainous proportions, which gave her the perfect excuse to send Maggie out to the front while she caught up with cleaning. Maggie looked only too relieved to get a break from Julie's relentless pace in the kitchen.

When Arrina had finally got through the stack of pots and plates, she turned around to find Julie whisking double cream past stiff peaks into crumbling defeat and staring at the clock. It was half past eleven.

'Come on,' Arrina said, sounding far brighter than she felt. 'Let's head to the police station. By the time we get to

Grindleford and find a parking space, it'll be officially afternoon.'

Julie's searching eyes filled with relief. She put down her bowl and whisk, left a note for Maggie to call if she had *any* questions about the café, and headed out of the back door.

Arrina followed into a crisp November day that felt like it could shatter to pieces around them.

7

Next to Grindleford train station was a café that Arrina and Julie visited often and loved dearly. Arrina wished she didn't have to park beside it now and connect the place with the current terrible situation, but she couldn't find another space anywhere near the police station.

The café there was nothing like Do-Re-Mi: this one sold tea by the pint, tray-bakes in clingfilm-wrapped bricks for hikers to take away, and chip butties so large they had to be prepared for. The two women had spent so many long afternoons in there that even the thought of it made Arrina happy. At least, it usually did.

As she got out of her car next to the cafe, frosted leaves crunched underfoot. Arrina's face stiffened in the cold. She wished she hadn't misplaced her coat in the hall the day before. Her hiking fleece was in the boot, though. That fleece was mud-stained and slightly torn from a losing fight with a blackberry bush, but it was warm, and that was all that mattered right then.

'They won't have fed him well,' Julie said. 'Should we take him something from the café? No, we can bring him here after we collect him. He'll appreciate a hot meal, and you know how he loves the signs in there.'

Grindleford café was covered in notices to customers: NO Mobile Phones; This is a Serving Hatch NOT a Viewing Gallery; No Omelettes on Sundays EVER. The staff were always friendly and helpful, so Arrina could never tell if the signs were a joke. Their vigorously underlined words suggested not, and she was never brave enough to test them.

The only good thing about parking by Grindleford café was the quiet footpath that led straight from there to the police station. Arrina and Julie walked along the isolated, tree-lined track, the rhythmic crunching of their footsteps drowned out by Julie's conversation with herself. She kept up a steady stream of reminders of what to tell Phil: the vet had called to ask them about the bill; the silage delivery was overdue; three of the cows were drying off ahead of schedule.

Arrina did her best to pay attention in case Julie needed anything. But her mind was still working over the question of why Phil had been arrested in the first place. The matter wasn't just strange because nobody could possibly believe that a gentle man like Phil would *kill* somebody. It was also that he'd been *arrested*, which was such a serious step. Phil had lived in Heathervale his entire life, and his family had farmed the same patch of land as far back as anyone could remember. Surely the police didn't need to lock him up to talk to him. He wasn't going anywhere.

An official arrest suggested something serious. Very serious. And the fact that Julie hadn't heard anything since Phil had been taken away made Arrina worry. Could the police know something Julie didn't?

But, in fact, Arrina realised, she didn't have a clue *what* Julie knew. Arrina had been walking on eggshells around her friend, too afraid of upsetting her by discussing the situation. The writhing snakes in Arrina's stomach whispered doubts about Phil's release. If he didn't get out, Julie would be a wreck of emotion, and Arrina wouldn't be able to get the information she needed to free him.

Arrina walked steadily on the frozen track towards the police station and waited for a chance to interrupt Julie's stream of farm updates.

'—And I swear that hinge has got creakier, even though Phil says it's all in my head.'

'But it's just been Halloween,' Arrina said, 'isn't he even a little suspicious that a ghost is trapped in there?'

'Apparently not!'

'Madness,' Arrina said. Then she spoke as gently as she could and asked, 'So, when the police came to the farm, did they explain much to you about what was going on?' The snakes of worry twisted tightly together in her gut at how Julie would react to this.

The track to the police station was narrow. At that point on the path, the tall, leafless trees crowded in from both sides, and the women walked in single file. Julie was up ahead, and when she didn't say anything, Arrina thought perhaps she hadn't heard. Then Julie turned her head slightly to reply over her shoulder.

'They explained a bit.' Her voice sounded strained, and Arrina hated that she'd upset Julie with her question. But then Julie cleared her throat and continued in her previous, determined tone. 'The body was found on the edge of the Yates family's land. You know the part that's above our farm and over the hill?'

Arrina didn't know that area well. No public footpaths crossed the Yates land. Arrina had walked along the unofficial track that led to the Morgan woods next door, but that only passed by a couple of large fields with no view of the rest of the farm.

'The part above your farm,' Arrina repeated, trying to picture the place. 'Is that the other side of the sheep pasture?' She knew there was a scrubby patch of common land across the road at the top of Phil and Julie's farm. But Arrina didn't really know what was beyond it.

Julie nodded. 'I thought the police were kidding at first. Nobody ever goes up there, not even the Yates family. But... but then they asked Phil if he was up there yesterday, and... and he said yes.'

'And the body was found there as well?' Arrina couldn't make sense of that either. The patch of land wasn't near anything other than farms. Kingsley was meant to be at the Careers Fair all day, so he wouldn't have been out on an Environment Agency investigation. What could he have been doing in that isolated place?

'The police said the body was discovered there in the early afternoon. A birdwatcher out chasing a rare yellow crested something found it.'

'Is that why Phil was there too? Birdwatching?' She knew the answer before she even asked the question. Julie shook her head. No, of course Phil hadn't been birdwatching. He was a farmer through and through. The only birds he cared about were chickens and the occasional goose. Arrina's mind filled with images of the man smiling in the sunshine, his ruddy cheeks turning a deeper pink as he worked with his dopey herd of Friesians. All he ever seemed to focus on was farming. What would he be doing on someone else's land, especially when nothing was up there?

'He told the police he was helping the Yateses put in a new fence.' Julie raked a hand through her tangled black bob, pulling free a brown oak leaf that had just tumbled from a branch overhead. 'He said they'd asked for his help as a favour. But I don't understand that. Phil's family and the Yateses have never got on. If they were going to ask anyone for a favour, it wouldn't be Phil.'

The Yateses didn't get on with *many* local families, in fact. They liked to keep themselves apart from everyone else, always seeming to think they were better because they were descended from some minor lord of the early medieval period. The only member of the family Arrina knew was Bill Yates. He was a geography teacher at the college, and the helpful man disliked his relatives as much as everyone else did.

'But even if he *was* there,' Julie continued, 'that doesn't explain what Kingsley Peters was doing on the land as well or why he died there. Wasn't he at the college all day?'

Arrina thought of Kingsley's broad smiles as she'd passed his booth on each lap of the hall the morning before. She also thought of how glad she'd been when he hadn't returned from lunch to continue smiling at her.

'He wasn't there in the afternoon,' Arrina said, realising then that the police would say he'd *disappeared*. 'I thought he'd just got tired of... of being there. He left leaflets for the students, and I assumed he'd be back at the end of the day to collect everything.'

Arrina's mind flashed to the Environment Agency's booth. It stood at the far end of the hall and was the only one that hadn't been packed up. She'd have to do that herself now and send the boxes on to the agency. Or would those things be evidence? Would the police come to take away scraps of paper and dust the hall for prints? Arrina didn't want to think of that.

There were a lot of things she didn't want to think about, though. If she was going to help Phil, she would *have* to face them. Julie seemed to think it was just a strange coincidence that Phil had been in the field where the body was found. But a coincidence wouldn't lead to an arrest that kept Phil in a jail cell overnight. She was sure the police knew something she didn't.

She was wondering what that could be and staring at her pacing feet when she and Julie reached the back of the police station. Out of the shelter of the trees, a strong, icy wind tried to knock the women down. Between them and the station, the large square of black tarmac was whipped by gusts that carried leaves and twigs across its surface at breakneck speed.

Arrina clutched her grubby fleece around herself more tightly, and she and Julie huddled together. They waited for a pause in the wind, and when it came, they dashed towards the squat, single-storey building. As Arrina got closer, she spotted something that almost made her stop in the middle of the exposed patch of ground.

Propped up in the shadow of the building was a black classic Norton Commando motorbike—one that she knew very well. The sight of it made her breath catch in her chest. The bike belonged to Tony Mellor, the man who'd broken her heart the year before and who she'd barely spoken to since.

She looked back at the footpath behind her. Its tunnel of trees was safe and inviting. As she crossed the last stretch of tarmac behind the police station, a vicious wind tugged at her. It was as sharp as a knife edge, and it cut between skin and clothes, pinching at every hint of warmth in her body. She couldn't turn back now, despite the cold and the risk of running into Tony. Phil was being held inside the small, red-brick police station, and Arrina and Julie were there to collect him.

8

Arrina and Julie pressed up against the red-brick back of the police station. The building provided some protection from the wind, and the women paused for a moment before heading around towards the side and battling the elements again.

Arrina only made it two steps before Julie called her name.

But no, it wasn't Julie. The wind-snatched shout was from someone else entirely. It came from Tony, standing up from behind his motorbike, a smear of oil darkening one cheek and a dirty rag draped over his shoulder. Tony looked as surprised as Arrina felt. He recovered faster, though, and he walked around his bike and came to stand with her and Julie.

'Has anyone been in touch with you?' Tony asked. Arrina couldn't imagine what he meant. But then he focused his attention on Julie and added, 'Anyone from the station?'

Julie shook her head. 'I don't know what you mean.'

'In touch?' Tony repeated. 'Has anyone called you? On the phone? Has anyone called or left a message... maybe a voicemail?'

'She knows how phones work.' Arrina had only meant to raise her voice above the howling wind, but her words sounded as hard as ice.

Tony's dark eyebrows drew together. 'Yes, of course. Sorry, I...' He looked around, as though checking for someone. But they were alone at the windswept back of the police station. 'It's just, I asked a couple of people if they were calling you, and nobody...' He trailed off and looked around again. Never before had Arrina seen the expression that was on Tony's face right then. It looked somewhere between confused and worried. But he was behind his workplace and had just been fixing his bike. Police work and bike repairs were Tony's two favourite things. So why didn't he look happy?

'Call me?' Julie asked in a voice that was almost lost beneath the wind. 'What's going on?'

'I don't know much,' Tony said. 'Maybe you should just call the station. I'm not on the case, but—'

'*Call* them?' Arrina's voice was loud and sharp still, but she didn't care. 'What are you talking about? We're right here. We've come to collect Phil.'

Now the look on Tony's face was one she *did* recognise. She'd seen this same expression on his face a year earlier, when he'd ended things between them without warning. This was the face that said he was keeping something from her. The difference was, this time, she would make him explain.

Tony rubbed a hand across the back of his neck. Arrina knew this gesture too. Tony felt bad about whatever he was about to say. Her stomach knotted with worry over what it could be.

'Phil's not in there,' Tony said, his sharp jaw tensing as he paused. 'He's not getting out today.'

Arrina's brain swirled with ideas of how this could be OK. Perhaps Phil wasn't getting out because it was a Sunday and there were strange opening hours that day. Or maybe he was out already. Or the police had just got an extension to their questioning time so they could get everything really cleared up properly, and he'd be out the next day instead.

'He's been charged,' Tony said, and Arrina's ideas were all whipped away in the wind. 'He'll have his first magistrate's hearing soon, and they'll keep him on remand until then.'

'On remand?' Julie repeated. 'I don't…I'm not…'

'In prison,' Tony said. 'He's being sent to prison until his hearing.'

'No,' Julie said, collapsing into the brick wall beside her. 'That can't be right. This can't be…'

Arrina wrapped an arm around her friend and held her up.

'I have to see him,' Julie said. 'Where is he now?'

'They won't let you see him until—'

'They have to!' Julie said. 'I'm his wife. They have to let me see him.'

'We'll sort this out,' Arrina said. 'Come on, let's—'

'Really,' Tony said. 'They won't let anybody see him. He's being transferred.'

'I have to try,' Julie said. She struggled to push away from the wall and stand up. Arrina could feel the shaking unsteadiness in her body, and she wrapped both arms around Julie.

'I'm coming with you,' Arrina said.

'They won't let you past the front desk,' Tony said. 'You could be here all day and—'

'I don't care,' Julie said. 'I don't care how long it takes. I need to—' Then she stopped and buried her fingers in her hair. 'The cows! They'll need their afternoon milking.'

'I'll sort it out,' Arrina said. She had no idea how to do that, but she'd find a way for Julie.

'No, it's OK,' Julie said. 'I'll ring Danny. He'll come over and do it, then I can stay here and sort this out.'

Julie pulled her phone from her bag.

'I can do that,' Arrina said. 'Don't worry. You just get in there.'

Julie glanced down at the screen, and her eyes widened. Arrina followed her gaze and saw that a reminder had popped up.

'The fundraiser,' Julie said. 'It's today.'

Tony stared over at her, his brow furrowed in confusion.

'The Lantern Parade fundraiser,' Julie said, as though this explained everything. 'I'm announcing the internship this afternoon.'

Arrina knew that the internship meant a lot to Julie, but surely it wasn't important at the moment. 'It's OK. You can do it another time.' The fundraiser was due to start in an hour, and Julie could barely stand up from stress. She couldn't present an internship in front of the whole village.

Her eyes brimmed with tears. 'It's all prepared. I just need to go there and announce it, and now I can't, and the whole thing is ruined, and all I wanted was to give someone a chance, just like you do all the time, and this is all... and everything's—' Julie fell back against the wall, her fingers scrabbling against the rough bricks.

'I'll do it,' Arrina said, tightening her grip around her friend and keeping her from collapsing entirely. 'I'll go to the fundraiser and make the announcement.'

Julie clutched at Arrina and mumbled something she couldn't make out.

'I know all the details,' Arrina said. 'And I've even got the draft of the announcement you emailed me. I can read that out and tell everyone about the internship.'

Julie managed to pull herself upright, though she still wobbled on her feet. 'Are you sure?' Julie's voice was tight and strained, as though something inside her was about to snap. Tears shone in her eyes, and Arrina wanted nothing more than to stay with her and find a way to fix all this.

'Yes. Absolutely.' In fact, however, Arrina was not sure. If Phil really had been charged with murder, then it would be the main topic of conversation at the fundraiser that afternoon. Arrina didn't want to stand in a room full of people who were spreading rumours about her friends. She didn't think she could be polite in the face of that.

And there was also the message from the Board of Governors, which forced its way to the front of her thoughts—the email had said the college couldn't be mixed up in the murder in any way. If Arrina went to the fundraiser and represented the wife of the accused killer, she was clearly ignoring that instruction. It was one thing to help Julie in her café, behind closed doors, and quite another to do so on stage in front of the entire village.

Arrina squeezed Julie tightly. 'Of course I'll do it. I'd do anything for you.'

'Thank you,' Julie said. She brushed the tears roughly from her cheeks and finger-combed her hair. 'Thank you. You make that announcement, and I'll go in here and sort things out with Phil.' She held up a hand to stop Tony's objections in their tracks. Then she sniffed and squared her shoulders. She nodded firmly. 'We'll get a taxi back to the village, and I'll let you know as soon as we're home. By the end of the day, it'll be like none of this ever happened.' She strode around the side of the building and disappeared from view.

Arrina stared after her friend, aching with the need to do more. She didn't want to go to the fundraiser. She didn't want to show up and make small talk when she should be with Julie, helping her through this terrible time.

But Julie wanted her to go, so she would. Before she did that, though, she needed to get some answers.

Arrina pulled her grubby fleece tightly around herself and stood face-to-face with Tony. He ran his eyes over the mud-stained, torn jacket, and Arrina did her best not to care that he was seeing her like this.

'What do you know?' she asked. 'Please, I know you're not supposed to talk about this, but you have to. If there's *anything* you can tell me...' Arrina stopped herself. She'd pleaded with Tony like this once before, and it hadn't brought her anything but pain. 'I'm trying to help my friends and clear up a miscarriage of justice. Is there any information you have that might help with that?'

Tony shook his head. He leaned in closer to her and lowered his voice, so she had to focus carefully on his words to hear him over the wind. 'They won't tell me anything. I didn't even find out that Phil had been arrested until this morning. I went straight home after the Careers Fair, and I only found out about the arrest when I came on shift.' She could feel his breath on her ear, the only warm point on her freezing body. 'I'm locked out of the computer files on the case, and when I started asking around, I was sent on my break. That's why I'm out here now. Nobody will talk to me about this. The official line is that it's because I was at the college yesterday, where both the victim and the suspect's wife were, but...' He shook his head.

They hadn't spoken in months, yet Arrina still knew what he was thinking.

'But you think it's something else.'

'I'm still under review over what happened this summer.' He didn't say anything more, and he didn't have to. Arrina knew what he was referring to—the murder at the college that he'd investigated and in which Arrina had got far too tangled up for the police's liking. Tony was under review because of what Arrina did.

'I'm sorry for—'

'Don't be. I didn't mean for you to feel bad. I'm just trying to explain why I couldn't stop this. I *can't* stop this. Even though I know...'

He couldn't say that the police were making a mistake. He was too loyal for that. But he leaned away to look at her then, and his eyes told Arrina the truth of what he felt. The wind died down around them. Arrina nodded.

'Perhaps after the fundraiser,' Tony said softly, 'you should...' He cleared his throat. 'You should try...' His dark eyes were locked on hers, and she knew he was trying to say something. 'Maybe you could do what you did this summer.'

Arrina didn't understand. That summer, she'd almost got herself killed by chasing down a murderer in the village. Tony had told her several times not to get involved in the case, and he'd been annoyed when she'd ignored him. But now he seemed to be saying that she *should* get involved. She couldn't ask him to explain, though. He would never come out and say any of this directly. She just had to trust she'd understood him.

'I wish I could help,' Tony said.

She felt the same. The distance between them seemed very small and shrank by the second. A gust of icy wind slipped down Arrina's neck. She stepped away from Tony.

'It's OK,' she said. 'I can do this by myself. I can find out what's happened and prove that Phil is innocent.'

Then, before Tony could say anything else, Arrina turned and walked away.

9

Life in Heathervale revolved around its High Street—one long road of chocolate-box buildings that sold almost everything a person could need. The Horse and Hound pub stood by the green at its end, and as Arrina drove past the pub, she felt a glimmer of excitement at the chalk-board sign announcing the first mulled wine of the season.

She wouldn't have any that day, though. In fact, she couldn't imagine savouring the sweet, Christmas-spiced drink until everything was sorted with Julie and Phil. Arrina hoped that would happen very soon. She drove on down a narrow, hedge-lined road, towards the other main focal point of Heathervale life—the village hall.

The monthly Parish Council meetings were held in the hall. The mood of these shifted from boredom to outrage and back again several times during the course of each evening. The Harvest Festival food drive also used the hall as its base, and that year's selection of donated tins had only recently been parcelled out to the less fortunate in the area. All manner of seasonal events were also held in the large, airy space, including the Easter bonnet competition, the Valentine's tea dance, and the preparations for the well-dressing festival.

However, Arrina's favourite events of the year were those held for Christmas. These started with the Lantern Parade, which was part of a long-standing village tradition. Children carried green and red lanterns through the village, while crowds of onlookers joined in with the carol singing. It was Arrina's idea of a perfect evening.

Before the parade, though, the village held a yearly fundraiser. Arrina looked forward to the fundraiser almost as much as she did to the parade itself. Or at least, she usually did. That afternoon, she was not eager to walk into the crowded hall, which would be filled with the standard bake sale, raffle, and gleeful exchanges of gossip.

Arrina knew there'd only be *one* topic of conversation on everyone's lips that day—Phil. And she also knew her presence there wouldn't stifle these conversations. Instead, chatter would fall to a polite, smiling hush whenever she came close. And the gossiping would start up again in flurried whispers as soon as she walked away.

Arrina did not want to face an entire afternoon of that. But she had to. Julie had worked so hard to set up the internship programme. She'd got funding from the county for it as part of a small-business initiative. Obtaining that funding had entailed a great deal of irate form filling and several calls to Arrina for assistance.

Julie had also talked to Arrina at excited length about the second chances she could give to people who'd fallen out of the world of work. The internship offered a real opportunity to local people who wanted to set up their own businesses. Arrina couldn't let these people down, just like she couldn't fail Julie.

Arrina pulled her XJ6 into the crowded car park behind the village hall. The crisp, clear morning had darkened into a muffled grey afternoon, and her car's distinctive mistral blue paint stood out like a shard of glacier ice against it. Arrina climbed out of her car and paused beside it.

She had been planning to wear her first Christmas outfit of the year to the fundraiser—perhaps a reindeer jumper paired with dark blue jeans, or a beautiful bottle-green dress to set off the hints of red in her hair. But after she'd returned from the police station and showered the cold from her bones, she'd put on a soft black jumper and matching black trousers, which were extraordinarily comfortable, while also looking—she hoped—strong and confident. She'd somewhat mitigated the seriousness of the look by stopping to cuddle Tinsel for a few minutes before leaving. Fine silver hairs covered the outfit, and Arrina could only hope they looked like a quirky festive touch.

Although the day was still freezing and sunless, Arrina left her muddy hiking fleece in her boot. It was bad enough that Tony had seen her in it. She didn't need the whole village to witness that spectacle as well. She would just have to hope that some of the draughts in the village hall had been repaired recently. Otherwise, she would hover around the warm tea urn for even longer than usual.

When she slipped in through the village hall doors, the fundraiser was already in full swing. A cold blast of air pushed in behind her, causing those nearby to turn and look. It was just her luck that Gillian DeViers was standing right there. And beside her were Eleanor Shale and Gertie Cooper. Arrina swallowed hard and forced a smile to her lips.

The three women were trussed up in their usual version of rural clothing—smart jackets and mid-calf-length skirts in various shades of brown tweed. These outfits tried to suggest an authentic pastoral quality that these women did not actually possess. Their dense clots of gold jewellery and frothed up, stiff-set hair made that very clear.

'Arrina,' Gillian said, stepping forwards from the centre of the trio, 'what an... unexpected surprise.'

Arrina's teacher-brain wanted to comment that all surprises were unexpected by their nature, and so the statement was redundant. But instead, she smiled. She knew that Gillian had chosen her words with purpose. 'You know I'd never miss a Christmas event.' Arrina smiled again and made sure to stand up straight, even as she felt the force of Gillian's intense stare.

As it was only mid-November, the full selection of Christmas decorations had not yet been put up in the hall. In fact, a horn of plenty still lay in the corner, which was left over from the recent harvest festival; Halloween bats were pinned to the noticeboard by the stage; and the youth group's wire-sculpture fireworks stood nearby as a reminder of the Bonfire Night just gone. Arrina fixed her gaze on the holly sprigs, tinsel ropes, and paper-cut snowflakes that dotted the room between these autumnal items, taking strength from the small nods to her favourite day.

'Yes,' Gillian said. 'I'm well-aware of your... fondness for the season.' Then she smiled indulgently, as though Arrina were a sticky-fingered child proclaiming her love of cakes and sweets. 'I had thought, though, that the connection between your college and the terrible events of yesterday might cause you to be... unable to attend.'

Arrina had to grind her teeth together tightly and force a smile to her lips to restrain her first, unutterable responses to this statement.

'Not at all,' she said after that pause. 'I am naturally *very* sympathetic towards the family of the poor man who died out on the Yates Farm.' Arrina paused for emphasis. Gillian DeViers and her wealthy set were the only locals the snobbish Yateses had any relationship with. 'However, I'm sure nobody involved would want this important fundraising event to suffer as a consequence.'

Arrina gave another wide smile. She blinked rapidly and tilted her head to one side, the picture of charitable innocence.

'Yes, of course,' Gillian said. The smile she returned was tight and pinched, making deep furrows of the lines around her mouth.

'Sadly, Julie won't be able to attend the event today. I know you two had gone to great lengths to arrange the internship announcement, and Julie sends her sincerest apologies.'

'Now that *is* terribly unfortunate.' Gillian turned to look at the clones on either side of her, who dutifully mirrored her expression of exaggerated pity. 'Though I had rather expected it. In fact, I've already taken dear Julie's name off the running order for—'

'No need,' Arrina interrupted. 'Julie absolutely wouldn't allow your careful planning to be disrupted. She's sent me in her place. I've got all the information from her. I'll be able to make the announcement in her stead without any trouble at all.'

'Well, as I said, I *have* actually taken her out of the programme, and we're just about to get started.'

Arrina's cheeks hurt from her efforts to be polite, and she could hear the strangled note in her voice that hinted that she couldn't keep this up for much longer.

'Right,' Arrina said. 'Then let me save you any trouble—I wouldn't want to cause you any scheduling bother. I'll just hop right up to the stage now, and then I'll let you get on with the rest of your arrangements.'

Gillian's face paled beneath her heavy make-up. 'I really don't think—'

But Arrina was gone before she could hear exactly what Gillian didn't think. Arrina strode to the front of the room and climbed up on the raised platform there. Gillian was frozen between her two cronies at the back of the room, each of them whispering in her ear. Gillian's pale face flushed a bright and festive red.

The microphone was set up in the middle of the stage. Arrina had helped out at enough talent shows, pantomimes, and auctions in the hall to know just how temperamental the sound equipment could be. She was nearly certain she could see Gillian eyeing the control panel for the microphone, but if she touched anything on it now, it would take an hour of squealing adjustment to wrangle the microphone back into working order.

'Good afternoon, ladies and gentlemen,' Arrina said, before Gillian could decide to take the drastic action of turning off the microphone anyway. 'It's wonderful to see so many of you out here for this marvellous cause.'

She looked out across the crowd of people who were squeezed in between the fundraiser's many stalls. The village hall was packed with people that afternoon, and it seemed as though every one of them leaned over in unison and whispered to the person standing next to them.

'I won't take up too much of your time,' she continued, trying not to let her awareness of the gossip shake her. 'I'm sure everyone is keen to get on with the festivities. However, I've been sent here to announce a very important, and incredibly thoughtful, new initiative from everyone's favourite baker, Julie Wen.'

She paused and scanned the crowd. Right then, she couldn't pick out a single friendly face—not over by the white elephant stall or the biscuit-decoration station or even the splat-the-rat game. Arrina leaned away from the microphone and cleared her throat.

'I know you'll all have heard some rumours over the past couple of days,' Arrina started.

'Too right, we have,' came a booming voice from nearby. Arrina looked down at the crowd to try to pick out who was speaking. All she found was a wall of stone-hard faces.

'As I was saying,' she continued, speaking faster now, 'I know you'll have heard some things, but until we have all the facts, it's best to—'

'I've got a fact,' the booming voice said. 'Phil has been charged with the murder of that man who was at your college.'

'The college really isn't—'

'Aye,' joined in another voice from the crowd. 'The police seem pretty certain, and we all know Phil wasn't a fan of the Environment Agency after their investigation of his farm this summer.'

'Seems like motive enough,' said a woman whose voice Arrina was sure she recognised but couldn't put a face to. 'And I've always said—'

'I really think—' Arrina butted in.

'We all know why you're defending that family.'

'And trying to keep your college out of it.'

The voices from the crowd called out from everywhere at once. Arrina's eyes darted around the room, trying to pinpoint who was talking, but she couldn't. She couldn't see any one person she thought could hate Julie and Phil that much.

Then her eyes fell upon the angriest face of them all. It belonged to Victor Stones, who stood against the wall halfway down the hall. The man was the chair of the Board of Governors—the group which oversaw the running of the college—and she was sure he had been the one behind the email telling staff and students to distance themselves from the murder. If looks could kill, Arrina would have been the village's second dead body that week.

Victor's clipped grey moustache twitched so much it looked likely to leap off his face. The buttoned collar of his white shirt stood in very stark relief against his tomato-red cheeks. Arrina was glad a large crowd of people stood between the two of them.

She took a step back from the microphone. A door behind her led to a short, dark corridor, and beyond that was the hall's back door. Arrina glanced over her shoulder at the door and thought of how very close her car was and how quickly she could jump inside it and race along the country lanes to get back to her cottage where she would find Tinsel, Julie's mince pies, and spiced apple tea.

But then she heard more people shouting and saying awful things about Julie and Phil. Arrina knew no better people in all the world than those two. They'd helped her make a home in the village and supported her through every up and down in her life since she'd arrived. They didn't deserve this.

Arrina stepped back up to the microphone and took it from its stand. Then she walked to the edge of the stage, leaned down, and held the microphone against one of the hall's huge speakers.

An almighty shriek of feedback cut through the room, silencing the voices. Everyone's hands flew to their ears. Arrina held the microphone in place for several long seconds then stood up and brought it to her mouth.

'Enough!' she said. 'That's absolutely the last I want to hear today about Julie and Phil and the murder of Kingsley Peters.' She felt her expression tighten into her disappointed-teacher face. It always worked extremely well on misbehaving teens, and it seemed to have the same powerful effect on the roomful of querulous adults before her right then.

She did not look at Victor Stones to see his response. She could imagine it very easily.

'I've had the good fortune to know Julie and Phil for five years now,' Arrina continued. 'But many of you have known them for your whole lives or theirs.' She paused and stared around at the room full of Heathervale residents, giving them a moment to consider this. 'I understand that the police have accused Phil of something awful. But he's our neighbour and our friend, and anyone who knows him should be well aware he'd never do this. Never.'

She left another conspicuous silence in the room, giving anyone who disagreed with her a chance to speak up. When nobody did, she knew that she could move on to the reason she was there.

'I'll hand the stage over to Gillian DeViers very shortly, and we can all get on with raising money for the Lantern Parade. But before then, I want to announce an important initiative from Julie, which, even during this difficult time, she insisted on going ahead with.'

Arrina slotted the microphone back in the stand and spoke with confidence.

'Julie is setting up a dedicated internship for local people in need. It's open to anyone who has fallen out of the world of work and will give that person an excellent chance to get back on their feet. The successful applicant will work side by side with Julie during the busy Christmas season, learning not just the daily operations of a small business but also the more complex financial aspects of running one. The internship is supported by the county, and so it will be well paid, and it will also come with a lump-sum award at the end, which can be used as seed money for a new business.'

The room was silent still, but Arrina saw nods and softened faces, which told her people were taking in what she was saying.

'I, for one, am very impressed by this new initiative, which offers a fantastic opportunity to the more mature residents of the village, who I am not able to reach through my work at the college. Julie has identified a key demographic of people with a specific need, and she has worked hard to serve them well. That is the hallmark of a good businesswoman, and I'm certain that the person who is lucky enough to be accepted as her intern is bound for great success. The application form for this internship can be collected from Do-Re-Mi... and I will also be putting it on the Heathervale College website.'

This last part was something Arrina decided only as she spoke. She flicked her gaze across to Victor Stones to see his reaction. But he was no longer standing at the edge of the hall. Instead, the swinging door at the far end of the room gave her a clue about where he'd gone.

Arrina squared her shoulders, ran her gaze once more across the crowd of people in the room, and dared them to say anything against her closest friends.

10

Arrina's adrenaline kept her heart pounding and her breaths short for several minutes after she got down from the stage. She checked out a few stalls in quick succession, keeping herself busy while she regained the composure she needed that day.

She spotted Nancy Morgan running the tombola and headed over to the girl. Nancy was the youngest of the Morgan clan, though there were rumours that one of her brothers—a pair of identical twins called Wilfred and Wallace—had a secret girlfriend with a baby on the way. Rumours always swirled about the Morgans, however, and so Arrina paid no attention to the story.

Before Arrina could reach Nancy, she was accosted by Fernella Anderson, who called to her from several feet away.

'Oh, Arrina!' Fernella trilled. She had once been a hair's breadth away from becoming a professional opera singer, or so she claimed.

Arrina rerouted and approached the woman, who would likely break into song to get her attention otherwise.

'What a lovely spread,' Arrina said as she approached Fernella's customary spot at the bake sale table. 'It looks like you've had some wonderful contributions.' Arrina pulled her purse out and ran her eye over the selection. The sooner she bought something, the sooner she could be on her way.

'Indeed,' Fernella said. She gazed down at the cakes and gave a theatrical sigh. The broad shelf of her bosom heaved. 'The people of Heathervale are such very generous people.

Very, very generous. Always looking for ways to help their neighbours. Never letting people down.'

Arrina knew the woman wasn't talking about cakes, but she also didn't seem to be talking about Julie and Phil. Then Arrina remembered, and she groaned internally. 'I've actually been meaning to come and speak to you, Fernella. I wanted to say how sorry I am that we couldn't find a place for Perry this year.'

'My Peregrine had his heart set on attending Heathervale College.' Fernella flung one end of her pashmina over her shoulder, looking every bit like the Puccini or Wagner characters she had once played.

Arrina put on her best sympathetic smile and nodded solemnly. She felt sorry for Fernella's son, not only for the awful name his mother had saddled him with but also because of the inflated ego she'd built up in him. The boy had handed his application form in to the college two weeks late, leaving off half the information it asked for, and proudly writing out GCSE grades that were only good for a high-scoring Scrabble game.

He'd waltzed into Arrina's office with the form, dropped it onto her desk, and told her that he was considering a number of options, but he'd still like a place at the college as a backup.

'As I said,' Arrina responded, 'it was unfortunate that we couldn't find him a place, but it was a very competitive cohort this year. I hope he's found somewhere else to continue his studies.' With Fernella's money, the boy had surely found a place willing to take on even *his* abysmal grades.

'Peregrine has realised that he doesn't require any further education,' Fernella said, casually picking up a slice of cake from the table in front of her and taking a bite. 'He's got a keen business mind, and he's not going to waste any further time in classrooms. He's already set up his first company, in fact, and he's got several employees working under him.'

'Oh,' Arrina said. She hadn't heard anything about this, which was odd given the small size of the village and its general fondness for gossip. 'Well, that sounds...' She could only finish the sentence with a friendly nod. 'Good for him.'

'Oh, yes, my Peregrine is just like his father.' Fernella smiled as though this were an excellent thing, and she took another large bite of cake. As far as Arrina knew, though, Fernella's husband had lost all of his own family's money on poorly considered business deals and saved himself from bankruptcy by marrying Fernella, whose wealth far exceeded his own. He worked through a good chunk of her money as well, and only the man's early death had kept Fernella's inheritance from being entirely frittered away. 'Peregrine has got a real nose for business. You know, he's here somewhere if you want to hear more about what he's doing.'

Fernella scanned the draughty hall and pointed at her son. Arrina was glad to find the boy engrossed in conversation with a group of people his own age. Perry was smiling widely, and, Arrina hoped, far too busy to notice her at all. She didn't have the patience for the boy that day.

In case Fernella called Perry over, Arrina planned to start up a discussion on Julie's internship with the ex-opera singer. The programme was aimed at women who had been unemployed long term, which certainly described Fernella. But any suggestion that the internship was applicable to *her* would leave Fernella short of words.

But Fernella didn't call her son over. She merely suggested Arrina say hello to him later. Arrina made a faint noise of agreement and quickly turned her attention to the table full of cakes. She made certain to compliment Fernella's own soggy offering and those of the woman's friends. Then Arrina bought Mrs Pangle's famous Dundee cake, which she knew from experience was well worth the eye-watering price tag. She also picked up a paper plate and contemplated which of the sliced cakes she wanted to enjoy as she walked around the fundraiser. She selected Maggie Lee's lemon drizzle, which was down to its last couple of pieces.

She had messaged Maggie before heading over to the fundraiser to ask if she would check on Julie. Arrina glanced quickly at her phone. Maggie hadn't replied. But she would probably be too busy in the café to check until later.

Arrina spotted a small stack of Julie's ganache-and-dashes at the far end of the table. She headed straight for them.

'Didn't you make those yourself?' Fernella asked as Arrina picked up one of the dark chocolate tartlets. Fernella wrinkled her nose, as though she could imagine no worse transgression than purchasing one's own cake from a bake sale.

Arrina glanced at the label and froze with the irresistible treat halfway between the table and her plate. The tartlet did indeed bear her own name, and she remembered then that Julie had brought the tartlets to the hall the day before and handed them in as Arrina's contribution to the bake sale.

She considered putting it back. But Julie's espresso and dark chocolate tartlets were delicious, and even the worst of days was made a little better by eating them. Arrina definitely needed one right then.

'I'm just heading over to see Nancy Morgan,' she said. 'I promised I'd save her one of these when I made them, but I completely forgot. I'd best take this over to apologise.'

Arrina handed over her money, waited until Fernella's back was turned to get change, and cut the tartlet in two with a nearby knife. She'd give Nancy *half*, so as not to make a liar of herself. But she needed at least a little caffeine-enriched chocolate goodness if she was going to get through the rest of the day.

Just as Arrina turned away, Fernella said something about having recently seen some very similar tartlets in Do-Re-Mi. But Arrina walked off quickly and pretended not to have heard anything. When Arrina reached Nancy, she offered the girl the rest of the tartlet and was extremely pleased when she declined.

'Not while I'm working,' Nancy said. Then she spun the large wooden box that contained the raffle tickets for the tombola stall. Her face was deadly serious as she turned the box, and Arrina covered her fond smile by popping the rest of the tartlet into her mouth. It was nice to be reminded that not all teenagers were like Peregrine Anderson. Even curly-haired Patience, whose 'help' with the signs the day before at the college had tried Arrina's own patience, was good at heart.

'Are you here to try your luck, miss?' Nancy asked, still spinning the wooden box.

Arrina swallowed. 'It's not *miss*, remember?' Arrina asked as brightly as she could. She'd had this same conversation roughly a hundred times since the girl started college that September, but somehow Nancy wasn't getting it.

'Right,' Nancy said, clapping her hand to her forehead. 'We're not in school now, are we?'

'Even when we're there though,' Arrina said, forcing cheeriness into her tone and a smile to her lips. 'Do you remember? It's just *Arrina*. At the college, you need to call teachers by their names.'

Nancy nodded slowly, clearly unconvinced. She tugged at one of her messy plaits. Then she flipped the hair over her shoulder and returned to spinning the wooden drum full of raffle tickets. 'So, do you feel lucky today?'

Arrina thought about doing a Dirty Harry impression, but she didn't want to confuse the sweet young girl any further. Instead, she fished a pound coin out of her purse and handed it to Nancy.

'You're looking for a number ending in a zero or a five,' Nancy said. She glanced over her shoulder at the array of prizes on offer, each of which had a raffle ticket stuck to them. The tickets up there did indeed all end in zero or five, and Nancy turned back and nodded to herself. 'You get three tries.'

Nancy opened a slot in the top of the box, and Arrina dipped her hand inside. She pulled out a pair of tickets and looked at them, but neither was a winner.

'Don't worry,' said Nancy, leaning over to Arrina and squinting hard at her tickets. 'You get one more try.' She shut the slot and twirled the box of tickets around. 'I'll give you an extra spin for luck.'

'Thank you, Nancy. I think I need all the luck I can get.'

Then the young woman opened the slot again and held up crossed fingers to show Arrina just how much she was hoping for a prize.

But this ticket wasn't a winner either.

'Oh,' Nancy said sadly. 'I really thought you'd get one. Do you want to try again? There's a really great set of Christmas lights up there—all sparkly and twinkly—and as soon as I saw them, I thought of you. Because of how much you love Christmas, you know?'

'That's very thoughtful,' Arrina said. 'But I think—'

'Really. Just one more go would do it, I'm sure. I'll give the box a really good spin and—'

'It's best as we let Arrina get on,' said a voice from the shadows. Arrina snapped her eyes over in its direction and was surprised to see Sampson Morgan standing there. He was the head of security at the college and also Nancy's uncle. A desire to look after the sweet girl must have brought him to the fundraiser that day—he normally gave village events a wide berth.

Sampson was dressed in his usual work clothes—sturdy black trousers and a dark-green shirt. Like many others in the hall, he also had a Remembrance Day poppy pinned to his outfit. The red flower on the green shirt looked almost festive, and Arrina wondered whether he'd worn the combination on purpose.

Arrina smiled gratefully at Sampson as he encouraged his niece to find some other customers. Arrina loved her students dearly, but they were very young and enthusiastic, and right then, she didn't have enough energy for Nancy by a long way.

Nancy didn't argue with her uncle. She simply followed his suggestion and stepped away to accost another passerby with her call of 'care to try your luck?'

'Thank you,' Arrina said. A wave of exhaustion passed through her. It really *was* time for her to be getting on. The effort of presenting a strong front before the whole of the village was very draining.

Sampson nodded. 'And so's you know, I've had to let the police into the college. Just the hall, mind. They poked about but didn't find nowt.'

'Right,' Arrina said. She'd known the police would have to come to the college, and yesterday, the thought had filled her with dread. But there, in the village hall, she was too tired to feel anything. She knew how much Sampson hated dealing with the police, though, so she thanked him before turning towards the door.

'Afore you go,' Sampson said in a low voice, stepping closer to Arrina, 'I've to gi' you summat.'

He rummaged in his pocket and pulled out a small, well-sanded piece of wood. Arrina took it and looked at it but had no idea what it was.

'It's fer Julie,' Sampson said with a nod. 'Our Sylvie made it.'

Arrina turned the small oval of wood over and over in her fingers. The piece was about the size of her thumb and had twists and spirals carved into it. Arrina had admired many of Sylvie's beautiful wooden sculptures on display in

Present and Correct, the gift and stationery shop on the High Street. But she'd never seen anything like this.

'Thank you,' Arrina said. 'I'm sure Julie will be very... grateful.'

Sampson reached out and took it from Arrina. Then he spread her hand flat and set the small piece of wood in its centre. 'Now close yer fingers.'

Arrina did as instructed. The carved oval settled into her palm just like her tongue nestled home against the roof of her mouth. She felt instantly calm and rested as she held it, and her breaths grew long and relaxed. 'What is it?'

'It don't really have a name,' Sampson said. 'We Morgans all carry one. They're made from a tree in our woods.' He reached into his pocket again and pulled out a darker, smoother version of the piece of wood Arrina held. 'Sylvie's the only one as can make 'em now. She calls 'em *heart woods*, though others call 'em different things. She wants Julie to have this 'un.'

Arrina nodded and thanked Sampson. She knew Julie would be touched to receive this small, precious talisman from Sylvie Morgan. The Morgans knew well enough what it was to be treated with suspicion in Heathervale. They'd been in the village as long as any of the old families. But they lived off the land and their wits. Many in the area thought them uncivilised because they made their home in the woods. Not Arrina, though. She'd seen often enough how much the Morgans really knew about the world.

'Mebee you might go gi' it to her right about now.' Sampson nodded at the door. Arrina turned and expected to see her good friend standing there. But of course, she wasn't.

Then Arrina heard a squealing from the speakers, and she looked at the stage. Up there, Gillian DeViers was getting ready to address the crowd. She was wearing one of her frostier expressions and glaring down at Arrina, who suddenly realized why Sampson was suggesting she leave.

'Good idea,' Arrina said. 'Say thank you to Sylvie. I'll see you at the college tomorrow.'

Then she strode out of the room, departing to the less-than-musical strains of Gillian's voice.

The last thing she heard was 'Victor Stones was *supposed to be here with me today. However...*' And Arrina was out of the hall before she found out exactly how many things Gillian could blame on her without directly saying her name.

She swung the dense but delicious Dundee cake from her wrist, carried a slice of lemon drizzle on a plate, and had one hand wrapped tightly around the heart wood that Sylvie Morgan had made.

For a day that had started out so abysmally, things seemed to be going OK. And, even better than that, now that the Lantern Parade fundraiser was underway, the countdown to Christmas had officially started.

11

Arrina strode out of the village hall with a strength she'd forgotten she contained. She had stood up to Gillian DeViers, and she'd also fulfilled her promise to announce Julie's internship in front of the whole village. She headed back to her cottage to wait for Julie's call with good news about Phil. And she waited and waited, but the call never came.

Arrina tried Julie's number several times, but the call went straight to voicemail. That wasn't uncommon in the countryside, where phone signal came and went with the wind, yet that night, a screw tightened in Arrina's chest with every unanswered call. She considered ringing Julie's parents. But she couldn't worry them. Mrs Wen's health got worse by the day, and Arrina couldn't add to the stress of that.

Julie had promised to call when there was news. Arrina clung to this thought as the hours ticked by. She distracted herself by writing to-do lists, scouring local news websites, and drinking more cups of tea than even *she* thought possible. Finally, late into the evening, Julie sent a message:

> *I couldn't get in to see him today, but I found out where he is. I'm visiting tomorrow. They said I need to wait a few days, but I'm going down there. Cross fingers and toes for me.*

Arrina pictured Julie scaling sheer prison walls with a grappling hook or bribing guards with mountains of cake. There was nothing she wouldn't do. Arrina planned and planned with the same dedication, making notes of how she would get Phil free. She sat in her kitchen, cold and hunched, until the early hours of the morning. Then she finally stumbled to bed for a fitful night of sleep.

Arrina was woken up by a buzzing against her forehead. The sound came from her phone, which soon increased its efforts to rouse her by playing the theme tune from *The Archers*. Her dry, tired eyes felt like Velcro as they opened. She answered the call as she struggled free from the tangle of her sheets. 'Hello?'

'Hello there,' came a bright reply that felt utterly out of place in her dark, chilly room. 'I'm just wondering if you're perhaps still planning to join us today?' The soft Scottish accent was easily recognisable as belonging to Linda, the head of chemistry at the college. But Arrina couldn't put the woman's question into any sort of context. There was no assembly planned, and Arrina never arranged meetings for Mondays, when everyone was stuck between their weekend and working selves.

'I've marked myself as working from home today.' Or at least, Arrina thought she had. She remembered meaning to do it, anyway, though she couldn't entirely recall logging into the college system the night before to do so.

'Aye, of course. You've a lot going on. It's just, with the interview this morning, I thought you might... Well, the Board of Governors has emailed the three of us to send feedback once we've seen the candidate.'

Arrina sat up. 'The interview!' She'd completely forgotten someone was coming in that morning to interview for a job at the college. It was a woman applying for the long-vacant position in the chemistry department. Arrina's mind scrambled for ways to push the interview back. But the board had told her last week that the substitute budget was coming to an end and that she either needed to hire a full-time teacher or cancel classes. The woman coming today was Arrina's only hope of avoiding that second, unacceptable option.

But still, she couldn't interview a chemistry teacher while her friend was sitting in prison, wrongly accused of murder.

Then Arrina thought over what Linda had just said. The Board of Governors had emailed the *three* of them. Three people were on the hiring committee for this position—Arrina, Linda, and Bill. And Bill wasn't just a teacher at the college. He was also Bill *Yates*, a member of the family who owned the farm above Phil and Julie's. That farm was where Phil had been working on Saturday, and it was also where Kingsley's body had been found later that same day.

Arrina told Linda she'd be right in, then she scrambled to shower and dress and make herself faintly presentable. After feeding Tinsel, Arrina decanted the dregs of last night's teapot, put it in the microwave, and then swallowed down a truly awful cup of tea. That didn't matter, though. She finally had a lead. She drove as quickly as she dared over the icy roads to the college. Bill was just what she was looking for. He would surely be able to help her on her quest to free Phil.

He *had to*, Arrina thought, as she pressed down harder on her accelerator. He was the only hope she had.

12

Arrina parked her car at the front of the college. Today was more of a day for sneaking in quickly from the back—avoiding anyone who wanted to chat about class schedules, submit equipment orders, or make yet another request for Wi-Fi at the college. But the car park there would have filled up hours earlier, so she had no choice.

She checked the time—it was OK, there was still a little time before the interview. Even better, it was the middle of a lesson period, so nobody would interrupt her purposeful stride along the corridors as she went to speak to Bill Yates. Or at least, Arrina hoped so.

However, as she passed her office—ignoring the siren call of comfy sofa, teapot, and bottom-drawer ginger biscuits—someone stopped her. The girl had been pressed into the doorframe, and her sudden presence took Arrina by yelping surprise. It was a moment before she recognised the long plaits and young-looking face of Nancy Morgan, who'd run the tombola stall with such care the afternoon before.

'It weren't me that did it, miss,' Nancy said, her voice quivering and tears threatening to roll down her red cheeks. 'I just found it like this and thought… and thought…'

Then the sobs overcame her, and Arrina followed the girl's pointing finger to the wall.

New murals had been painted all along this corridor at the start of the school year. They depicted scenes from local life. The ones Nancy pointed at showed seasonal celebrations in Heathervale—spring maypole dancing, summer well dressing, an autumn harvest festival, and a winter Lantern Parade.

But something wasn't right about the people watching these events. Arrina leaned in closer and inspected the small, well-painted people who lined the High Street in one of the scenes. Then she saw what Nancy was pointing at and what had got her so upset.

All the tiny, unique people in the murals had stickers on their faces—red, smiling lips that parted around cartoon-white teeth. Arrina gasped. She stepped back and looked around. The caricatured grinning lips were everywhere, stuck to each of the murals' small, delicate faces.

Arrina couldn't believe someone would do that. The murals were beautiful. How could someone want to disfigure them like this?

'It's awful,' Nancy said. 'I know how much you like these pictures, and someone's spoiled them.' She sniffed heavily and wiped her face.

'Who did it?' Arrina asked faintly.

Nancy shook her head and looked grief stricken that she couldn't provide the answer Arrina needed. But she was the niece of the college's security head. Even if *everyone* in the building knew who'd defaced these murals, nobody would whisper a hint to Nancy.

Arrina reached out to peel off one of the stickers. She got her nail under an edge and pulled, but the flimsy paper tore in an instant. She tried again. White paper backing stuck fast, and just a sliver of the smile came away. Arrina rubbed at the remains of the sticker. It loosened, and then the paint underneath chipped, and a piece of it fell from the wall.

'No!' Arrina cried. She touched the white spot in the mural that she'd made. Half of an old man's face was missing.

Tears welled up in Arrina's eyes. She loved these murals. They'd been created to celebrate the end of a difficult summer just gone. Arrina felt terrible for the painter too. He was a student at the college, and he'd thought so hard about the designs and worked diligently to get them ready for the start of term. He was hoping to go to art school at the end of that year, and the murals were a big part of his portfolio.

She traced her fingers over the beautiful, detailed paintings that Olly had created. She wanted to go into her office to find the boy's schedule—she should speak to him about this and make sure he was OK.

Arrina looked down at her watch. Several minutes had already passed since she'd arrived at the college. She didn't have time for this. But she couldn't just walk away.

'Do you know Olly?' Arrina asked, turning back to face Nancy. 'He's the blue-haired boy in the year above you.' Arrina thought the girl's face blushed even redder as she nodded.

'I'm in his coursework movie,' Nancy added. A shy smile crept to her lips. 'We're filming the fight scene at lunch.'

Arrina's feet were already itching for her to take off. She hesitated at the mention of this fight scene. But *Olly* was organising it. She knew for certain that he was a good kid, and she did her very best not to worry about whatever his newest artwork involved.

'Can you tell him that I'm very sorry someone's done this? I'll have it fixed as soon as I can. Tell him not to worry.' In fact, Arrina realised that Olly might quite enjoy that someone had stuck the smiles on his paintings. He was always trying to push boundaries and try new things in his art—he'd probably take the defacing in his stride and see it as engagement with the piece. Arrina didn't feel nearly as positive—there was a vandal in the college, and she didn't know who. Plus, she *loved* those murals. Looking at them was often the only point of calm in her busy workday.

Nancy played with one messy plait and promised to pass on Arrina's message.

'Can you also tell your uncle to get the maintenance crew to fix this and ask him to... to find out who's responsible?' She bit back the harsher words about what she wanted Sampson to do to the vandal. Arrina started to walk away then stopped and turned. 'Thank you for waiting here to tell me about this. It was a very thoughtful thing to do, and I appreciate it.'

The girl puffed up with pride, tossing a plait over her shoulder and squaring her narrow shoulders. Arrina allowed herself a moment of pleasure at the sight, and then she was off, racing towards the staffroom where she was sure she'd find Bill Yates.

13

Bill Yates was a creature of routine. On Monday mornings, he eased into the week with three straight periods of essay marking in the staffroom, drinking awful instant coffee from a plain white mug, and eating precisely two plain digestive biscuits at eleven on the dot. Bill was a single man with no pets and no children. As far as Arrina knew, his main hobby was collecting antique maps. She had no idea why he needed such a quiet start to his week, and she'd never quite wanted to ask.

The reason didn't matter right then. All that mattered was that Bill would be in the staffroom as always. Only, when Arrina burst into the room, he wasn't sat in his usual seat. The mountain of essays lay stacked on the table, and a half-drunk cup of coffee was beside it along with the waiting pair of biscuits, but Bill wasn't there.

Instead, he stood over at the noticeboard—a rectangle of chipped cork that usually bore sign-up sheets for college activities, invitations to book groups and aerobics classes, and passive-aggressive notes about washing-up fairies. That morning, only a single piece of paper was pinned on the thing, and Bill was staring at it.

Arrina had a sinking feeling—if something had pulled Bill Yates from his routine, it had to be big, and in Arrina's life at the moment, big just seemed to mean awful.

The piece of paper on the noticeboard was tacked up with four neatly placed pins. The notice was perfectly placed in the very centre of the empty space. At first, Arrina thought that Bill himself had put it there. But then she recognised it.

It was the email that the Board of Governors had sent out on Saturday night. The one telling all staff and students to keep well clear of anyone or anything connected to the murder of Kingsley Peters. The one that Arrina had ignored so very conspicuously as she'd stood on stage at the Lantern Parade fundraiser the day before and publicly defended Julie and Phil.

At the top of the page, a large, hand-written note had been added in heavy black pen: *This notice is for* all *staff at the college. Disregarding the official policy outlined in this email will have serious consequences.*

Arrina knew immediately who had written it—Victor Stones. The retired GP had a natural doctor's scrawl, which turned into shaky block letters when he tried to be neat. Arrina read the note again, thought for a second, and then reached up and ripped it off the board. If Victor Stones wanted to threaten her, he'd have to do it to her face.

Bill turned to stare at her. She'd expected him to look shocked, or perhaps even disapproving. But instead, he simply smiled.

'My father has a favourite quote,' Bill said, as he and Arrina sat down beside his towering stack of essays. 'It's from Abraham Lincoln: "Character is like a tree and reputation like a shadow."'

Most conversations with Bill started in a similarly confusing way, and Arrina usually interrupted to bring Bill around to the thing she had to discuss. But that morning, he'd started in just the right place. 'I actually wanted to ask about your father.'

'He says that even a small tree can cast a long shadow, so we ought always to be aware of our reputation's reach.' Bill nodded at Arrina, as though this was a perfectly reasonable response to what she'd just said. 'However, he's missing the second half of the quotation. "The shadow is what we think of it; the tree is the real thing."'

Arrina forced herself to breathe. There was usually a thread to Bill's line of thinking, but she wasn't sure she had the patience to hunt for it then.

'The Board of Governors is like my father.' Bill adjusted the pile of essays on the table while Arrina tugged his ideas into some sort of sense in her brain.

'They care more for reputation than character,' Arrina said.

'Indeed.'

She ran her eyes over Bill's thick, brown cardigan, his large glasses, and his fine, shaggy hair. She could imagine how his family regarded him. 'As I said, I do actually want to speak with you about your father before we go into the interview. About your whole family, in fact. Well, more about their land and what happened there this weekend.' She didn't add, *About the murder there*. She couldn't bring herself to say those words in the staffroom with its everyday smell of instant coffee in the air.

'My father called upon me at home yesterday,' Bill said.

Arrina glanced down at her watch. They didn't have long before the interview. 'Did he tell you anything about what happened?'

'He informed me that Phil came to him at the end of summer asking for work. My father had the impression that Phil was in rather dire financial straits, as he was offering to do any work at all which my father needed, at any hour of the day or night. My father took up this opportunity and asked Phil to do several tasks for him.'

Julie hadn't mentioned that to Arrina, and in fact, she'd been confused when Phil told the police that he was volunteering on the Yates family's land, given the relationship between the two families. Now it seemed that he wasn't volunteering but working there. Phil had lied to Julie.

'On an estate the size of my father's,' Bill continued, 'there is always work to be done, and good help is hard to find. That's how my father explained it, anyway. That's the closest he could come to demonstrating sympathy for a neighbour. He considers displays of emotion to be vulgar.' Bill pursed his lips. 'He was also rather discreet when talking about the work Phil was doing on Saturday in that far corner of the land. It's a section of the estate that my family prefers to keep out of sight and out of mind.'

He didn't add anything to this, and so Arrina was forced to ask what he meant.

'Nobody speaks of it openly, but that corner is known as a…' He cleared his throat and adjusted the pile of essays again. 'Well, as a place of some disrepute. Illicit activities and so forth.' He shifted in his seat and rearranged his long limbs like an umbrella folding away. 'People meet up there for business that cannot be conducted in the open.'

Arrina saw Bill strain to explain what actually happened there. His features were pinched tightly as he tried to find the words to explain. But he couldn't. Arrina was starting to get an idea, though. Even a quaint village like Heathervale had its secrets and its illegal activities.

'My father asked Phil to put up barbed wire fences around the area as well as signs to scare away trespassers. That's what he was doing there that day. Phil had estimated the work would be completed by noon that day, although nobody actually saw him leave. It's an isolated spot which is near his own land, so it was assumed that Phil simply went home when the work was finished. According to my father, that was their usual practice, and Phil invoiced him weekly for the work completed.'

Bill's explanation of Phil's work made sense, but Arrina still had no idea why Phil hadn't told his wife what he was doing.

'And Kingsley?' Arrina asked. 'What was he doing there?'

Bill shook his head. 'My father didn't know.'

Arrina considered what Bill had just told her about that patch of land and why people usually went there—illicit activities. That could mean a lot of different things. Her mind spun with possibility at what that meant about Kingsley. 'Could your father have been... less than honest about that?'

Bill shook his head. 'My father is a discreet man, but I know him well enough to tell if he's lying.'

After a knock on the door, a round head popped around the corner. It belonged to Linda, the short, Scottish chemistry teacher, who very politely asked if Arrina and Bill wouldn't mind possibly, maybe, if it was no bother at all, coming to meet the waiting interview candidate.

'Yes, of course,' said Arrina. 'We're just on our way.'

As she and Bill walked over to the interview together, Arrina leaned towards him and asked, 'Why did your father come to your house to tell you all that?'

Bill's faint eyebrows lowered into a frown. 'He asked me to leave my position here. He insisted the scandal of the death on our land was already too great, and to have me work in a place with further connection to the murder was unthinkable.'

Arrina almost stumbled over her own feet. She couldn't lose Bill. He was one of the best teachers in the college, and he helped out in innumerable small ways around the place. She'd already been searching for two months for a chemistry teacher. She didn't want to start a hunt for a geography teacher as well.

'I told him the matter was not up for discussion,' he continued. 'I would never consider leaving my position here, and I certainly wouldn't entertain the notion in order to save my father from social embarrassment.'

Then, before Arrina could reply, he ducked through the doorway to the room where the interview candidate was waiting. Bill greeted the woman with his usual stiff formality, but underneath that, Arrina could see the fiery passion of a man who stood up for his beliefs. She hoped that passion included giving her any future information she might need about his family that would help her get Phil free.

14

The interview was likely to be a fast one. When Arrina, Linda, and Bill had received the woman's CV the week before, they'd wanted to put it in the reject pile. But by then, they were too desperate to have a reject pile, so they'd called her in. The almost two-decade-long stretch on her CV with nothing but occasional part-time or substitute teaching hadn't filled them with hope.

Arrina assumed they'd go through the motions of an interview without finding any reason to justify hiring her. As much as Arrina wanted to sort out the chemistry teacher shortage, she was also eager to get away from the college and get on with freeing Phil.

However, when Dee walked in that morning, Arrina was instantly impressed by her attitude. She'd been out of full-time teaching for several years while raising four kids. But she was eager and dedicated, and Arrina was sure she'd work hard and catch up with any training she needed.

Bill and Linda didn't seem so convinced. They questioned Dee's ability to retrain, to keep up, and to fit back in with a workplace.

'All I can say is, I'll try my best,' Dee said. 'I always face up to a challenge. I've got four teenagers at home. It might look as though I've been out of teaching, but for the past eighteen years, I've helped with homework, dealt with difficult behaviour, and done it all with a smile on my face. I'm confident I'll be able to do a good job here, if you give me the opportunity.'

'I'm sure you will,' Arrina said. Then she stood up with a sharp scrape of her chair, extended her hand, and asked if Dee could start next week.

She could feel Bill and Linda's shocked eyes on her. They were supposed to discuss this afterwards as a group and give feedback to the Board of Governors before making any decision. But Arrina didn't have the patience for that today. She simply thanked Dee, asked Linda to notify the board of the decision, and left the room.

Arrina and Julie had spoken a lot lately about helping people back into work after a break. Julie had many customers who struggled to overcome that hurdle, and her experiences with them had inspired her to set up an internship. Arrina would do anything for Julie. Right then, she still wasn't sure how to get her friend's husband free. But it felt good to continue Julie's mission of helping people back into work, even if the Board of Governors would disapprove of it.

In the corridor, Arrina allowed herself to pause and take a deep breath.

She had hired a chemistry teacher, dealt with Victor's irritating notice, and assigned people to fix the murals, find the vandal, and comfort Olly. She'd also spoken to Bill, who had told her everything he knew about what had happened on his family's land that Saturday.

Bill hadn't told her who the real killer was. Arrina had secretly been crossing her fingers he knew who it was. But he'd given her plenty to think about—Phil had been desperate enough for money that he'd approached the head of the Yates family and begged for work. Also, the corner where Kingsley's body had been found was a place of secrets and illegal activities. Arrina had no idea what Kingsley had been doing out there, but it couldn't have been anything good.

She walked down the corridor, and, when she reached a turning, she took it. She paced around the college at random, taking advantage of the quiet during the last ten minutes of the lesson period. Arrina often liked to do this when she had something to think about. The corridors were long and wide—designed for mass movements of boisterous teens but also ideal for someone who processed their thoughts by moving their feet.

If Arrina was ever *really* stuck on something, she would head through the back exit of the college and continue walking across the farmland there, up over hills, and as far as she needed to go to solve the issue in her head. But she wouldn't do that today. Thoughts of Kingsley drew her feet to the last place she'd seen him—the hall.

Kingsley had been in her college just a couple of days earlier. But she didn't know anything about him. Or at least, not enough to solve his murder. Arrina scanned her mind for every fact she knew about the man.

Kingsley had a picture of himself with a smiling blonde woman on his phone, a woman Arrina was almost certain was his wife. He was an Environment Agency Officer who'd worked local cases and didn't care much for farmers. Arrina searched her brain for anything else. He'd worked on the Drabble case. She was grasping at straws when she pulled up the fact that he drank coffee, or at least he had done so the morning she met him.

That wasn't enough. The only other hope of finding clues about him lay on the other side of the hall doors. Kingsley had been there—right *there* in her college for the Careers Fair. And he'd left suddenly, without packing up his stall.

When she'd seen Sampson at the fundraiser the day before, he'd told her that the police had been to the college. They'd poked through Kingsley's belongings but hadn't found anything.

Arrina wasn't sure she could find anything that the police had missed, but she had to try. She glanced up and down the corridor—suddenly sure that Victor Stones and the rest of the Board of Governors would be standing there, waiting to catch her disobeying their instructions to stay away from the murder. But the hallway was empty, and Arrina headed in.

She could tell them she was looking for her lost coat if they caught her there. But as she strode across the hard floor, her heels sending up a clatter of echoes, she knew she wouldn't bother with this lie. She was there to help Phil and Julie, and she would turn her hardest teacher-stare on anyone who questioned her for that.

She did, in fact, glance around the space for her warm winter coat, which was new that year, but she saw no sign of it. She made a mental note to check in lost property. Then she scanned the rest of the hall. The room was empty except for a single booth at the far end. It was Kingsley's table, with everything just as he'd left it.

Not *exactly* as he'd left it, Arrina saw as she walked over to it. The table was messier than it had been when she'd last seen it. The police had rifled through the leaflets there and moved things around. That seemed to be the extent of their investigation. There was no fingerprint dust and no crime-scene tape to keep people away.

The police must be convinced they'd got the right man in Phil, as they weren't looking hard for another suspect. Arrina knew they'd got the wrong man, though, so she went over the items in the booth carefully. She leafed through details of rural legislation and images of damaged farms. She glanced behind posters about recent court cases, including the Drabble one that she and Kingsley had spoken about.

Nothing there quite counted as evidence, though. Of course, there *must* have been people who disliked Kingsley—she could see the many posters around of the farmers he'd fined or helped put in prison, including the father of the red-headed Drabble tribe. But nobody stood out as more likely to hurt him than the rest.

Arrina found a book of newspaper clippings of the cases he'd worked on—it was richly bound and had his name stamped into the cover in smart, dark-green lettering. Kingsley had presumably brought this to show the students the sort of work he did at the Environment Agency.

Arrina flicked through it, seeing just how many cases he'd been involved with. He really had done a lot to protect the environment of the Peak District. Even if he had seemed a little untrustworthy, he'd also done a lot of good. He hadn't deserved to be killed in some lonely corner of a field.

She ran her eyes across several of the articles. Kingsley had rescued animals, protected rivers and trees, and put damaged fields under government ownership. The clippings in there went back years. This tome must have covered his whole life. Everything important he'd done, all neatly cut out and bound in a single book. Arrina flicked to the recent articles, and she was glad not to find any mention of Julie and Phil's farm there. Perhaps she could show this book to the police and convince them that others had better motive than Phil to hurt Kingsley.

She hoped for a name that would stand out. But then she found something perhaps even more useful. It was a clipping from *The Longnor Gazette*—the local paper from a village at the bottom end of the Peak District, not more than half an hour away. The clipping was a profile of Kingsley written earlier in the year, and it said he lived in that very village! Arrina peered at the grainy photo that went with the article. The laughing blonde woman from Kingsley's phone was with him again. The caption confirmed she was his wife.

Arrina felt awful for the woman. Her husband had not been very honourable in life, and now he'd been murdered in a place connected with the sort of illicit activities Arrina didn't even want to think about.

But the pity soon slipped away beneath a tide of excitement that she had another lead. If she could find out more about Kingsley, she might be able to solve the case. And if he and his wife lived in Longnor, learning more about him wouldn't be hard. The village had been a bustling market town once and still had a charming cobbled square and a grand brick hall from the Victorian era. But it wasn't busy anymore. Its population was only a few hundred people, and Arrina was certain she could easily find Kingsley's wife among them.

Arrina clutched the expensively bound book of newspaper clippings and walked out of the hall. She would take the book to Kingsley's wife. It had obviously been important to Kingsley, so Arrina was doing a good thing by returning it.

A small grumble from deep in her gut told her that this wasn't a nice thing to do. The woman was a grieving widow, and Arrina wasn't exactly a mourner going to pay her respects. But she couldn't worry about that. Not with Phil's freedom on the line and with it, Julie's future happiness. No, Arrina had to push aside her sense of discomfort and do what needed to be done.

Arrina raced through the corridors of the college just as the bell sounded the end of the lesson. She ran past open-mouthed students, many of whom she'd shouted at for running in the corridors themselves. But she didn't have time to stop and set a good example that day. She had a lead. She had a chance to help Phil.

15

Arrina had visited the village of Longnor before. She and Julie liked to take summertime day trips there when their own tourist-friendly village was overwhelmingly busy. She remembered Longnor as a golden, glowing hamlet, resting in a nest of green and embraced by a gently trickling brook.

As she drove towards it now, though, she barely recognised the place. A deep frost gripped every tree and field, icing over any trace of colour in the world. Longnor had faded into white and grey. Arrina blinked hard as she drove, trying to clear her eyes of the pale haze that blinded them.

She reached the bridge that crossed the Cound Brook. On their first visit there, Julie had told her of the White Lady of Longnor—a jilted bride who was said to haunt the crossing and throw herself into the water as people passed by. Arrina slowed to a crawl. She saw no ghostly bride there, only slick, treacherous ice. Though in the harsh world of white, Arrina wasn't sure she'd see the woman anyway.

The Cound Brook covered over any sound the White Lady might have made as well. What Arrina had previously seen as a lazy summer stream was now a torrent of snowmelt. Its roar pounded through Arrina's windows and made her shiver in her seat.

She parked in the centre of the village and got out into the world of ice. The freezing air bit through her thin clothes, and Arrina wished she'd tracked down her coat before leaving the college.

The cold air also chilled the optimism she felt about following this lead. Was it really OK to visit Kingsley's widow under the pretence of returning a book? Surely, the police would have spoken to the woman already. What more could Arrina find that they hadn't?

Arrina thought about dialling the number stored as DO NOT CALL on her phone—Tony Mellor's number. Perhaps he could tell her what the police had got from the widow. But Tony would never give out confidential information like that. And besides, he'd told her the day before that he was being kept out of the investigation. He wouldn't know anything. Arrina's only option to learn more was to speak to the woman herself.

She shivered in the ice-white world, the fog of her own breath the only sign of movement in the hibernating village. The pale streets were utterly deserted, with nobody around to ask about Kingsley.

There was a pub and a café in the village, though, just like in Heathervale and every other small Peak District village. She could ask in either of those places. But Arrina had been there with Julie and shared good food and long conversations that hovered like ghosts she didn't want to disturb. It would hurt to go inside those places and be reminded of that summertime Julie, who had become as bleak as this winter day.

Arrina turned towards the Longnor Village Store. With its walls of hand-chiselled stones that hugged large, plate-glass windows, it looked like something plucked out of a history book. This store seemed the sort of place that would be run by a single old lady in drooping stockings and a faded, flowery apron. But Arrina had lived in the Peak District long enough to know this wouldn't be the case. For little shops to survive in these villages, they had to keep up with the times. Indeed, as she walked closer, she saw posters in the window for a cashback service, electronic bill payments, and an e-reader lending library.

The thickly painted door swung open with the tinkle of a bell, and Arrina stepped through it. Her eyes took a moment to adjust from the bright white outside to the dim golden glow of the shop. When her vision cleared, she realised she was looking straight at someone. She hopped back in surprise. She was even more shocked when she felt a flicker of recognition as she looked at the person in front of her.

'Can I help you?' asked a bright-eyed woman who looked about Arrina's age but whose rainbow-striped tights and bright yellow dress were unlike anything Arrina would ever wear. 'My name's Ophelia, and whatever you need, I can get it for you. Unless it's the sun, that is. I think it's on an extended holiday.'

Arrina blinked again. She didn't know where she'd seen this woman before, but she couldn't shake the sense of recognition. The only Ophelia she knew was in Shakespeare's Hamlet. Surely, she'd remember meeting a real-life person with that unusual name. This woman's chirpy demeanour, too, was something Arrina wouldn't easily forget.

Then her mind flashed to the picture on Kingsley's phone and in the grainy photo in the newspaper clipping she'd just seen. The huge smile and golden blonde hair in the photos matched this woman in the shop.

Was this that woman? Was this Kingsley's widow?

No. It couldn't be. Kingsley had died just two days earlier. The man's wife wasn't working in a corner shop, dressed like a toddler given free rein over her outfit, and smiling like she didn't have a care in the world.

'Tea,' Arrina stammered, buying herself time to think and make sense of what she saw.

'You've come to the right place,' Ophelia said. 'We've got a great selection.'

She led Arrina to the far side of the room. This single room was the only shop in the village, and it stocked all manner of necessities, from eggs and milk to birthday cards and sunglasses. There was also, Arrina was astounded to find, a whole wall given over to tea. The area Ophelia walked to was stacked high with tea in boxes, in bags, and even loose in jars that were labelled with names like Morning Frill, Peppered Lords, and Ladies in Waiting.

'Most folks think a place like this will just have a dusty box of PG Tips,' Ophelia continued, straightening the display. 'But those in the know come for miles to get something new or to pick up an old favourite.' Her singsong voice was the type Arrina herself used only when talking to very young children. She felt strangely comforted now to hear it talk through the many varieties of tea the small shop stocked. 'We've got a lovely young Darjeeling. Or there's this English rose, which looks beautiful and isn't too fragrant. And if it's a floral blend you're looking for, this new afternoon tea has got some delicious jasmine undertones.'

Arrina stood and listened while she ran her eyes across the display. There were small brown bags tied up with yellow ribbons, huge glass jars with crisp twists of dried leaves, and wooden boxes with slide-open lids that promised treasure. She couldn't believe she'd never heard of this place before. The tiny supermarket in Heathervale was nothing like this. That place's tea supply was crammed onto the end of the cereal shelf, and the owner considered it an extravagance to offer two varieties. Arrina had to restock her own tea cupboard on visits to the nearby cities of Manchester and Sheffield. How had she never been in here?

She thought of her tea cupboard carefully then, comparing its contents with the astounding array in front of her. She could see a box of Ceylon orange pekoe that she'd recently run out of and an elderflower Earl Grey that looked tempting.

'Now let me guess…' said Ophelia, running her eyes up and down Arrina slowly. 'I reckon you're a lapsang sort of lady. Am I right?'

Arrina glanced at the woman's eager grin, startled once again by the hint of familiarity. The jolt reminded her that she wasn't in Longnor that day to buy tea. She had a job to do. Arrina focused on her real reason for being there and came up with a plan.

'You're close,' Arrina said with a smile. 'I do like lapsang, but Russian Caravan tea is my favourite.'

'Oh,' said Ophelia with another mega-watt smile. 'You like a little oolong and Keemun in there. That's a great blend!'

Arrina returned the beam as best she could. She glanced over at the tea wall and then back at Ophelia, wishing she could find a more natural way to move the conversation on.

'So,' she started slowly, 'I suppose you must know the favourite teas of everyone in the village.'

Ophelia nodded, and her blonde hair bounced and swished.

'That's great. I could actually really use your help choosing a gift for someone who lives here.'

The woman's smile grew even wider.

'I'm going to visit...' Arrina realised in that very instant that she didn't know Kingsley's widow's name. Her heart clenched in panic. Her thoughts raced as she tried to find any trace of the name in her mind. But there was nothing. 'I...' Arrina started again. She had nothing to say. So she did the only thing she could think of—she blinked rapidly and brushed a hand across her cheek.

'I'm sorry,' Arrina said in a tight voice. 'It's all a bit overwhelming. I feel so awful for her. The death must have come as a shock.' The strain in her voice was not entirely fake. She hated lying like this, but she knew she had to, for Phil and Julie.

'Oh dear,' said the woman. 'Oh my goodness. I didn't realise you were a friend of Callie's.'

Arrina pressed her lips together to keep the eager smile from them. In a village this small, there could only be one person who'd suffered a loss recently. Or at least, Arrina hoped so.

'Callie's my sister,' Ophelia said. 'Kingsley was my brother-in-law.'

Arrina's heart clenched. The excitement at finding a connection to Kingsley was replaced by a sharp stab of guilt. She imagined Callie in a back room behind the shop, crying and waiting for her sister to comfort her. 'I'm sorry. I didn't realise.'

This wasn't right. Arrina shouldn't be bothering the man's family just after he'd been killed, even if it was for Phil and Julie. She would find another way to do this.

Arrina stepped away. Her mouth moved as she searched for a better apology, but nothing came. She could just run away—leave now, get in her car, and drive back to Heathervale without stopping. But Ophelia wrapped Arrina in a tight hug before she had the chance. 'Thank you for coming. It's so thoughtful of you.'

Arrina stared over the woman's shoulder at the door. Ophelia's arms tightened around her, leaving Arrina no chance to get away.

16

When Ophelia let go, Arrina stepped a little closer to the wall of tea and its familiar, comforting scent. She would have given anything for a cup of it right then—hot, steaming and milky. Nothing less would soothe her frazzled nerves.

'Callie's your sister,' Arrina said, repeating the smiling blonde's revelation. Ophelia nodded and blinked expectantly. Arrina's guilt eased a little as she saw the woman was still as cheerful as ever despite the mention of Kingsley's death. Perhaps Arrina could get some information from her and not have to bother poor, grieving Callie. 'So you're *that* Ophelia.' As though there could be more than one.

'The very same,' Ophelia said. 'And before you ask, no, I never climb the willows by the brook.' She laughed with a light, tinkling sound.

'I'm sorry?' Arrina half-remembered something about Ophelia and a willow tree in *Hamlet*. But the play certainly wasn't set near the Cound Brook of Longnor.

'It's about the *other* Ophelia,' the blonde explained. 'There's a Shakespeare society that meets near here, and they all ask me that when they come into the shop. It's something about climbing a willow tree over a brook and falling in.'

Arrina remembered the scene in the play. The lovesick Ophelia had climbed a tree, and when a branch broke, she tumbled into the brook and drowned. That Ophelia was another woman in white, Arrina realised, another jilted, drowning woman, just like the White Lady of Longnor. They were both just as white and bleak as the village itself.

Arrina shivered despite the stuffy warmth of the shop. Something about this place was very strange and confusing.

'Calliope got the far better end of the stick being named after a muse; don't you think?' Ophelia continued. 'Where did you say you knew her from?'

Arrina took another step away and found herself pressed up against the wall of tea. A stream of possible lies flowed through her head, but none would stand up to questioning.

'You know, I'm not really sure,' Arrina said, certain that her face gave her away. But Ophelia didn't look over at her. Instead, she was gazing up at the selection of tea behind Arrina, perhaps contemplating making a pot. If she did that, Arrina would come clean. She could explain everything with a cup of tea in her hand.

'Well, I'll pass along the message that you came by,' Ophelia said. 'I know she thought she'd be back by now, but apparently, Venezuela's very popular this time of year. All the flights are fully booked for another couple of days.'

'She's in Venezuela?' Arrina repeated, unable to quite make that information real until she said it. Had Callie fled the country after Kingsley's death? Surely, the police would count that as suspicious. Maybe *she* had killed him and hopped on a plane. Perhaps the tale about fully booked flights was a lie to keep people away while she made her escape.

Arrina's heart raced with excitement as these thoughts raced through her head. Did she finally have something that would get Phil free?

'You didn't know?' Ophelia looked closely at her now, the bright smile slipping from her face. Arrina thought she had a matter of moments before Ophelia realised that Arrina had never met Callie. And she wasn't ready to go just yet. She wanted to learn more about this trip to Venezuela. She should also find out the reason behind Ophelia's good mood. Before then, Arrina had been too busy worrying about upsetting the woman to think much about it. But she should have stopped to wonder why Ophelia was so chipper in the wake of Kingsley's death.

'I'm actually more of Kingsley's friend,' Arrina said. 'Or, I mean I *was*. I saw him on Saturday morning, and I was shocked to find out that he'd died later that day. After I heard about what happened, I thought he'd want me to come and make sure Callie was OK.'

Ophelia's eyes narrowed. Clearly, Arrina had said the wrong thing.

'You're a friend of Kingsley's?' the woman asked. Arrina nodded slowly. She regretted this when Ophelia added, 'A very *good* friend of his, I imagine. You're just his type.'

Arrina stuttered as she realised what Ophelia meant. 'I... No, it wasn't...We weren't...'

'Callie and Kingsley were meant to go to Venezuela together a week ago. They'd planned the holiday of a lifetime there. But then Kingsley changed his plans at the last minute, and Callie flew out alone. He said he'd got something very important to do on Saturday. Wouldn't say what it was, but now I can see.'

Arrina opened her mouth to speak, but Ophelia silenced her with a sharp glare. 'Do you know how your precious Kingsley died?' she asked. 'The police just told Callie, who called me about it in tears.'

Arrina shook her head.

'He was strangled to death,' she spat, 'with a length of twine.'

Arrina backed away, her thoughts racing with the realisation of what this revelation meant.

Ophelia followed her to the door. 'If you ask me, it couldn't have happened to a more deserving guy.'

17

A length of twine. The phrase repeated like a stuck record as Arrina drove away. *A length of twine. A length of twine.* The bleak, frost-bleached landscape of Longnor matched the hollow shock she felt. Arrina hadn't known how Kingsley had died. Not until Ophelia told her. Now she wished she'd never found out.

Strangled by twine. Arrina couldn't get that image out of her head. Not just because it was an awful way to die but also because of what it meant. She knew who always carried twine—who she'd seen with it on the morning of Kingsley's death.

It was Phil.

He'd told her he had nothing more important on his toolbelt. He'd said so when he came to fix the heating at the college. He'd stood there with the twine in his hands, snipping off a piece and tying up a loose pipe so the system wouldn't explode over the weekend.

And a length of twine had been used to strangle Kingsley Peters right in the field where Phil had been working later that day.

But Phil couldn't have done it. Arrina told herself this again and again as she drove away from Longnor and back towards Heathervale. It couldn't have been Phil. It was just a coincidence that he'd been there in the corner of that field. And just another coincidence that the murder weapon was something he always carried.

Arrina shivered in her seat as she assured herself that *both* these matters were coincidences. But then she thought of something else she knew about Phil.

He had a connection to Kingsley that some might call a motive. Arrina didn't want to think about that, but a small voice in the back of her head insisted on it.

Phil had been desperate for money. He'd begged the Yates family—who he normally avoided—to give him work. Arrina also remembered the day before, when she and Julie had walked along the tree-lined track to the police station. Julie had been making a list of things to tell Phil, and several of them were related to money. Arrina remembered an unpaid vet's bill and an overdue restock of silage. Phil's farm had been struggling for a while, but it seemed like recently things had got much worse. *Very recently*, the small voice in the back of her mind said. *In just the past couple of months*, it insisted. *Ever since the milk spillage that Kingsley Peters had investigated.*

As Arrina drove away from the bare landscape of frosted fields and into the northern part of the Peak District, she thought about this. Perhaps Phil had only *told* Julie they'd been cleared by the Environment Agency for the milk spillage. It seemed unthinkable that he'd lied to her about something like that. But it was the only thing that made sense to Arrina. If he'd lied, and he *had* been fined, it would explain his desperation for work and the farm's money issues. And maybe it would also explain what had happened to Kingsley. Perhaps Phil's anger over the situation had driven him to...

No, Arrina couldn't even think it. She *knew* Phil hadn't done this, no matter what the evidence suggested. But other people would be quick to call him guilty. She'd already seen people turn against him in the village hall the day before, and they hadn't even known all the details then. Things would only get worse when they did. But Arrina couldn't let that happen.

She drove straight to her cottage, not stopping at Julie's farm as she'd intended, not stopping for anything. She rushed towards her cosy house, already imagining herself curled up in the window seat with Tinsel and a huge mug of Yorkshire tea.

But when she reached the end of her road, she had to slam on the brakes to avoid crashing into a car. It was parked in her usual spot at the top of the dead-end road that stopped halfway up the hill. There was only one reason for a car to park there—someone was waiting for her. As Arrina peered through the gloom under the trees, she saw the blue and white of a police car.

Her thoughts split in two—half excited that Tony had come to help solve the case or to say he'd freed Phil already, half petrified that something even worse had happened to the poor man or to Julie. Arrina leapt out of her car, and the driver side of the police car opened. Out stepped, not Tony, but the detective inspector of the local police. Arrina hadn't even considered the visitor could be anyone but Tony.

Ian was a large man, leaning back to balance his beer belly. This tilted stance was further exaggerated by the way he lifted his chin to hide the expanding bald patch at his crown. Arrina knew this distinctive figure well. The detective inspector was a good friend of Tony Mellor's. Arrina had spent countless evenings at the Horse and Hound with him, back when she and Tony were together. He had an endless store of bad puns, could best anyone in movie trivia, and maintained a very soft spot for corgis.

Arrina had got on well with him, but he was really Tony's friend, as well as being his colleague. Thus, over the past year, she and the inspector had drifted back to nodding terms and packed away the knowledge that they'd ever been friends.

'Ian,' she said. The name sounded strange after so long. 'What is it?'

'Perhaps we should…' He gestured up to her house.

'What's happened?' Arrina asked. 'Is it Phil? Or Julie? Are they OK?' Strength drained from Arrina's legs. She stumbled on acorns as she crossed the last few feet towards Ian, but she didn't fall.

'It's nothing like that. Nothing at all. This is just routine.'

'They're OK?' Her heart pounded in her ears, and it took a few seconds to make sense of what he said.

He nodded. 'I'm just here to ask you a few questions. Shall we head up to your cottage?'

'You're sure? Everyone's fine?'

'Yes.' He shuffled from foot to foot on the icy ground. 'I'm sorry to call on you so late.' The afternoon was dark, but the hour wasn't late at all. This was probably as close as he'd come to apologising for making her worry. 'So, do you want to…?'

Again, he gestured up towards her cottage. But Arrina crossed her arms across her chest and stayed still. 'It's just a couple of questions?' she asked. 'I don't want to keep you.'

Her headlights bathed them in stark blacks and whites. 'What is it you want to know?'

When she'd spoken with Tony behind the police station the day before, he'd sounded worried. He'd given the impression the police weren't acting quite as he thought they should. Arrina didn't know if Ian was part of the problem, and until she found out, she didn't want to sit down over tea and tell him everything she knew.

Ian's face didn't reveal his feelings about this, though he stamped his feet and rubbed his hands together before he spoke. 'OK. I just need to ask about your relationship with Kingsley Peters.'

'Our relationship? I've only met him once.' In Heathervale, *once* was enough to start rumours of anything. Several people had seen her and Kingsley together at the Careers Fair. Any one of them could have whipped that encounter up into a torrid romance that had spread around half the village. 'We talked about his work at the Environment Agency.'

'I just mean your connection to him. We're checking in with everyone who's been in contact with Kingsley recently. We want to get a clearer picture of his recent movements and interactions.' The white cloud of Ian's breath plumed out in front of him. 'Can you tell me anything about that?'

Arrina stared at him, trying to work out what he knew. Did he know she was investigating the murder herself? Did he know she'd been to Longnor that day? No. How could he?

'I met Kingsley Peters once,' she said, 'on the morning of his death. Our interaction was limited, but if it would help your investigation, I can provide a written statement detailing everything I recall about that morning and deliver it to the station within 24 hours.'

'I...' Ian started, a flicker of what must have been surprise finally breaking through his hard face. 'No, I don't think that's necessary.'

'Is there anything else?' She gave the smile she usually reserved for school inspectors. The one that was wide and friendly but entirely failed to reach her eyes.

A breeze whipped up the hillside and through the bare branches of the trees. Arrina and Ian both shivered. He stamped his feet once again, loudly. 'Let me know if you remember anything important.'

Arrina nodded, then she walked back to her car and locked up while Ian drove away. Once he was gone, she ran up the hillside and into her cottage. Within minutes, she was on her window seat with Tinsel and a much-needed cup of tea. She finished the drink quickly and got up to make another.

Only then, away from Ian's gaze, could she think about why he'd come all the way out to her cottage that afternoon. Surely, he could have called her if he'd had nothing more than a couple of routine queries. Had she missed something? Had Ian been trying to tell her something? Or perhaps, more worryingly, find something out without her knowing?

She reached into her bag. The heart wood that Sylvie Morgan had made for Julie was in there. Arrina wrapped her hand around it and took long, slow breaths.

Arrina didn't understand why Ian had come to her cottage that evening, but she had no time to dwell on it. She still had a murder to solve and a friend to exonerate.

Tinsel lifted his head from a cushion nearby and meowed. He fixed his blue eyes on her and twitched one ear.

'I know what you're thinking,' Arrina said. 'How am I going to complete this investigation when I've entirely run out of leads?'

Tinsel looked over at his empty food bowl and meowed once again.

'I know,' Arrina said. 'It's a very tricky case. But as always, I'm happy to have any input from you on this.'

The sleek silver cat leapt down and paced in front of the food cupboard.

'I'm not sure there's a clue in there, but I can check. And while I'm at it, I'll get you some dinner. You're not going to solve this murder on an empty stomach.'

Arrina's own stomach growled, and she pulled out blocks of Wensleydale and crumbly Cheshire cheese as well as her favourite chunky pickle, put the kettle on for a fresh cup of tea, and once again thought over the scant facts she knew about the case.

18

As the dark afternoon drifted into a hard, icy evening, Arrina looked through the leather-bound book of clippings Kingsley had left behind in the hall. This was her only link to the man, and she hoped it would provide some sort of clue. But nothing leapt out at her. Arrina jiggled her foot as she read, tapped her fingernails on the kitchen table, and finally gave up and shut the book.

She paced around her small cottage, trying to make sense of everything she knew. Nothing would settle in her mind. Each scrap of information was like a snowflake, swirling in a flurry, too weightless to land.

Twine, Venezuela, milk, frost, watery ladies drowning in white—everything blanketed her mind in confusion. Nothing settled. Nothing connected.

Arrina wanted to have *something* to tell Julie. But she'd got nothing. Still, she needed to talk to her best friend and try to give her hope.

She tried calling Julie but got no answer. A few minutes later, a message came through that simply said: *Milking*. Arrina replied offering help and asking Julie to let her know if she needed anything at all. But Julie's only response was a quickly dashed-off reply saying she was exhausted from her failed efforts to see Phil and maintaining daily operation of the farm. She thanked Arrina and said that after milking, she was heading straight to bed.

Arrina thought about jumping in her car and going over there. She just wanted to make everything OK for Julie. Julie always did that for her.

But this problem couldn't be fixed with their usual cake and cups of tea. If Julie was able to sleep, that was probably the best thing for her.

Arrina continued pacing around her small cottage, glancing out of her windows at the black night that pressed in on all sides. She wished she was back at the college, where the long corridors were like a track she could unravel her thoughts around. In fact, she *really* wished it was summer, so the sun would stretch out for hours and she could range across the rolling hills around her small cottage. In the confines of her home's cramped rooms that dark evening, she had to turn around just as tightly as the jumbled thoughts that churned in her head.

She found herself digging out her torch and all the warm clothing she owned—perhaps she could still walk that night. But she put everything away again. It wouldn't help anyone if she broke her neck trying to hike the icy trails.

Instead, she made a plan. Arrina set her alarm for bright and early the next morning. She would head out as soon as the first rays of sun peeked into the world. She would wear her hiking boots and her warm clothes and even take her torch. She was going to investigate the murder of Kingsley Peters properly. And the only way to do that was to go to the scene of the crime.

Arrina was going to the hidden corner of the Yates family's land—the one that Bill could barely bring himself to speak of. He had stammered over telling Arrina that it was a place of disrepute and illicit activities. Though she didn't like to admit it, she had some experience of those things from her work at the college. The vast majority of her students were good, hardworking kids. But a few each year did get into trouble.

Arrina had learned a thing or two about what the young people of Heathervale got up to when they thought nobody was looking. She was certain she'd be able to find something in the corner of the field that the police had missed. She would find a clue to lead the case in a clear direction, and that direction would be *away* from Phil.

As soon as Arrina finalised her plan, she felt a weight fall from her shoulders. She lay down on the sofa bed she'd shared with Julie just a couple of nights before and put on *Little Women*, one of her and Julie's favourite films. She curled up with it and imagined Julie was beside her, watching as well. This was one of the few Christmassy films that Arrina could ever persuade her friend to watch before December.

Arrina focused all her attention on the film, willing it to lull her into a restful night. Her mind grew quiet as Marmee read the letter from her absent husband aloud. Sleep was already tugging at Arrina before the four young March girls were huddled together on Christmas morning and wishing for presents.

Arrina couldn't believe that in the real world, Christmas was just a matter of weeks away. It didn't feel that way at all. But in the film, it was already Christmas Day—the landscape was deep with pristine snow, and a fire crackled in the hearth.

The sound of the fictional sisters' chatter lulled Arrina to sleep. She strained her ears to hear them talk about the Christmas presents they'd got their mother. Their light, happy voices quieted the last squirming worries in Arrina's mind for the evening.

That was all she needed right then—to ease herself into oblivion within the March family's warm embrace.

Then tomorrow, she'd carry the strength of all those girls with her as she trudged through the fields to continue her investigation in the corner of the Yates family estate. That was where she'd find answers, she was certain. She'd find answers there, and everything would be OK.

19

The ground was hard and unyielding beneath Arrina's boots as she crossed the dawn-lit Peak District landscape. The once-muddy trails had captured the footsteps of those who'd walked there before her. Each imprint was a frozen hollow—a leaf-stuck rut that tried to trip Arrina as she walked.

It took all her effort to stay upright. But this strain was exactly what she needed. Arrina focused her thoughts on the ground directly ahead. She stared at it in the grainy dawn light and stretched and strained her muscles as she walked over the hills towards the Yates family land.

She was also walking in the direction of Julie and Phil's farm. But Arrina pushed thoughts of the place from her mind. That was where the milk spill had happened—that accident of fate that had brought Kingsley Peters into Phil's life and must have been the reason the police had latched onto him so firmly. The farm was also where Julie would be, waiting desperately for a phone call from Phil or a piece of good news from Arrina that she didn't yet have to give.

Arrina was also walking past the Morgan woods. Technically, the woodland there belonged to the Yates family, just like all the land around it. But the Morgan family—including the college's head of security, Sampson, and his young niece Nancy—held a strong claim that even the Yates family couldn't fight against. The Morgans had lived in those woods for hundreds of years, and they had no intention of moving.

Sampson Morgan's rustic cottage lay just a few minutes into the woods there. The man would certainly be awake, even at that hour. Arrina was tempted to go around for a cup of his deliciously strong tea and to ask if he'd found the mural vandal. But she couldn't let herself be sidetracked by that. As much as she wanted to know who'd stuck those ugly, smiling stickers along the corridor of the college, she would have to trust that Sampson was handling it. He had his nephews to help him—Nancy's brothers, Wilfred and Wallace. They often lent Sampson a hand with anything he needed—even things he was looking into on Arrina's behalf, such as the college's events that summer. The Morgan family was close like that. Arrina left them to it. She had to focus on finding out who had killed Kingsley Peters.

Arrina pushed herself faster as she climbed the last hill to the corner where the murder had happened. She arrived out of breath and with her heart pounding in her ears. Pulling off her mud-stained hiking fleece, she stood and panted, letting the sweat on her brow cool to a chill.

Then she looked up and saw the view that spread out before her. She knew it well—a wide stretch of the Hope Valley, with the River Derwent down below, and on the far side of that, the majestic cliffs of Stanage Edge.

The heather on the rock formation's flat top still clung to its late, purple blooms. And the sloping hillside below was aflame with the red rust of autumn ferns. The cliffs themselves were tinted pink in the earliest light of the day. So much colour shone in the world right then, and Arrina was glad of the reminder that not everything was the bleak white and grey of the past few days.

Arrina's breaths grew calm, and her heartbeat slowed as she stood there. The whole of the Peak District was beautiful, but the small patch she lived in was breathtaking. She loved looking out over Stanage Edge whenever she could. There, she beheld the same view that could be seen from Julie and Phil's farm. Arrina hoped Phil would be able to look out upon it soon.

Before that could happen, though, Arrina needed to find the evidence to set him free.

She looked around at the untended scrap of land she stood in. This corner was just above the common pastureland that marked the edge of the Yates estate. This was apparently the place people came to for illicit activities and things that needed to be concealed. But as Arrina gazed around at the few stunted trees and the dark, rocky earth, she couldn't see anything significant about it.

She wondered at first if she'd got the wrong field. But then she saw a snagged scrap of police tape in a gorse bush a few feet away. And she noticed the wire fences at the edge of the field. They were taut and shiny, clearly brand new. That must have been Phil's work.

She also spotted one of the signs that he'd put up, bearing the words No Trespassing in large, black letters. But that wasn't *all* that the sign bore. There were several small red stickers on the painted metal.

Arrina stepped back in shock. She knew these stickers well. She'd seen dozens, perhaps even hundreds of them, already. They'd been stuck all along the walls of her college. These were the same grinning, cartoon lips that had been stuck to the murals there.

She stared at them in disbelief, unable to work out what it meant that she'd seen the stickers in both places. Was it significant? It certainly felt that way. Did these stickers mean one of her students had been up here? Surely none of them were connected to the murder.

Arrina turned away from the sign to look for evidence—preferably something that didn't link back to the college or her students. She couldn't bear to free Phil only to see one of the teens she worked with locked up in his place.

She looked all around the cold and wind-blown outcrop of land. A few weathered crisp packets were half-buried in the scrubby earth. Names had been carved into the bark of a crooked tree. And somewhere there, Kingsley's body had lain on the ground as the man's life slipped away.

Arrina bent down and examined the icy soil. The earth was sandy and pale here. This dirt was the sort that would fly up in a fine dust in the summer months, sticking to skin and scratching at eyes. Arrina could see why the family ignored this corner. It wasn't useful farmland at all. Arrina examined everything. She wasn't sure what she was looking for, but there had to be something.

Over by a gorse bush, Arrina found a churned-up patch of earth. It was rock hard from the recent frosts, so she had no idea whether the disturbance was related to the murder or something else from weeks or months ago. But it was something. Arrina crouched down and nudged aside a pile of leaves that had blown against the bush. There was another crisp packet, a single red glove, and a soggy mess that might once have been a newspaper. None of those items seemed relevant to Kingsley's death.

A sharp wind cut across the landscape, slicing into the gaps between Arrina's clothes and skin. She shivered and put her fleece back on.

The wind grew stronger, driving skittering leaves across the patch of ground she'd thought was significant. She wondered what on earth she was doing there.

As she stood up and braced herself against the strong gusts of wind, a loud voice echoed her thoughts: 'What on earth are you doing here?'

Arrina yelped in surprise and turned around. Her foot caught on a tree root and threw her off balance. Arrina stumbled, reached out for a branch, missed it, and tumbled to the hard, frozen ground.

She looked up and saw the looming mountain of a beer belly hovering over her. It was Ian, the police officer who'd been at her house the evening before. He bent stiffly and offered her a hand. Arrina didn't take it. Instead, she pushed herself up on aching muscles and bruised bones. As she brushed down her clothes, she tried to think of a good answer to Ian's question. What *was* she doing there, bent over inspecting the ground at a recent, grisly crime scene?

'I'm on my way to visit Julie,' Arrina said finally, pointing down the hill in the direction of her farm. This was not entirely a lie, since she'd been planning to visit Julie after this excursion.

'I'd ask why you're not driving over there, but I've been in your car.' He gave her a gentle smile, but it didn't last long. 'I will ask why you've chosen to walk *this* way, though, when it's not the easiest route and when in fact, there is no path here.'

Arrina glanced over at the fence which now blocked off access to the main road. She thought about telling Ian that she *always* walked this way. But claiming that she often visited this disreputable corner of Heathervale wouldn't help matters at all.

'I just thought that on the way there, I might...'

She gazed down at the ground. What *had* she thought she'd do? The night before, she'd needed a plan, and she'd latched onto the idea of visiting the crime scene as though it was the answer to everything. But Kingsley had been murdered on Saturday. There wouldn't really be any evidence left out in the open by Tuesday morning.

'Look,' Ian said gently. 'I understand it must be difficult to see your friend accused of something like this. However, I can assure you that the police are doing a thorough job with the case. I'd strongly advise you against getting involved.'

His statement didn't seem to be true. Even Tony, who Arrina had never known to doubt his own beloved police, seemed to think there was something going on. Arrina didn't want Ian to know her suspicions, though, so she looked away and said nothing.

She swiped the toe of her hiking boot through a pile of leaves. Beneath it was the hard knot of tree root that had caused her to fall. Arrina glared at it, resisting the urge to kick it. Then she spotted a familiar, carved oval by her foot. It was the heart wood that Sylvie had made for Julie! The talisman must have fallen out of her bag when she tripped.

Arrina bent down and grabbed it. But her thick gloves fumbled and failed to grip it. She tried again to pick it up. It seemed to be half stuck in the solid earth.

'Arrina,' Ian said. 'Are you listening to me?'

But Arrina was too focused on trying to get the heart wood free to say anything. Ian gave a heavy huff of effort and bent down beside her. 'Arrina—'

'I dropped this,' Arrina said. 'I just want to get it back, and then I'll leave.' She brushed away more of the leaves around the precious talisman. 'I just need to...' The heart wood looked like it was frozen into the ground. But that wasn't possible. It hadn't been out of her bag for more than a minute, and she'd felt firsthand how hard the earth was. How could the piece of wood have sunk into the dirt and frozen in there?

'When exactly did you drop this?' Ian asked.

Arrina needed to get the heart wood back. She needed to give it to Julie. It was the only good thing she had to give to her friend. 'Just now. But I don't... I can't...' Arrina tried to work her wool-covered fingers into a gap between the heart wood and the earth around it. But there were no gaps. She picked up a rock nearby.

'Wait,' Ian said. But she couldn't wait. She had to get the heart wood back.

Before he could stop her, Arrina banged the rock against the frozen earth, crumbling it enough to get the heart wood free. She laid the small talisman gently into the palm of her dark-green, woollen glove and stared.

There were rumours in Heathervale that the Morgans possessed mysterious powers. Arrina had never believed the tales of the all-seeing Grandma Morgan, and she hadn't thought the heart wood was anything more than a comforting curio. But now it seemed that the tiny thing had burrowed halfway into the frozen earth, as though it had felt a deep connection with the Heathervale land.

Arrina stood up and stared at the piece of wood in her hand.

'I'm going to have to ask you to give that to me,' Ian said, his red face staring hard at Arrina. When she didn't move, he added, 'I don't want to arrest you for tampering with evidence, but I will if I have to.'

'What? No, it's not evidence. I told you, I just dropped it a minute ago.'

'I saw how hard that thing was stuck into the ground. It must have been down there during the frosts of the last few nights.'

'It was in my bag.' Arrina opened her handbag with her free hand, as though doing so would somehow explain. And *there* was the heart wood.

The small, carved oval of wood was right there where she'd left it.

'I don't understand,' she said, holding two heart woods now—one clean and smooth, the other dark and dirty. 'I thought I'd dropped it, but it's here.'

'Did you have two of them?' Ian asked.

'No. It's not even really mine. It's Julie's.' Quickly she added, 'Julie doesn't have another one either. She hasn't even seen this one yet. Sylvie made it for her, and I was supposed to pass it to her on Sunday, but I forgot. It's been in my handbag ever since.'

'Sylvie Morgan?' Ian asked. Arrina nodded. 'Does she sell these in Present and Correct?'

Arrina shook her head. She looked again at the two heart woods she held.

'No,' Arrina said. 'Sylvie only makes them for her family. And Julie.'

'So, Phil doesn't have one?' he asked.

'No. They're just for the Morgans usually.'

'For *all* of the Morgans?'

Arrina held the two ovals of wood in her cupped palms. She didn't like the tone of Ian's voice. He sounded far too interested, and Arrina didn't know why.

'I...' Arrina started. She knew that the answer to Ian's question was yes. But she wasn't sure exactly why that was important. She needed a moment to think about it.

The police had arrested Phil for the murder of Kingsley Peters. Arrina desperately wanted to find some evidence to set him free. And now it seemed as though Ian suspected one of the Morgans instead of Phil. Sending the police after the Morgans would be easy. They were always high on the suspect list whenever anything went wrong in the village.

Arrina didn't want to be yet another person who pointed a finger in their direction, but if it helped get Phil free, did she really have a choice?

'I shouldn't tell you this,' Ian said, 'but we have DNA evidence belonging to someone other than Phil.'

'You mean one of the Morgans.'

Ian gave the slightest up-tip of his chin but said nothing.

'If you have DNA, then why haven't you arrested the person? You can let Phil go if you've got another suspect.'

His eyes stared directly into hers, trying to tell her something. 'DNA can't always point you at a person. Not only *one* person, anyway.'

Arrina didn't understand what he meant. That was the main purpose of DNA in forensics. Every person's DNA was unique. But when she thought about it, she realised that wasn't *always* the case. Identical twins had the same DNA, and when Arrina thought about that, she realised why Ian had been asking about the Morgans. 'Wallace and Wilfred,' she said quietly. Sampson's helpful nephews were identical twins.

'If that's a special family charm, I doubt it would get lost very easily.'

'No,' Arrina said, looking down at the carved piece of wood.

'Perhaps someone might drop it under certain circumstances, say perhaps, during a fight.'

Arrina's mind flashed onto an image of Kingsley grappling with one of the Morgan twins. Yes, she thought, the heart wood could get lost in the midst of that.

'And it also,' Ian continued, 'seems like the sort of thing that might have a person's fingerprints on it.' He held out a small evidence bag.

The dirt-stuck heart wood suddenly felt very heavy in her palm. Ian had said there was DNA linking the brothers to the crime scene. Arrina had always defended the Morgans when people were rude or cruel about them. She'd only ever found the members of that family to be honest and kind. But now one of them was linked to a murder scene.

Arrina extended her hand slowly, holding out the piece of wood she'd just found. It was for the best, Arrina promised herself. She had to do this to get Phil free.

As Arrina dropped the piece of wood into the evidence bag, she pictured Julie's smile—wide and bright. Arrina hadn't seen it in a while. Once she heard that Phil was free, Julie would be smiling for days.

Then Arrina allowed herself a smile. She'd got Phil free! She felt bad for the Morgan family, who'd soon be going through what Julie had been experiencing. But if one of the twins was a murderer, then they had to face what they'd done.

The smile wavered as she thought about Sampson Morgan and sweet, young Nancy. That smile dropped completely when she looked over at Ian and saw the grim expression on his face.

20

'You can let Phil go now, can't you?' Arrina asked, her voice straining against the wind that whipped across the landscape. Ian didn't say anything. 'Will he be let out today, or...'

She forced herself to focus on Phil's release and not on how the Morgan family would react to what had happened.

She'd done the right thing. Phil was innocent. The police had found DNA evidence against one of the Morgan twins, and the fingerprints on the heart wood could confirm which one was guilty.

Ian still didn't say anything, but the furrow in his brow didn't look good.

'You said there was DNA on the murder weapon,' Arrina persisted. 'If the DNA isn't Phil's, and you've got evidence pointing to someone else, surely you can let him go.'

Ian shook his head and refused to meet Arrina's eye. 'The DNA isn't on the murder weapon.'

'But you said—'

'I said DNA was found here at the scene, but it wasn't on the murder weapon. It was on a lemonade bottle next to the body.'

Arrina looked around at the litter-strewn landscape. The DNA evidence suddenly didn't sound so strong if it was just an empty bottle that could have blown in on a stiff wind. 'But...' She didn't know what else to say.

'We didn't find any DNA on the murder weapon. The killer must have worn gloves.'

'So you don't know who did it?' Arrina thought about the various legal shows she'd watched over the years. She had no idea what would happen in a case like this, but she knew doubt was usually a good thing. 'Then when does Phil get out?'

Ian sealed the evidence bag and labelled it. 'We can't clear him with the evidence we have. Both suspects will go to trial.'

'What?' Arrina closed her fingers around the remaining heart wood in her hand. She could barely feel the talisman through her woollen gloves, and it did nothing to slow her racing heart. 'But they can't both be guilty.'

The large man took another step away. 'I should let you know that you may be called as a witness to testify about what you found here this morning.'

'That can't be right. You can't drag two people through court cases when you know... when they can't...This isn't right.'

Ian didn't answer. He simply turned and walked away. As he did so, he spotted the same smiling stickers Arrina had seen earlier—the red, grinning mouths on the sign at the edge of the field. The large man walked closer and peered at them. He pulled out his phone and took a photo. Then he turned back to Arrina, as though he wanted to ask what she knew about them. But he must have seen the look on Arrina's face and thought better of it. He said nothing and walked away.

Arrina almost wished he had asked her. She wanted to shout that she wouldn't help him with anything ever again.

Even if he threatened her with arrest right then, she wouldn't tell him what she knew about the stickers. It was bad enough that she'd failed to help Phil and had also got one of the Morgan twins in trouble at the same time. In no way would she point a finger in the direction of her college.

Arrina watched the large man stride away, forcing herself to stand still until he was gone. She couldn't trust her legs, and she didn't want him to see her stumble once more. She let the wind gnaw through her clothes. Soon, she was frozen to the bone.

When she was finally alone in the corner of the field, Arrina realised she had no idea what to do next.

She turned towards the path she'd walked down just a short while earlier. That path led past the Morgan woods—past the house that Nancy shared with her parents and also the one that Wallace and Wilfred had built for themselves a few summers before.

The Morgan family had been kind and friendly to her since she'd first moved to the village. They were good, hardworking people. And now she'd sent the police after one of them. Were a lemonade bottle and a dropped piece of wood enough to suggest one of the Morgans was a murderer? Arrina didn't think so. But then again, she couldn't imagine any Morgan would lose their heart wood—unless they were in an extreme situation.

Arrina considered going to the Morgan woods and telling them what had happened. But she'd never be able to explain. She barely understood it herself.

She turned the other way and faced towards Julie's farm. Arrina hadn't done anything to help poor Phil either. How could she face Julie with nothing to give her but a small piece of wood and an apology because she'd tried her best and failed?

No. She couldn't go to either of those places.

She looked around at her bleak surroundings. Then she hopped over the fence, proceeded down the steep, tree-lined track to the main road, and walked home.

21

By the time Arrina reached the hill she lived on, her joints creaked, and her feet had hot patches that would soon swell into blisters. She'd walked home at a punishing pace. She hadn't even looked up to see the beauty of her surroundings—just stared at the pendulum tick of her brown boots and tried not to think about anything.

She took a deep breath and trudged up the road, passing her silver-blue car at the end of it, and then continued along the footpath that led right to her door.

Tinsel would be inside. Her tea cupboard was there. A Tupperware box full of mince pies was waiting in her freezer. And there was a whole library of Christmas films that Arrina could use to escape from the terrible morning.

She knew she ought to change and head into the college—she'd left a message to say she'd be late, but there were still things she needed to do. She should go in, but she couldn't. That day, Arrina knew she wouldn't be able to show her face to anyone, least of all to Sampson and Nancy Morgan at the college.

Arrina was going to hide from her work and from the whole village, and nobody could stop her.

Well, almost nobody.

As Arrina crested the last rise to her house, she found someone waiting at her door who would certainly have a thing or two to say about her plans to skip work that day.

It was Victor Stones, the chair of the Board of Governors. In his position, he could fire Arrina if he really wanted to. And Arrina had often thought that he *really* wanted to. Over the last couple of years, he'd fought against her on countless issues regarding the college. And then there was Arrina's recent defiance in front of the entire village. Victor's face had looked like a storm cloud when she'd stood there and proclaimed her support for Julie and Phil. She seriously considered turning around immediately and walking away.

But she had nowhere to go to. And apparently, even when she tried to hide at her cottage, people would just track her down there. Victor raised his hand in a neat little wave, and, giving up thoughts of running away, Arrina returned it. She was too tired to run then anyway. Trudging the last stretch of the hill to her cottage felt like a momentous effort.

'Arrina, my dear,' Victor said, sounding far more cheerful than she'd expected. Indeed, as Arrina drew closer to the man, his small, clipped moustache twitched above an eager smile. Her racing heart felt heavy at the sight. Perhaps her impulsive hiring of a chemistry teacher the day before had been the final excuse he needed to get rid of her. That would certainly make Victor happy.

'I hope you've not been waiting long,' Arrina said as she covered the last few feet of ground between them and tried to slow her panting breaths.

'Not at all,' Victor said. 'I've been out for a stroll—got to keep the old ticker in shape—and stopped here a mere minute ago.' He tapped his chest and smiled proudly. Arrina, in her panic at seeing Victor outside her house, had not properly noticed what the man was wearing. But the tap on his chest brought her attention to the fact that he wasn't clad in his usual crisp shirt and well-pressed trousers. Instead,

Victor wore a strange baggy Lycra outfit, which looked far too cold for the weather that day. He also had on a pair of brand-new trainers with thick cushioned soles. He bounced lightly from foot to foot. 'I rang the college looking for you earlier, and when they said they weren't expecting you for a while, I thought I'd get my steps in and head over here.'

'Right,' Arrina said. She couldn't think of a single thing to say that wasn't related to Victor's outfit. It was all she could do not to stare. Sweat cooled on her brow, and she wondered if the cold would seep through and numb her brain entirely—if the shock of what she was looking at didn't do that first.

She tried to force her thoughts onto important topics, such as why Victor was looking for her and what terrible news he was bringing her way. But then he bent one leg behind himself and grabbed it by the ankle. She lost hold of the last scrap of sensible thought as Victor pushed his hips forwards and told Arrina about his trouble with stiff quads.

'Tea,' Arrina said loudly. She fumbled in her bag for her keys, feeling adrenaline-fuelled heart beats right down to her fingertips. 'Let's go inside and get warmed up with a cup of tea.'

'Arrina, dear, that sounds delightful, but I'm afraid I can't.' He tapped his watch. 'This snazzy piece of kit is tracking my vital signs, and if I don't start walking in the next... six minutes, it's going to start making a beeping sound that I don't yet know how to stop.'

Arrina nodded and gave a smile that she hoped looked sympathetic. Inside, she still felt utterly scrambled. She and Julie often referred to the man as Victorian Victor. Arrina had never previously seen him without a tie on. Now, he was wearing an outfit that clung in all the wrong places, and he was jogging on the spot like a schoolboy stuffed with sugar.

Even stranger was Victor's friendliness. He had stormed out of Sunday's fundraiser because Arrina had stood up for Julie. He'd been the one to forbid a connection between the college and the murder of Kingsley Peters. He'd circulated an email about the subject and tacked a copy to the staff noticeboard as well. He'd promised serious consequences for anyone who ignored his instructions. And now he was standing on Arrina's doorstep, looking as though he was about to skip with her through the woods for a picnic.

Perhaps this was all a dream, Arrina thought. Perhaps she had fallen down while hiking and hit her head on a rock. This was just the sort of strange delusion her unconscious mind would serve up.

A bright, strobing light hit the backs of her retinas and cast doubt on that idea. The light's sharp shock felt far too real.

'Oh, goodness,' Victor said, peering at his watch. 'It's flashing. That means we're down to five minutes. I'll have to make this quick.'

Arrina nodded. She had no idea what *this* was.

'Firstly, I wanted to commend you on your bravery in facing down those hooligans on Sunday. Standing there in the village hall that afternoon, I could not believe what I was hearing. You're a stronger person than I to have spoken in tones of such civility. I could not even bear to be in the same room as those people in the end. To know that one's friends and neighbours can turn on a person in their time of need...' He shook his head. 'It beggars belief.'

Arrina nodded slowly. *Was he really praising her for supporting Julie and Phil?* This was the polar opposite of what she'd been expecting.

'My father was the village doctor here before me, and he delivered young Phil himself. And everyone in Heathervale has known Julie's lovely family for decades. And now to...' He shook his head again. 'I'm sure you know, dear, that both Julie and Phil were absolute angels when my Rayna got sick. Sweet Rayna wouldn't eat anything, until one day, she asked me for Lumpy Tums, and *oh*, what a pickle that put me in.'

Victor's eyes watered as he told her this, and Arrina wanted to say something sympathetic, but she could make no sense of what he was saying.

'Her grandmother had made them when she was a little girl,' Victor continued. 'And when poor, dear Rayna was nearing the end, all she wanted was Lumpy Tums. Have you ever had them?'

Lumpy Tums sounded like an unsightly disease of the abdomen, but Arrina was almost certain that wasn't what Victor meant. She simply shook her head.

'Porridge oats with a little water in. Roll them into a ball and boil them. Then serve in warm milk and honey. That's what my Rayna told me, and it sounded easy enough, but I couldn't get it to work at all—the oats kept separating into a thin sort of soup. I mentioned the problem to Julie, and she came around the very next morning with a thermos full of Lumpy Tums in her farm's own milk. She and Phil did that every day until my Rayna passed on.'

Arrina didn't remember this at all, though Victor's wife had only died the year before. But it didn't surprise her. Julie was always delivering cupcakes on people's birthdays, recreating half-remembered family recipes, and making food for sick people around the village. For that reason, Arrina had been so very shocked by the angry shouts that Sunday in the village hall. The smile on Victor's face right then should have been *everyone's* response when thinking of Julie.

The cold air gnawed at Arrina's bones, but she didn't interrupt Victor as he talked about the generosity of her friends. It was nice to find someone else in the village who supported them. Then another beep from Victor's watch brought his reverie to an end.

'Anyway, my dear,' Victor said, 'I just wanted to come here to tell you that I'm on your side, and I hope you won't let anyone stop you in your fight to help Julie and Phil.' His clipped moustache twitched sharply. 'I am aware that the rest of the Board of Governors haven't been quite so supportive. They voted almost unanimously in favour of emailing staff and students to officially warn about connections between the college and the murder. Of course, I am obliged to send out communications in line with the board's decisions, but I'm sure you saw that the email and notice about the matter were both written in a tone that conveyed my displeasure at being forced to do so.'

Arrina hadn't noticed any hint of that in Victor's writing, but his usual stiff and stern communication style made it hard to see where a note of displeasure could be conveyed.

However, she couldn't say that. She simply said, 'Thank you.'

A blush rose in Victor's cheeks, which he tried to hide by fussing with his moustache. Then he glanced at his watch and continued. 'There is another pressing matter that has brought me here today. It's regarding the plummeting student numbers.'

Arrina was caught entirely off guard. Her mind had been full of porridge balls, honeyed milk, and Phil and Julie. 'I... I'm not sure I'd say plummeting. In the first term, we naturally expect—'

'Have you seen the numbers this week?'

Arrina shook her head. She *had* noticed slightly more dropouts than usual this year. She'd been meaning to follow up on the matter after the Careers Fair. But she'd been far too distracted in the days that followed it.

'Forty-six students have left the college since the start of term.'

'Forty-six?' That didn't seem possible. The college held just over a thousand students. The loss of forty-six of them within the first two months of the year was too high a number to make sense. 'I know things on the local farms have been difficult. Perhaps some students have left to—'

Victor shook his head. 'I know *exactly* what the students are doing.'

'Really?'

Victor was a retired GP. He didn't usually have his finger on the pulse of the local young people. But his expression was certain. 'They're going to work for Peregrine Anderson.'

Arrina glanced around the sparse winter woods that surrounded her cottage. She could make no sense of what Victor was saying, and the dark, leafless trees were no help, no matter how hard she stared at them in disbelief.

Peregrine Anderson was the son of Fernella Anderson, who had run the cake stand at Sunday's fundraiser. The operatic woman had told Arrina that Perry was setting up a business. But Arrina hadn't taken the claim seriously at all. She'd assumed Fernella was simply covering for her lazy, entitled son.

'They're working for him?' Arrina asked. 'Doing what?'

'That is indeed the question. When I saw Fernella last night at Wolferton Manor's wine tasting, she told me that over 30 of our students had gone to work for her son. She did try to explain what they were doing, but...' His moustache twitched again, and Arrina got a sense that the wine the night before had been more than *tasted*. 'I think it's best you hear about it firsthand. I've asked Fernella to set up a meeting between you and Peregrine. Ideally, you can develop a way in which to coordinate your efforts and somehow keep more students from leaving the college entirely.'

'I'm not sure I quite follow you. You want me to work with Perry?'

'Not just you. The whole college. Let's see if we can't bring him on board as the new business mentor. I know the position is still vacant since Barbara retired last year. If we bring Peregrine in and set up some form of apprenticeship for students who want to work with him, perhaps we can—'

'You want him to be the business mentor?' Arrina was now *sure* this discussion was a hallucination. She was lying in the woods somewhere, bleeding into her brain, and imagining this crazy conversation.

'Indeed. Fernella assures me he'd do a splendid job of it. And I think the students would respond well to a peer in the position. It would really inspire them.' He glanced down at his watch and tapped it. 'The things these young people know about the future of technology! Would you believe this gadget can...' He continued talking about his watch, but Arrina didn't listen.

She had never heard a more ridiculous suggestion than hiring Perry to be the business mentor at the college. Peregrine Anderson was arrogant, careless, and conceited. Arrina never wrote off a young person entirely—there was always a chance they could change—but she doubted he'd changed much in a matter of weeks.

At the first break in Victor's watch monologue, she said, 'I'm not really sure Perry is—'

A loud klaxon blast from Victor's wrist caused them both to jump. Victor jogged up and down on the spot. He lifted his knees to a surprising height, and Arrina knew she'd never get this image out of her mind.

'I've set up a meeting for the two of you at eleven,' he said. 'Do you know where the Andersons live?'

'Yes, but—'

'Excellent. I look forward to hearing all about the meeting. I have to dash now though. It's time to get my heart rate up, or the sirens will start wailing.' He gave Arrina a wide smile, turned from her, and set off into the woods at a surprising clip.

He was out of sight in a matter of moments, leaving Arrina feeling utterly lost while standing on her very own doorstep.

Her keys were warm and coppery in her fist. She walked inside and had the hottest shower she could stand. There was only half an hour before her so-called meeting with Perry. She considered forgetting the whole thing and staying under the stream of water until she turned lobster pink.

But she couldn't do that. If the student numbers were as bad as Victor had said—and she knew in her gut that they were—then she needed to fix the problem as quickly as possible. She'd already given the board enough of a reason to turn against her when she'd stood up for Julie at Sunday's fundraiser. Then she'd hired a new chemistry teacher who didn't fill the requirements of the position.

She didn't need to give them any more ammunition against her. If they kicked up a fuss and called her in for performance reviews and retraining, that would only distract her from helping Julie and Phil. It was best to sort out the declining student numbers as quickly as possible. If Perry could help with that, then she had to give the boy a shot.

Plus, Arrina had a bad feeling about Perry that deserved investigation. She wondered if there was a connection between his poaching of students at the college and the recent vandalism of the murals outside her office. It was a bit of a stretch, but Arrina couldn't believe that one of her own students had defaced the walls of the college, at least, not without a little encouragement. And if Perry was linked to the vandal who put the stickers in the college, then that also linked him to the stickers in the corner of the Yates field. Maybe the boy knew something about the murder that could help her free Phil.

Arrina stepped out of the shower and got dressed in fresh work clothes. She felt ludicrous putting on a smart outfit to meet with a sixteen-year-old who wasn't even clever enough to get into her college. But right then, she didn't have a choice. She didn't bother with her heels, though, which would have been unbearable on her newly blistered feet. She slipped on smart black pumps and dashed down the hill.

Her car started on the first turn of the key, as though it knew the importance of her task. The wheels crunched over pebbles, dry twigs, and frost-stiffened leaves. Then she set off to meet Perry Anderson, the last person she'd thought she'd ever be asking for help.

22

The Anderson house was set in an area of well-maintained woodland, high, clipped hedges, and long gravel driveways. It was one of a group of properties that had once formed a sprawling ducal estate. Several people who lived in that area, including Gillian DeViers, claimed it to be the Chatsworth of Heathervale. However, nearby Chatsworth House was a grand palace with cascading fountains, drawing rooms fit for queens, and gardens designed by Capability Brown. The stable block alone at Chatsworth House was larger than any home in Heathervale.

Still, Fernella Anderson's house did have a certain stature to it. It had probably only been a gate house or a garden folly on the old duke's property. But the sense of history about the place made it truly impressive. The house's walls were made of enormous grey stones, which were cut in sharp, imposing lines. Full-length leaded windows took up most of the front of the house. These were framed by long velvet curtains, which were tied with gold-tasselled ropes. Arrina peeked into the room to the left of the door. From there, she could see dark wooden furniture, stiff-looking sofas, and portraits that were at least three times life size.

Everything about the house spoke of wealth and history, both of which were entirely absent from Arrina's family tree. She wished she had worn her heels now, so she could stand a little taller as she walked through the place. But it was too late. And besides, she was only there to chat with Fernella's sixteen-year-old son about the supposed business he was running. Arrina couldn't imagine that was nearly as impressive as his family's pedigree.

She rapped the large black knocker against the door. Peregrine himself answered, with a wide grin and a sharp suit that did little to hide his youth—the boy had barely started shaving, and a hint of puppy fat remained in his cheeks.

'I'm so glad you were able to come today,' Perry said. 'I hope you didn't have any trouble finding the place.' He held open the tall door and extended an arm to welcome Arrina inside.

'Not at all.'

'With this weather we're having,' he said, 'the roads are becoming terribly treacherous. And when there's even the barest hint of snow, we're quite cut off down here as these private roads don't get cleared.'

He might *look* young, she realised, but he was making a significant effort to act like a grown-up. She remembered her own teenage self—a bookish, awkward girl who'd blushed easily. She wouldn't have felt confident welcoming a head teacher into her family's home, let alone setting up a business meeting with one.

'Is it your first time here?' asked Perry. 'Let me give you the grand tour. There are several original features, including a quite impressive stained-glass window at the back.'

The young man turned to walk down the portrait-lined hallway, but Arrina didn't follow. She wasn't the same nervous teenager she'd once been.

'I think it's best if we get straight to business,' she said. 'I'm afraid I've got several other meetings booked in today.'

She looked at her watch pointedly and hoped that Perry wouldn't ask for more details.

He stopped and turned to face her. He glanced at one of the thickly varnished portraits of long-faced men on the wall, as though about to explain some feature that might engage her interest in his house's history. Then he shifted his weight from foot to foot and gave her another wide grin. 'Next time, perhaps.'

'Indeed. Are we through here for the meeting?' Arrina gestured at the sitting room that she'd seen from the driveway. The room was dimly lit despite the long picture window at its front, but Arrina could just about make out a tea service on the table in there. Her last cup of tea had been hours ago, and it was almost all she could think about.

'No, my mother has one of her groups coming.' Perry's voice was full of teenage petulance then, and Arrina found herself pleased to see his polish slipping. The boy noticed his mistake and quickly added, 'She assists with *many* worthy organisations. She's such an inspiration. I hope to be able to add a charitable arm to my own endeavours before too long.'

'That's very admirable,' Arrina said. 'I look forward to hearing about all of your... endeavours.' If Arrina remembered correctly, Perry had earned a D in his GCSE English exam. Where had this vocabulary been then?

'Great.' He cleared his throat and shuffled again on the hallway's thick carpeting. 'If you'll follow me, I'll be able to tell you everything. I'm using the annex as my office at the moment but hoping to expand into my own space very soon.'

That was the second mention of his future plans in as many minutes. Whatever Peregrine Anderson was working on, he clearly had big ideas for it.

As they reached the back door, a loud musical call filled the house: 'Peregrine!' Arrina would know that voice a mile off—she could probably hear it at that distance too. It came from Fernella Anderson, Perry's mother and a former opera singer.

Arrina expected the boy to duck through the back door and dart away. That was the usual response of boys his age to the presence of parents. But instead, he turned and walked towards the staircase, where he met his mother coming down.

Fernella wore one of her many voluminous velvet dresses that day. This one was a sickly shade of dusky pink that reminded Arrina of her grandparents' old bathroom.

'Arrina,' the woman said as Perry escorted her down the hallway, 'I'm so glad you could make it for this meeting. I'm sure you and Peregrine will have a very fruitful discussion.'

Arrina could find no words to respond to this assertion. Instead, she smiled and said, 'You have a lovely home.'

'Thank you. Has Peregrine here given you the tour? There's a simply marvellous—'

'Arrina doesn't have time for a tour, unfortunately.' Peregrine and his mother shared a smile, one that pitied those who couldn't appreciate the value of beautiful architecture and well-preserved historical features. Arrina expected to see the smile drop from Perry's face as soon as his mother looked away. But it remained.

'That *is* a shame,' Fernella said. 'I hope you've at least directed her towards the facilities, as the annex is currently without.'

Arrina was not entirely sure what Fernella was talking about. But then Perry explained that the 'facilities' were along the side corridor and to the right, and Arrina guessed he meant the toilet.

'Thank you,' Arrina said. Then she gestured to the back door. 'Shall we get started?'

'Of course,' Fernella said, nudging Perry down the corridor towards Arrina. 'I'll leave the pair of you to it.'

Perry led Arrina through a large and well-maintained garden to a wood-panelled building that was almost as big as her cottage. 'It's a little crowded today, I'm afraid,' Perry said. The hum of voices in nearby rooms confirmed this. 'We've got several new starters in, and they're going through their training with some of our more experienced team members.'

'How many people are working here?'

'I'd need to take a look at the records to get an accurate number, but we're growing far faster than expected. It's really quite incredible. We can pop our heads in and say hello to some of the trainees if you'd like. You should recognise several faces, and I'm sure they'd be happy to see you.'

Arrina realised that he was talking about her students, or rather, *ex*-students, who had left the college to come and do whatever it was that Perry's business did.

She tapped her watch. 'As I said, I really am quite pressed for time.'

'Of course. Let's head straight to the nerve-centre of my operation, then, and we'll see what synergy we can establish between our two pursuits. My mother briefed me a little on what your board is considering, and I agree that a mentorship programme does sound very interesting. Very interesting indeed.'

Arrina tried to keep her expression as neutral as possible. She had several reactions to Perry's marketing-speak nonsense and mention of his mother's arrangement of their meeting. None of those would make this interaction go better, so it was best to keep them well concealed. She merely gritted her teeth and made plans for several hours of Christmas movie watching that evening. She lined the films up mentally as Perry led her into his office: *It's a Wonderful Life, White Christmas, Elf...*

The first thing she saw inside was a poster with the word Success beneath a picture of an ocean sunrise. Arrina added several more films to her list, took a deep breath, and stepped into the room. This was going to be a very trying morning.

23

'I must apologise for the mess,' Perry said. Piles of paper sat on every surface. Most of the documents looked like invoices, and all of them bore strange, unreadable words that Arrina wasn't sure were even English. 'As I said, we're expanding far faster than I'd anticipated, and it's all I can do to keep up with the business side of things. Mummy says I should get an assistant, but that takes so much time to arrange. I'm sure I don't have to tell *you* about the pains of the hiring process.'

'Not at all,' Arrina said. She thought of the chemistry teacher she'd employed on impulse the day before. In another meeting, she might have mentioned this decision so she could break the ice before getting down to business. But not with Perry.

The boy sat down in a high-backed leather chair and gestured for Arrina to take the noticeably smaller seat that faced it. 'So, I'm not sure how much you've heard about my little operation here.' He wore a wide grin that said that of course she must have heard *something*.

'Your mother mentioned you were setting up a business, but she didn't give me any details.' Arrina wondered how long she had to stay. She wasn't really going to make Perry the business mentor at the college. She'd known that before even driving over here. She just had to make a show of looking into the idea.

'A number of your students are keen to get on board,' Perry said, leaning back and interlacing his fingers behind his head. 'There's a real buzz around the venture. A lot of groundswell. I'm surprised none of it's reached you.'

'Running the college keeps me quite busy.' Arrina gritted her teeth again and smiled.

'You know, there have been huge developments in the tech field in the last few years. I can send you a list of solutions to make your job easier. Things have really changed since your day.'

Arrina cocked her head to the side. Had he really just said that? 'Thank you. It's good to hear you're so connected with the tech world. I know it's a little friendlier to those without a... traditional background.' Her overly sympathetic smile made her meaning clear—since he'd got such terrible grades, most jobs weren't an option for him.

Perry's hairless cheeks flushed red. He picked up a pen and twirled it around his forefinger in quick, jerky twists, looking like a student who'd failed an exam after trying his absolute best.

Arrina felt glad for all of three seconds before her stomach clenched to see a young person looking hurt. 'It seems like it's going well for you, though. You've clearly captured the attention of the young people of the area, a goal in which we're both interested. Shall we see if there are any more points of commonality between our work and find out what we can do together in the future?'

Perry stopped spinning the pen and sat a little straighter in his seat. He opened a drawer in his desk and pulled out some papers. Before Arrina could look at them, the sound of a key in the lock caused her to turn towards the door.

'Here you are,' came a voice Arrina recognised but could not place. 'Are you working on the new order?'

The door opened, and in walked Maggie Lee. She was the sweet young family friend of Julie's who lived on the farm behind the college. Maggie had originally moved to the village to work as a chemistry teacher but had changed her plans and was now setting up a natural pesticide company.

At least, that was what Arrina had thought she was doing. Now she appeared to be working with Perry.

'Oh,' Maggie said. 'I'm sorry. I didn't know you had company.' Maggie kept her eyes fixed on Perry and didn't glance at Arrina even once. Arrina couldn't understand this. Just that Sunday, they'd worked together in Julie's café, and now Maggie was acting like they didn't even know each other.

In fact, Arrina couldn't understand a lot of what was going on. Maggie was almost a decade older than Perry, and she was a professional, hard-working woman who had a business of her own. Arrina had spoken to Maggie at the Careers Fair about her new natural pesticide company. The two women had also helped out at Do-Re-Mi together that Sunday morning, and Maggie had mentioned nothing then about working with Perry.

Arrina had thought Maggie was *still* helping out at the café for Julie. It made no sense that she was there in Perry's office that day, nor that she had a key.

'It's good that you're here, actually,' Perry said, smiling and standing up to welcome Maggie in. 'I remember you mentioned that you once thought about working at Heathervale College. Arrina is here suggesting that I do the same—not as a teacher, of course, but as a business mentor. You'd be an excellent facilitator for our new joint venture.'

'I didn't know about this,' Maggie said. Her voice was soft, but it had an edge that Arrina couldn't understand.

'It's a new development,' Perry said, his smile still wide even though Maggie didn't look happy at all. In fact, Arrina thought she saw Maggie subtly shake her head.

'I wish I'd known you were in a meeting now. I've just had a message about that video call you were waiting for. I told them you'd be with them in two minutes.'

'Can it wait?' Perry flicked his gaze between Maggie and Arrina.

'I'm afraid not. I've got to get back to my farm shortly, and I promised them I'd get this sorted before I did.' Maggie focused her stare hard on Perry. Slowly, she asked, 'So are you free?'

Perry paused a beat too long. 'The video call. Absolutely.' Then he held out his hand to Arrina. 'I'm afraid we're going to have to pick this up another time.'

Arrina paused as well, then she slowly reached out her hand in return. 'Right, yes.' She looked between Maggie and Perry, trying to read the crackle of unspoken matters between them. 'Another time.'

Arrina leaned down to pick up her bag. Her face was inches from the desk, and she peered at the paperwork that Perry had left on it. The document closest to her was some sort of organisational hierarchy. Sales assistant, crew manager, and team leader each climbed up the chain on the piece of paper. There were no names on it, though, so it didn't tell her anything useful.

As she tried to glance at the other documents, Perry swiped them from his desk and tidied them into a drawer. 'Maggie here can show you out.' He spoke as though Maggie was his assistant. But he'd told Arrina just a minute ago that he hadn't hired one. If not that, then what *was* Maggie doing there?

Maggie finally looked over at Arrina, but her eyes darted quickly away. Arrina remembered a hint of this same evasiveness in Do-Re-Mi that Sunday. She'd thought Maggie was just upset by Phil's arrest and unsure how to act. But perhaps she'd actually been avoiding Arrina's gaze because of her secret work with Perry.

Before Arrina could ask about this, Maggie opened the door and waited beside it. She kept her eyes fixed on Perry. 'Actually, Patience is just out in the corridor. Let me grab her and she can show Arrina out.'

After the shock of finding out Maggie was working with Perry, Arrina felt only a small fizz of surprise that Patience was involved as well. The young girl, whose energy filled every space she was in, struggled with the order and routine of college. It made sense that she'd be tempted to try some other, more immediate option for herself.

Within a matter of seconds, Arrina found herself out in the hallway, face-to-face with the curly haired girl. Patience turned bright red and rushed Arrina from the building without saying a word. Arrina couldn't tell whether the silence was because the girl was still embarrassed to have hung all the signs in the wrong place that Saturday, or because she was panicked at seeing Arrina now that she had, presumably, dropped out of Heathervale College. Whatever the cause, Patience's tight lips gave nothing away.

Back in the freezing morning air of the garden, Arrina saw several other teenagers she recognised from the college. They were standing in pairs having animated conversations. Arrina only caught snippets of these—*excellent results, unbeatable prices, effective on all crops*—before Patience rushed her back through the main house and deposited her by her car.

As she rummaged through her bag for her keys, Arrina pieced together what she little she'd learned about Perry's business that morning—it was something to do with crops, teenagers were being trained as salespeople, and it involved Maggie Lee. Then Arrina realised what all of it meant—*this* was Maggie's natural pesticide company. She'd got Peregrine involved, presumably because of his connections with the young people of the village. That made a lot more sense than the young man setting up his own successful business in a matter of weeks. And now he and Maggie were stealing the students from her college to work for them.

How could Maggie do that? Arrina had thought they were friends. And even worse, Maggie was supposed to be helping Julie this week. Had she really deserted the woman she called aunty? Arrina had only known Maggie for a couple of months. Now it seemed like she'd never really known the woman at all. Though perhaps that was the new normal for Arrina—missing things. She hadn't seen what was going on with her own students. She hadn't noticed that so many of them were being lured away from the college to work here.

Arrina stared around at the bare, winter landscape, and wondered what else she'd missed recently. Had there been signs that Phil was struggling? Surely there'd been hints that he was stressed and taking on extra work. Why hadn't she seen them?

Arrina's thoughts were interrupted by a loud horn and the crunch of tires on gravel. She turned just in time to see a car heading towards her, swerving aside at the last minute, and then stopping on the ice-hard lawn beside the driveway. She strode over to the car to chastise the reckless drivers. But when she saw who got out, she was too surprised to speak.

24

Distinctive red hair and four matching, flinty expressions faced Arrina on the driveway. These people were the Drabbles—the youngest siblings from the family, to be precise. Arrina recognised them from Kingsley's book of clippings. She also remembered what the family had done—burned kitchen waste and spread poisonous ashes on their land. Only the father was in prison for it, but Kingsley had said the rest of them were involved as well.

The four family members standing on Peregrine Anderson's driveway—two boys and two girls—all looked to be in their late teens or early twenties. From what Arrina knew about their family's recent trouble with the law, it shouldn't have surprised her that they were involved with Perry. There was something very untrustworthy about Perry's slick suit, corporate-speak, and workforce of eager teens. The Drabble family—who treated their farm like a landfill—fit in with that perfectly.

She was still surprised that Maggie Lee was connected to that world as well, but Arrina hadn't known the young woman very long, and Arrina was coming to see she'd never really known her at all.

'Is Perry in?' asked the smallest of the Drabble siblings. She was a short, athletic-looking girl of about seventeen. She wore a striped crop top and no coat, yet she showed no sign of shivering in the below-freezing day.

'He's in,' Arrina said, 'but he's on a video call.' Actually, as she thought about it, Arrina wondered if Maggie had just said that as an excuse to get her out of there. Arrina would be rethinking a lot of things related to young Maggie Lee, she suspected.

'See,' the Drabble girl said, punching the arm of the brother by her side, whose bulging muscles didn't flinch. 'I told you we couldn't trust him. *Clearing his whole morning*, you said. I told you he was full of it.'

The tall, muscular brother said nothing. Another brother was standing nearby, who was the chalk to his cheese. That boy was a twitchy, skinny young man who looked like he'd just gone through a growth spurt and wasn't used to his towering perspective on the world. He squinted and bobbed his head before saying, 'Maybe it just came up. Could have been an emergency. He *did* tell Nate the morning was clear. He promised it.'

'He had an eleven o'clock meeting with me,' Arrina said, still not exactly sure what had happened back in Perry's office a few minutes earlier and feeling stuck for a moment from the surprise of it.

The short girl punched her well-muscled brother once again—the one apparently called Nate—even though he hadn't said anything. 'I told you. I told you, didn't I?' She looked over at her sister, whose slumped shoulders gave a faint shrug, then she thumped Nate once more for good measure. 'I knew as soon as we saw Kingsley Peters walking out of here that Perry was no good. Only a snake, no, a *rat*, would have anything to do with that man.'

'Kingsley Peters was here?' Arrina asked. *That* was why she was there. She'd known there was some link between Perry and the dead man. 'What—'

'He explained that,' the string bean brother said, ignoring Arrina entirely. 'Perry said the guy must have been seeing his mother about some charity thing.'

'Yeah, right!' the girl replied. 'The only charity Kingsley Peters has ever cared about is his own pocket.'

'When was—' Arrina was cut off again by the two squabbling siblings, who pushed and shoved each other on the gravel driveway. They called each other names and kicked up a scattering of cold, hard pebbles.

'Stop,' Nate said in a low voice. The pair instantly stood still and stepped away from each other.

Arrina turned her attention to Nate. 'Was Kingsley Peters really here?' she asked.

He nodded.

'When?' Arrina hoped he would say Saturday, which would give her a new line of investigation after so many dead ends.

'A few weeks back.'

Arrina felt disappointed at first, but then realised that this answer was just as significant. And she hoped, given how much the Drabble family must hate Kingsley Peters, they'd tell her all about it. Indeed, she didn't even have to do more than look interested for them to explain what they knew. The short, crop top-wearing sister started, 'We was here a few weeks ago to talk about joining the business.'

'Yeah, we all came down,' added the skinny brother. 'But as soon as we pulled up, we saw that scumbag Kingsley Peters walk out the door, and we drove away. Perry called up later and promised he didn't know anything.' He then turned to his angry young sister and repeated those words. 'He *promised* he didn't know anything.'

'A likely story,' the shorter sister said. 'But Nate said to give him another chance, and Perry was calling us all the time asking us to come down.'

'Drabbles give second chances,' said the slump-shouldered sister in a voice almost too quiet to be heard.

'Yeah,' said the other sister. 'Not like everyone else.'

'Perry's giving us a chance,' said Nate.

'I still reckon he's dodgy,' the short girl muttered. 'Any friend of Kingsley's can't be trusted. That man was a crook, through and through.'

Kingsley was responsible for putting their father in prison. Arrina didn't know how much she could trust their assessment of him. But she had suspected a connection between Kingsley and Perry herself, so she had to find out what the siblings knew. 'Why is he a crook? What did he do?'

'What did he do?' the young girl repeated, looking shocked. 'What did he do? He only stitched up our dad and sent him to prison for something he never did.'

The other siblings all nodded at her assertion. Though, of course, they *would*. Arrina needed much more than that to work out what had really happened to Kingsley. 'I'm sorry to hear it.' She smiled politely.

'I know you don't believe us,' the young girl said. 'Nobody does. But Kingsley Peters was a liar and a thief, and whoever killed him did the world a favour.'

'And before you ask,' said Nate, stepping between Arrina and the rest of his siblings, 'we didn't do it.'

'I wasn't—'

'We were visiting our dad in prison, like we do every month.' He stepped closer. 'The whole family goes, even though only three of us are allowed in each time.' He took another step towards Arrina, his feet crunching on the icy gravel. 'We make a day of it. Take our mum for a nice meal. It's the least she deserves.'

Arrina stood her ground. She looked up at Nate and nodded. As a head teacher in a sixth form college, she spent her days around boys who were newly becoming men. She knew this type of behaviour well, and she knew the fear that lay behind it. The best way out of the situation was to keep calm and make it clear she understood what he was saying. She held eye contact with the tall, muscular man until she sensed him relax.

'My friend is being held in prison as a suspect in Kingsley's murder,' Arrina said. 'He didn't do it, and if there's anything you can tell me that you think would help me prove that, I'd really appreciate it.'

Nate stepped away and exchanged glances with his siblings. They didn't say anything but seemed to come to a quick agreement.

'Kingsley Peters wasn't a good guy,' Nate said. 'Every family we know has been threatened by him with either a fine or a prison sentence. He had his own cut-price deal to get out of that, and most people took it. Our dad didn't, and you know what happened to him.' The young man turned and started to walk towards his car, his band of red-headed siblings in tow. 'I know it wasn't a Drabble that killed Kingsley, but I'd bet good money it was one of the farmers whose lives he ruined.'

Then the siblings drove away, leaving Arrina to stand in the drive and process what she'd just learned. Kingsley Peters was blackmailing people and threatening to prosecute them if they didn't pay him off. If she'd heard that said about any other Environment Agency Officer, she wouldn't have believed it. But she'd met Kingsley Peters, and very little would surprise her about that man.

She thought about what the Drabbles had just said. *Every family we know has been threatened by him.* That meant an awful lot of suspects in the man's murder.

Of course, if she told anyone what she'd just learned about Kingsley, they'd say it was more evidence against Phil. He could very well have been threatened by Kingsley, just like the others. Phil might even have paid the man off, Arrina realised. That would explain his desperation for extra work from the Yates family. And when one combined that with the fact he was working in the very place the murder had happened, Phil looked guiltier than ever.

But not to Arrina. She knew there had to be another explanation for everything that had gone on. She just had to figure out what it was.

Arrina stood alone in the driveway and thought about this. The sun broke through a gap in the clouds and bathed her in pale light. But still, she shivered.

25

Arrina desperately wanted to go home and bury her head beneath the covers on her huge, cosy bed. Every new fact she learned about Kingsley Peters was darker and more complicated than the last. Each step she took towards finding out who'd killed the man plunged her deeper into a world she couldn't understand.

Kingsley had blackmailed local farmers; Perry Anderson was tied up with the corrupt dead man; Phil had lied to his wife; Maggie Lee couldn't be trusted; the *police* couldn't even be trusted. The list went on and on, bringing Arrina nothing but pain as she thought of it.

If she went home to bed, she could stay there all day, listening to Christmas music and drinking cups of tea. She thought of Tinsel's soft fur warming her fingers. She thought of the delicious mince pies waiting in her freezer.

But *Julie* had made those mince pies. Arrina wouldn't be able to eat them without feeling awful for failing her friend. As she reached into her bag for her car keys, her fingers brushed against the heart wood. She'd even failed to give *that* to Julie.

At least she could do that one thing. She could give her friend the heart wood and bring her a little peace as she clutched the comforting talisman. Julie would be in Do-Re-Mi—Maggie wasn't looking after the place, and Julie would trust no one else to run it properly. Arrina got into her car and headed over to the café on the High Street.

She was surprised not to see Julie's bright yellow Mini parked in front of the building. Julie only hid it around the back when she closed up to work in the kitchen undisturbed. But it was the middle of a Tuesday, so the café would be open and preparing for the lunch rush.

Yet it wasn't. The lights were off, and the front door was locked. Arrina rattled the handle to check, but she saw nobody inside.

Arrina peered in through the full-length window at the front of Do-Re-Mi and saw the chairs up on the tables from the previous night. Or perhaps the night before that. There was a stillness about the place that Arrina had never felt before.

She knocked hard on the window. She knocked until her knuckles turned red. But there was no sign of movement inside. She stepped back, intending to head to the kitchen door around the back.

But she stepped neatly into the path of Gillian DeViers. The woman tottered on her low heels, let out a cry of surprise, and stopped several feet short of actually running into Arrina. Gillian pressed her hand to her chest and looked as though she'd had a brush with death.

'Sorry,' Arrina said. 'I'm sorry. I wasn't paying attention.' An irate Gillian DeViers was the last thing she needed. But it looked like that was exactly what she would get.

'This is a public thoroughfare,' Gillian said. She brushed down the front of her dense tweed jacket and skirt. 'Many of the village's elderly residents are not as nimble as I, and they would not be able to remain safe in the face of your careless behaviour.'

'Nimble' was the last word Arrina would use to describe Gillian DeViers. The woman was in her late fifties, and the combination of her tight tweed outfits and stocky frame made her about as nimble as a combine harvester. Arrina didn't say that, though. Instead she apologised again and headed for her car.

But Gillian intercepted her. 'I'm actually glad to have run into you.' She pursed her lips to remind Arrina of how literal their run-in had been. 'I wanted to tell you in person that the Parish Council is cancelling this year's Lantern Parade.'

'You're cancelling it?' Arrina said.

'Yes. I know you're fond of it, but I do hope you won't cause too much fuss. That's why I wanted to speak to you about it in person. Due to recent events, we really feel it's in the village's best interest not to go ahead with the event this year.'

'You can't cancel it.'

'I assure you that we can. This—'

'It's a tradition.'

Gillian pursed her lips once more. She stared at Arrina and sighed. 'The Parish Council has not taken this decision lightly.'

'But the Lantern Parade has been around for hundreds of years.'

Gillian looked up and down the High Street, which was empty despite the approach of lunchtime. 'If that's your main concern, I can assure you that you needn't worry. The parade was started in 1986. Missing one year won't harm anybody.'

Arrina was speechless for several seconds. 'But all the posters say it dates back centuries.'

'Not exactly.' Gillian folded her arms across her chest. 'What they say is that *records* of it date back that long. Indeed, there are several references to Christmas lanterns in the parish documents, and a local historian has unearthed a short story from the Victorian era that describes a ceremony close to the current parade. However, as I said, the parade itself...'

1986! Arrina couldn't believe it. 'So it's a lie?'

'It's good marketing, which, I must say, recent events in the village are not. Nobody wants to spend an evening in the murder capital of the Peak District.'

'I'm sure nobody's calling it that.' Given the local area's love of gossip, however, Arrina wouldn't be surprised if the salacious name had already spread. 'Anyway, the parade is still two weeks away. People will have forgotten about the murder by then.' Arrina winced. She hadn't meant her thoughts to come out quite so bluntly. 'I mean, it's very sad, obviously, but Kingsley Peters wasn't even from Heathervale, so it doesn't seem disrespectful to hold the parade. And the children will be devastated if the parade's cancelled.'

'Kingsley is not the issue here.'

Arrina's mind scrambled to figure out what Gillian meant. Had there been *another* murder in Heathervale?

Gillian unfolded her arms and planted her hands on her sturdy hips. 'It was bad enough when *one* local man was arrested over this, but now *two*. Nobody wants to visit a place where every other person is a serial killer.'

Two! That meant the police had already been to the Morgan woods and made their arrest. Arrina drew a slow, deep breath to fight the panicked guilt at the knowledge that she had caused this. 'It's a mistake. It will all be cleared up before the parade.' Arrina hoped more than anything that this was true.

'We can't take that risk. As chair of the Parish Council, it is my duty to uphold our village's good standing. At this stage, it's best that we cancel public events and avoid drawing too much attention to the terrible situation.'

'But you know Phil didn't do this.'

'And Wallace? Are you equally sure about him?'

'I...' Arrina's mouth dropped open in surprise. Wallace was Wallace Morgan, one of Nancy's identical twin brothers. It was shocking enough that the police had already made their arrest, but Arrina couldn't wrap her mind around the idea that the evidence had pointed to *Wallace*. He and his brother Wilfred were identical in looks but very different in personality. Wilfred, with his thickly clustered tattoos and quick wits, was who Arrina had thought of when the police said a Morgan twin was involved. But Wallace? He was a soft-hearted young man who was too trusting for his own good, but he certainly wasn't a murderer.

Gillian looked around the street once more. Old Mrs Pangle was shuffling down the pavement on her Zimmer frame, but she was only level with the supermarket. At her pace, she'd be out of earshot for several more minutes. 'If the Lantern Parade were to go ahead, our usual visitors would likely stay away, and the only people attending would be those looking to gossip about our village's misfortune.'

'But—' Arrina started. Then she stopped, knowing that she couldn't make an argument that would persuade Gillian DeViers. Nothing would help other than Phil and Wallace being released.

Arrina's every effort to solve the murder so far had made things worse. She wasn't sure she could do it now, not even to save the Lantern Parade. Arrina got back into her car and tried to start her engine. The vehicle seemed to feel as awful as she did right then, and it coughed and spluttered every time Arrina turned the key. After Arrina spent a full three minutes trying, the car finally roared into life. By then, Old Mrs Pangle had drawn level with Arrina, and she jumped up in surprise at the sound.

Arrina readied herself to rush out to help the ninety-three-year-old woman, but Old Mrs Pangle was sturdier than she looked. She clutched her Zimmer frame and continued shuffling along the pavement. Arrina watched her move slowly but surely across the village green. Then Arrina was once again alone on the High Street. She sat in her idling car for several minutes, feeling the thrum of the engine and trying to gather some of its powerful energy into herself.

Julie needed help. Arrina had been trying for days to give it to her, but nothing was working. She glanced over at the dark café once more and knew she would never give up. No matter how hard things were getting, Arrina would keep going for Julie.

She gunned her engine and roared along the narrow country lanes. She headed to the farm to find *something* she could do to help Julie.

26

It was lunchtime when Arrina reached Julie's farmhouse. Her stomach rumbled, and she hoped that Julie was dealing with stress in her usual, food-based way. But then Arrina heard the lowing of cows from the parlour and realised her friend must be doing the milking.

Arrina took several steps towards the large building before realising this situation wasn't right. The cows shouldn't have been in the parlour then. They were milked first thing in the morning and again in late afternoon.

Now that it was lunchtime, the cows should have been doing nothing more than chewing cud and contemplating.

Arrina looked around the yard between the farmhouse and the parlour. There was no sign of Julie's yellow Mini. But there *was* a pink bicycle propped against a nearby gate. Purple ribbons streamed from the handlebars, and a glittery bell completed the child-like look. Arrina wondered if Barbie herself was inside with the cows. But then she remembered where she'd seen the bike before. It was parked in the rack at the college most days, and it had been locked up by the village hall that Sunday as well.

The bike belonged to sweet, young Nancy Morgan. Coming to milk the cows of a neighbour in need was just the sort of thing the kind-hearted girl would do. Arrina knew she had a full schedule on Tuesdays, and lunchtime was the only free moment she had to help.

Nancy chatted to the cows inside the barn, her thin, girlish voice drifting on a frosty breeze to where Arrina stood.

Nancy sounded cheerful, and Arrina wondered if she hadn't heard about her brother. Poor Wallace Morgan, Nancy's older brother, had just been arrested, and it was all Arrina's fault.

Arrina took a step towards the parlour. Then she stopped.

How could she tell Nancy what had happened? Arrina had thought she was doing the right thing when she handed the heart wood over to the police and told them it belonged to a Morgan, but Nancy wouldn't see it that way.

Arrina looked back at her car. But she couldn't just drive away. Her limbs felt heavy even thinking about this. Out of the corner of her eye, she spotted a robin hopping along the frozen ground. The bird stared at her and cocked its head. Arrina watched it for a few seconds, then she turned back to the parlour. She would find a way to tell Nancy what had happened. Arrina always encouraged her students to be honest, even when it was hard. She could do that now herself.

But when she looked over at the parlour entrance, she realised she wouldn't have to.

Nancy Morgan was standing there, glaring at Arrina with a face as frosty as the season.

Tears wobbled in Nancy's eyes, just as they had done the day before in the college. But *then* her tears had been on Arrina's behalf, since the murals she loved had been ruined by vandals. And now the tears were *because* of Arrina, who'd helped the police pin a murder on her brother.

Arrina walked towards Nancy. The young girl held up a hand and stopped Arrina in her tracks. The cold air felt brittle between them. Any sound threatened to shatter it into a thousand knife-edged pieces, but Arrina couldn't stay silent. 'I'm sorry.'

Nancy crossed her thin arms across her body and glanced at her bike.

'I'm really very sorry,' Arrina said. 'It wasn't my intention to get your brother in trouble.'

'He didn't do it,' Nancy said. And Arrina knew in her heart that this was true. Wallace Morgan shovelled snow from the paths of the elderly residents of Heathervale. He made props for village plays. He had even, once, jumped into the freezing water of the River Derwent to save a drowning lamb.

That morning, when Ian had suggested that the evidence against a Morgan twin could set Phil free, Arrina had been sure it would be Wilfred Morgan who'd be tied to the murder. Wilfred was a silent, burly man, who combined his strength with a sharp mind in a way which hinted at danger.

'I didn't mean to...' Arrina started. Then she stopped herself. She sounded just like a teenager at the college. 'It was a mistake. I'm sorry, and I'll do everything I can to fix it.'

Nancy chewed on her lower lip and then blurted out, 'He's having a baby.'

Arrina pictured the muscly, tattoo-covered Wilfred Morgan flat on his back with his legs up in stirrups. Then she realised that Nancy meant *Wallace* was having the baby. But that still didn't make any sense.

'I'm not meant to tell anyone,' Nancy said. 'But it doesn't matter now. Not if he goes to prison. It won't matter anymore because those poncey Yateses will never let him see the baby. Probably *none* of us will see it, and they'll just say that Imogen had some sort of immaculate contraception.'

Arrina was confused but then understood that Nancy had meant to say immaculate *con*ception. Arrina stopped herself from correcting the girl. This wasn't the time to be worried about terminology. What mattered was that Imogen Yates was pregnant, and, if Arrina was following correctly, Wallace Morgan was the father. There had been rumours that one of the Morgan twins had got a baby on the way, but Arrina hadn't believed them. The look on Nancy's face said they were certainly true.

'Wallace and Imogen?' Arrina asked. Imogen was Bill Yates's niece, the apple of her grandfather's eye, and certainly not someone the Yates family would want involved with a Morgan.

'They were planning how to tell her family,' Nancy said. 'That's what they were doing down in the corner of the Yates land on Saturday. Wallace wanted to marry her. He tried to give her his heart wood to seal their engagement, but she ran away crying because she was too scared to tell her parents about it. She dropped the heart wood, and Wallace couldn't find it. Then you found it and gave it to the police so they'd think one of our lot did it.'

A chill seeped into Arrina right down to her bones. But the fire of guilt burned through her chest. 'I didn't mean for it to happen like that.' Again, she felt like a teenager making excuses, but she had nothing better to give the distraught girl. 'I'm sure the police will let Wallace go when he explains what he was doing there.'

Nancy looked at the ground and shook her head. 'The police never listen to Morgans.'

Arrina opened her mouth to deny this, but it was true. The police always checked with the Morgans first when a crime was committed in the village. She'd heard enough tales of Morgan mistreatment to believe that Wallace would be locked up without a chance to explain himself.

And Arrina's suspicions about the police were growing every day. First, Tony had been kept out of the murder investigation, and now Ian was poking around in Arrina's business in a way that didn't make sense. She didn't even know what Ian had been doing at the Yates farm that morning. She hadn't thought about it at the time—she'd been too stricken with panic and then guilt to wonder what he was doing there so early in the morning, especially when the crime scene had already been scoured for evidence.

He could only have been there following Arrina. A shiver ran through her that was not brought on by the icy air.

Had it really been a coincidence that she'd discovered the heart wood on the Yates farm? Or had Ian planted it? Perhaps he set up Arrina's discovery to pin the murder on a Morgan.

But that didn't make sense if the police already had Phil in custody. Why would they want to frame a second person? And this was Ian she was thinking about—a man who'd once won a pub bet over the number of pork scratchings he could fit in his mouth. He wasn't the malicious conspiracy type. But then what was going on?

Arrina looked at Nancy, whose cold-pinked cheeks were streaked with tears. Arrina had to fix this. Something strange was going on in Heathervale, and Arrina was determined to get to the bottom of it.

She apologised once more to Nancy, but the young girl just shook her head and walked back into the milking parlour. Arrina almost chased after her. The Morgans had always been good to her, ever since she'd first arrived in the village. It had even been a Morgan who—in a roundabout way—had brought Tinsel into her life five years earlier.

Arrina's heart ached knowing that she'd hurt the Morgan family. But Arrina couldn't keep apologising for that. She wanted to, but apologies wouldn't get Wallace free, and they wouldn't help Phil either. All Arrina could do now was solve the murder of Kingsley Peters.

She was completely out of leads, but she wasn't going to let that stop her. She contemplated flying to Venezuela to track down Kingsley's widow, Callie. She thought about tunnelling into prison to speak to Phil and Wallace. But in the end, she decided to start a little closer to home and talk to Julie. She still had many unanswered questions about what had been going on between Phil and Kingsley, and Julie might have some of the answers, even if it would upset her to talk about them. With enough luck, something she said would lead Arrina to the corrupt man's killer.

Arrina had already spent a good part of the day looking for her best friend and hadn't found her yet. Julie wasn't working at the café, and she wasn't on the farm. There was one other place she was likely to be. Arrina got back in her car and headed to a small cottage down by the churning River Derwent—down to a cottage that in summer was trellised with yellow roses and in autumn was covered in pale pink cherry blossom petals. In winter, the outside of the cottage lost its sweet, flowery welcome, but the inside was kept cosy with wood fires, and tins of cakes lay within reach of every seat.

The cottage belonged to Julie's parents. Arrina headed over there and felt warmed at the thought of the friendly welcome she'd get. It was exactly what she needed right then.

27

Down at the bottom of the Hope Valley, frost lay thick and white in the shadows of the trees. The cold air had a stillness which the wind-whipped peaks never knew in any season. The only movement came from the roaring River Derwent as it cut sharply through the middle of the valley. Summer games of Pooh sticks and trouser-rolled paddling were distant memories to that steel-grey stretch of water which ran slick with speed.

The only bright spot down by the river was Julie's yellow Mini, which was parked at the front of her parents' cottage. The sight of the car made Arrina's heart leap in her chest. She parked her own silver-blue Jaguar beside it and headed down the mossy path to the Wen's cosy cottage.

But before Arrina could reach the door, Mr Wen came rushing out. He was a short, soft-featured man, whose smile was usually just as wide and warm as Julie's. But not that day.

His small feet skipped along in house slippers that offered no protection from the frozen ground. Mr Wen didn't let that slow him down. He dashed over to Arrina and managed to hug her and turn her in one smooth motion. She was facing her car when he let go. He kept one hand lightly on her back and led her towards her Jaguar, moving her politely but firmly away from the cottage.

'It's so nice of you to visit,' Mr Wen said. 'So nice. We will be sure to tell Julie you have called.'

Mr Wen always spoke as though his wife was standing right beside him—always said *we* instead of *I*—even though

Mrs Wen's poor health meant she rested in bed most days. Arrina's stomach clenched as she worried why he was hurrying her away.

'Is everything OK?' Arrina asked. 'Is it Julie? Is it Mrs Wen? Is she—'

'*Aunty*,' he interrupted, as he always did. Then he lay a hand flat on his own chest. '*Uncle*. And everything is OK. We are having a strong day today.'

'I'm so glad.' Arrina had known the Wens for over five years by then, and she certainly considered them as close as family, but she'd never quite been able to call them aunt and uncle as they wanted. Usually, she tried to explain that calling them 'Mr' and 'Mrs' was how she was raised. Using these titles was her way of showing respect and signalling their importance. But she didn't have time right then. Mr Wen was opening Arrina's car door and stepping back to usher her inside.

'Mr Wen, I'm here to see Julie. It's important.'

'We think maybe not today. Julie has been trying to do too much all by herself.' Mr Wen did not look at Arrina when he said this, and he would never want to make Arrina feel bad, she was sure, but the ache of guilt was as hard as a punch.

'I've been trying to—'

A door banged open behind them. Arrina and Mr Wen turned to look. It was Julie, who raced down the path towards them.

'Dad, why didn't you tell me Arrina was here?' Julie's feet were shoved into large wellies over fluffy, knee-length bed socks. She was wearing a faded Bananaman T-shirt and fleecy pyjama bottoms. And on top of this combination, she clutched a crocheted blanket around herself like a housecoat.

Arrina could see why Mr Wen hadn't wanted any visitors, not even her.

'Jujube,' he said, 'you must go back inside.'

'Dad, I—'

'June-bug, we will come and see you in a minute.'

'I just want to say hi to Arrina. She's—'

'Julie,' Mr Wen said.

Julie fell silent. Her father had a thousand nicknames for her, and he only called her Julie when things were serious.

'We have told you that you must take better care of your health. The tea we made will help. Please go inside and drink it.'

Julie looked from her father to the cottage. Her dark eyes struggled to settle. One hand let go of her blanket and raked through her hair, which was more tangled than Arrina had ever seen. The blanket slipped off Julie's left shoulder and trailed on the frosty ground.

'Will you tell her?' Julie said softly. 'Will you tell her... you know?'

Mr Wen shuffled in his slippers. His thin eyebrows knitted together, and he nodded. 'Yes, Juniper-pea. Please go in now and drink your tea.'

Julie looked at Arrina but didn't quite connect with her gaze. Then she slowly walked back into the house, the trailing blanket collecting leaves and twigs in her wake.

After the front door closed, neither Arrina nor Mr Wen said anything for a long while. They stood together in the pale winter light as small birds twittered overhead and the river raced nearby.

'I didn't know she was...' Arrina started. But she couldn't say the words out loud. Couldn't explain how entirely unlike herself poor Julie had been. 'I saw her on Sunday, and she was OK then. I've been following some leads while she's been tracking down Phil. I didn't know she was...' Arrina cringed at the word *leads*. It sounded so foolish, like she was a kid playing at being detective. Mr Wen didn't say anything. He simply nodded slowly.

'Did she... did she manage to see Phil?' Arrina asked.

'No, but she has found some other things, which have upset her greatly.' He looked back at the house. Julie's mother was the original baking genius in the family, but Mr Wen was the eager host who'd made their café a success. Arrina could see how much it unsettled him not to be able to offer tea or cake, or even a sample from his famous baijiu supply. He must also have been cold in his thin slippers, with only a smart red jumper to keep out the chill. He started to shiver but made no move to go back inside.

'Is that what Julie wants you to tell me about? The things she's found?' When he nodded, she gestured at her car and suggested they get in.

Mr Wen's eyes widened. He shuffled from foot to foot and eyed the vehicle suspiciously. The man often left circled adverts for new cars in Do-Re-Mi, hoping that both she and Julie would replace the spluttering old bangers they loved so dearly.

'We can just sit in it,' Arrina assured him. 'The heating works well, and we're going to freeze if we stay out here.'

Arrina thought he would refuse. But he reluctantly nodded and walked around to the passenger seat.

He and Arrina shut the heavy doors behind themselves and left the frosty world behind. Arrina had to switch on the engine for the heating to work. Before she tried it, she thought of Julie's egg-yolk scooping tip and smiled. She scooped as she turned the key, and the engine started the first time.

Then she cranked up the heating and sat in silence while Mr Wen told her what Julie had found.

28

'This has been very hard on Julie,' Mr Wen said. His hands were folded neatly in his lap, which was an extremely rare sight. Arrina thought it might have been the first time she'd ever seen him without a plate of cakes to hand out or a pot of tea ready to pour. 'It has been hard on all of us.'

'It doesn't feel real,' Arrina said.

'Yes. That is the feeling. This weather, too, it seems like we're frozen here. Trapped. Like we're...' He gazed out of the window and trailed off. And again, this was not the Mr Wen that Arrina had known for five years. Normally, he was never without a cheery word or a piece of gossip to keep the conversation flowing.

He was right, though. It really did feel like they were frozen there in some cold, nightmare version of the world. A quote from *The Lion, the Witch and the Wardrobe* popped into her head: *Always winter, and never Christmas; think of that!*

It felt as though they had fallen into the story, but there was no parcel-carrying faun waiting by a lamp post and no sacrificing lion to save the day. Nobody was coming to fix this.

Arrina and Julie had sat in this very car just a few months earlier and joked about the White Witch of Narnia. Julie had teased that she'd cancel Christmas, too, given the chance. She'd filled the car with laughter at Arrina's reaction. Now Julie seemed like she would never laugh again.

Mr Wen stirred in his seat, breaking Arrina from her memories. He reached into his pocket and pulled out a white paper bag that he rustled open to reveal pink and yellow pear drops, thickly sugar frosted.

'Julie's favourite,' Arrina said, reaching into the proffered bag. She didn't really like pear drops herself. Their smell reminded her of nail polish remover. But she took a small one and popped it in her mouth. She thought of every time she'd gone hiking with Julie and had sweets pressed on her to keep up her energy.

'You hold onto these,' Mr Wen said, folding the bag shut and putting it in her glove box. 'Just in case.' That was something Julie would do. The whole family was so thoughtful and giving. It seemed impossible that the village had turned its back on Julie and Phil. 'There might be some blackcurrant and liquorice in my other pocket too.'

'Thank you, but I'm fine,' Arrina said, knowing how easily accepting one thing from Mr Wen could turn into him loading her entire boot with chopped wood or enough eggs to feed an army. 'I really just want to know what Julie has found. It sounds important.'

He pulled out a second bag of sweets from his other pocket. Arrina sucked her pear drop and waited while he smoothed and folded the paper with his nimble, busy fingers and finally began to speak.

'Julie has been thinking about Phil's actions over the last few months.'

'Since Kingsley investigated their milk spillage?'

'Yes, she is sure now that Phil was different after that. She had thought it was just the stress of the cows and milk prices and somehow the investigation. However, Phil said everything was quite OK. He even showed her a letter of the investigation results. There were no problems—no fine and no court case. Everything OK.'

'He didn't seem OK,' Arrina said, then she crushed the pear drop between her back teeth. She thought of the mix-up on the morning of the Careers Fair—she'd made an accidental joke about his enormous toolbelt, and instead of laughing or blushing or anything she might have expected, Phil had stammered awkwardly and rushed away. He had seemed unable to engage, as though his thoughts were entirely elsewhere. In the last couple of days, Arrina had remembered some other similar occasions, all of them coming in the months since Kingsley Peters had first been to the farm.

'Julie, when she thought of his change after the investigation, she went to look for some letters she remembered. There were letters she had seen, from a bank not theirs. The letters were to Phil, and he has take them and said something about that they were just junk mail. Julie forgets it. But now she remember, and she go... she find...'

Mr Wen's speech stumbled to a halt. He'd lived in England almost his entire life, but when he was stressed, his words fractured and sometimes failed him. Arrina could always tell when his wife's health was very bad as Cantonese words slipped into his speech and Julie had to translate them into English.

Mr Wen crumpled the bag of sweets in his hands. Those hands, which usually delivered cakes and pots of tea, shook now with what could only have been his frustration at trying to explain.

Then Arrina remembered something. She reached down into her door well and rummaged for a battered tin that Julie had put in it a few weeks earlier. After the first reports of frost on the way, Julie had moved aside Arrina's maps and manuals in favour of this flat, book-sized tin. Arrina had laughed at her then, but now she was very grateful.

She passed the tin to Mr Wen. He pulled off the lid, and the air suddenly filled with the fragrance of treacle and ginger. The smell came from Julie's parkin, a sticky, chewy cake made with oats, ginger and dark, smoky syrup. Mr Wen's face lit up the moment he saw it.

The small squares of parkin were stuck together and squashed into one end of the box. Mr Wen nudged them apart carefully, arranging and neatening them with great care then offering the display up to Arrina. She took a piece, and he prodded the rest of the parkin into a new, orderly arrangement.

'There was a letter from the bank,' Mr Wen said, speaking slowly and turning the tin of parkin in his hands to check his display. 'Several letters. Phil told Julie they were junk mail, but she noticed he kept them separate from the other letters, and he didn't throw them away.'

He paused to offer Arrina a second piece of parkin, but she was still chewing that heavenly first square. 'She found them in the house this morning,' he continued. Then he took a deep breath. 'Phil has taken out a loan for several thousand pounds.'

Arrina swallowed. 'And Julie didn't know?'

Mr Wen shook his head.

'And was the loan for...' Arrina didn't quite know what to say. A *bribe*? Was that it? The Drabble siblings had told her just a few hours earlier about Kingsley's corruption. She hadn't wanted to really believe it. But they'd said that Kingsley threatened huge fines or jail time and that he took pay-offs to prevent such outcomes. Would Phil really have given him the money?

'There are no records of where the money went,' Mr Wen said. 'Nothing Julie could find. But Phil took the loan out a few days after the milk was spilled at the farm. She is sure it was that man Kingsley who made him pay it.'

Arrina held the last bite of Julie's parkin between her finger and thumb. The sticky brown cake had a gentle balance between comforting sweetness and fiery ginger. Julie had worked for years to perfect her recipe. It seemed impossible that someone as good and hard-working as her could exist in the same world as corrupt men like Kingsley Peters.

'That isn't the worst of it,' Mr Wen said, his voice low and his eyes fixed on the tin in his hands. 'There is... there was...'

Arrina forced herself to eat the last of her parkin, although her mouth was suddenly very dry. She took another neat square from the box and watched Mr Wen keep his hands busy with rearranging the dark brown cakes in there. He slowly explained the worst part of what he knew.

29

'Millions of pounds are missing from the Environment Agency's banks accounts,' Mr Wen said, putting the lid back on the parkin.

'Millions?' That didn't sound possible. She now knew that Kingsley had been taking bribes from farmers to make his investigations go away. But those bribes were a few thousand pounds each, and they hadn't gone to the agency's accounts. What were these missing millions? And how were they connected to Phil and Julie? Arrina tried to wrap her head around what was going on.

'Yes.' Mr Wen shuffled in his seat. 'Millions. Kingsley got a promotion recently that gave him access to the agency's accounts, and then on Saturday morning, several of the accounts were cleaned out remotely.'

Both Mr Wen and Arrina looked out at the small cottage in front of them. Down here in the bottom of the Hope Valley, it was easy to forget that the rest of the world existed. Nearby, a blackbird hopped on a bare branch, a single cloud drifted overhead, and the frosty ground sparkled in the weak sun. And somewhere out there, people were stealing millions of pounds from government agencies.

'This was on Saturday morning, you said?' Arrina asked finally. 'Kingsley was at the college. There's barely enough phone signal there to receive a message, let alone transfer millions of pounds. So he must have had help.'

The despair on Mr Wen's face told her he knew this already and that *this* was the problem. 'There is a money trail.

The money was put in one of those cryptic currencies. Is that the name?'

'A cryptocurrency.'

'Yes. I don't understand this—it sounds like Monopoly money, but the police say it is very real.'

'And they can trace it?' Arrina had heard about huge computers mining for these cryptocurrencies, which, as far as she knew, were just long strings of numbers on screens. She'd thought cryptocurrencies were designed to be untraceable. But that was about the end of her knowledge about them.

'They can trace the address of the computer... Its AD, no, ID...'

'I think it's an IP.'

'You young people are always so good with these things.'

Arrina imagined her students hearing this conversation. They'd laugh at the idea she was any more in touch with cryptocurrencies than Mr Wen. She had the barest smattering of technical terms she'd overheard on the news and from her students about cryptocurrencies, but other than that, she was clueless.

'They traced the cryptic money,' Mr Wen said. 'It was transferred by a computer in Do-Re-Mi.'

Arrina knew the police would claim Phil had taken the money. But that wasn't possible. Perhaps somebody was trying to frame them, or... But then she realised something. 'That can't be right. The money can't have been transferred in Do-Re-Mi. There isn't a computer there. Julie has that ancient thing on the farm for her accounts, but she doesn't have a computer at the café, and—'

'It was the internet address of the café,' Mr Wen said gently. 'The transfer was done with the Wi-Fi.'

Arrina's heart sank, but she couldn't let go of the hope that this could somehow be good news. 'Then it could have been anyone. The café's Wi-Fi password is *cake*. Everybody in the village knows it. And Julie and Phil weren't even *in* the café that day.'

'Phil's location is—'

'In fact, Kingsley Peters was there! He brought drinks from the café to the Careers Fair. *He's* the one who took the money himself.'

'Really?' Mr Wen asked, pulling a small pencil and notepad from his pocket. 'I will tell the police this. They are sure that Phil must have been at the café and made the transfer after... getting the passwords from Kingsley. They want the café's CCTV so they can see if he was there.'

Were the police suggesting Phil had forced Kingsley to give up the passwords before killing him? That idea sounded like something from a TV show, not the actions of a dairy farmer in Heathervale. Plus, it made no sense—the money had been taken in the morning, but Kingsley wasn't killed until the afternoon, so surely the man had taken it himself. 'Phil was at the Yates farm all morning. He was working on their fences.'

'Nobody knows what time he was there. Phil has told the police he was there until noon, but there is nobody who saw him.'

'It can't have been Phil,' Arrina said, shaking her head so vigorously that her fringe fell into her eyes. 'I don't think I've ever seen him on a computer.'

'No, he is more interested in cows than computers.'

'Where's the money now?' She tried to picture Phil staring at an account showing millions of pounds. But she couldn't do it. She could only see him out in a field with his Friesians, herding them down the lane to be milked.

'The money was in a purse, or a bag... no, a wallet. Is that right?' Arrina had no idea, but it sounded familiar, so she nodded. 'From there, the money has disappeared.'

'Disappeared?'

'The police can't find it. They're still looking. They have told Julie she cannot go back to the farmhouse until they finish their search for it.'

Arrina couldn't imagine what the police could be searching for in the large, messy house. A printout of number strings? A computer file marked 'stolen millions'?

No, the money couldn't be there. Kingsley must surely have taken it himself. He'd set up his table at the Careers Fair, gone to Do-Re-Mi, and transferred the millions while picking up coffee, then spent the rest of the morning chatting to kids about careers in the Environment Agency he'd just embezzled from.

She couldn't believe anyone could do something so awful. Why had he even gone to the Careers Fair though? That seemed like an odd thing to do on the same day as stealing a fortune—unless he was using the college as his alibi.

Arrina couldn't quite get her head around that. If the Careers Fair was his alibi, why would he leave it and go to a place the transfer could be linked to? Maybe, like Arrina, he'd thought that cryptocurrencies were untraceable.

And if Kingsley was the one who *had* taken the money, then where was it? Arrina still didn't know much about the man. She hadn't even managed to talk to his wife, Callie.

Then it clicked. Kingsley's wife was in Venezuela. Callie was meant to be on the *holiday of a lifetime*, according to the woman's sister, Ophelia. But perhaps that wasn't quite right. What if it was a holiday *for* a lifetime? Millions of pounds would go a long way in Venezuela. And, Arrina was fairly certain, Venezuela had no extradition policy with the UK. A criminal could live there without worry of being captured by the police or sent back to England to face prison.

Kingsley and Callie must have been planning to take the money and live out their days on white sand beaches, drinking cocktails and laughing at the foolish police back in England who couldn't touch them for their crimes.

Arrina looked over at Mr Wen. His nimble fingers were flicking through the notebook in his hands. The handwriting on those pages was shaky. There were lists of lawyers with prices by their names, as well as other lists that looked like doctors and medicines. He turned over several pages, nodding, underlining, and checking through all of his many responsibilities. Poor Mr Wen didn't need these stresses in his life. He was a good man who'd spent his life working hard for his family.

He should be the one relaxing on a Venezuelan beach. How could he have a son-in-law wrongly imprisoned and a daughter on the brink of collapse?

Arrina kept quiet about her theories regarding the money trail to Venezuela and Kingsley's wife. Knowing Mr Wen, he'd hop on a plane to track down the woman himself. Arrina didn't think he could really handle that. Instead of saying anything about the clues she'd pieced together, she thanked him for telling her what Julie had found.

'Thank you also,' Mr Wen said. 'You are always such a good friend to Julie.'

'She's a good friend to me,' Arrina said. 'She helps me with everything. Phil as well. They...' Arrina couldn't continue. Tears had sprung to her eyes suddenly. Now that she'd realised what was going on with Kingsley and the embezzled money, it all seemed so huge and impossible. She didn't feel like she'd ever be able to free her friends from this predicament.

'And Maggie too,' Mr Wen said fondly. 'Her help with the café is so wonderful. I don't know how she has been running the place on her own, but we're very grateful. Please be sure to thank her from us.'

Arrina opened her mouth to say something. But she stopped, remembering that Mr Wen didn't need any more stress. She didn't know exactly what Maggie was doing at the moment, but it wasn't running Do-Re-Mi. Arrina had just come from the closed café, and when she'd seen Maggie earlier that day, the young woman had appeared to be working with Perry Anderson and his mysterious new company of teens.

Mr Wen said goodbye, but before he got out of the car, Arrina dug through her handbag and pulled out the heart wood. She put Sylvie Morgan's carved little talisman into his hand.

'This is for Julie,' Arrina said. 'The Morgans would like her to have it.'

She was about to explain more when Mr Wen's hand closed around it, and a look of serenity passed over his face. 'Thank you. I'm sure Julie will appreciate it.'

Arrina tried not to think of the *other* heart wood she'd held recently and the consequences of its discovery. This heart wood was the only one that mattered right now—the one that would help Julie find a little peace.

Mr Wen walked along the path to his house. At the door, he turned and waved. Then he went inside and returned to his wife and Julie.

Arrina was left alone in the frosty world. She felt the enormous scale of the challenge she faced rising on all sides like cliff faces. She had no idea where to start.

The only small task she could think of—the only thing she could actually tick off her to-do list without the help of Interpol or MI6—was to get Do-Re-Mi open again. It certainly wasn't something she could do on her own—not with her baking skills. But Maggie would be able to do it. All Arrina had to do was speak to her and get her to stop messing around with Perry's gang of teenage salespeople. She remembered Maggie had said she was heading back to her farm that afternoon. Arrina knew her way around the place well, and she could track Maggie down easily.

She looked at her phone before setting off. There was a string of emails and messages from the college. She wasn't surprised by this one bit, and she skipped through the messages, deleting or deferring them as quickly as she could. But then she saw one that made her stop and read it properly.

It was from Bill Yates. Arrina could have guessed that even without his name at the top of the screen. His message style always reminded her of a telegram.

Dee arrived. Claims you promised tour and induction today. Nobody free. Send her away?

Arrina's mind raced. For several seconds, she couldn't place the name Dee. But then she recalled the new chemistry teacher she'd hired. Arrina also remembered an eager promise to give the woman a tour, though she had no memory of suggesting a time or date. Perhaps she had though. It wouldn't surprise her at all. The way her week was going, Arrina could have promised the moon. Giving someone the moon wouldn't have been the hardest thing on her to-do list right then.

She dashed off a quick reply to Bill and then reworked her plan for the afternoon.

'OK,' Arrina said as she wrestled her temperamental car into gear, 'I know you're nice and cosy now and you just want to sit here by the river and watch robins, but we've got to get going. We're heading to Maggie's farm to give her a piece of our mind, but we're just going to make a quick detour on the way.'

With that, she backed onto the road and drove towards the college. She pressed her foot down hard on the accelerator. She realised then that she had quite a few pieces of her mind to hand out that day. She couldn't give Kingsley the one she owed him, but she would make her feelings heard to the rest of the people who were getting in her way and hurting her friends.

30

When Arrina arrived at the college at half past two, she expected the quiet hum of busy classes to be the only noise she encountered. She was utterly confused to find the halls filled with cheering and clapping that came from the back of the building.

Arrina paused at the entrance and listened.

Then she realised it was Tuesday—*still* Tuesday, somehow—the longest day in the longest week she'd ever lived through. And Tuesday afternoon in Heathervale College was a noisy occasion.

There were no classes during the period after lunch. Instead, the entire student body was invited to go to the hall to take part in Trying Tuesday. The event wasn't mandatory, but almost everybody attended the fun hour to blow off steam, and they tried out new skills or talents that were chosen from a list at random. It didn't matter if their performances weren't any good. That was the point—they were just trying.

Over the years, Arrina had seen some amazing things happen in that room: ungainly rugby players twirling in ballet tights, shy girls reciting passionate soliloquies, and a group of self-proclaimed science nerds discovering a love of improv.

She thought about going down there now—the encouragement that the students gave one another just for trying was always a boost that carried them on a high all week, and it did the same for Arrina. But she didn't have time for it. She had to track down the new chemistry teacher, Dee, and make her feel welcome. Then she had to dash off and find the *old* chemistry teacher—though in fact, Maggie had never even become the chemistry teacher at the college, only promised to do so and not followed through. She had done the same with Do-Re-Mi that week. Not following through was a pattern for the young woman, it seemed.

Arrina headed down towards the chemistry department, which was close to the front of the building. She'd told Bill to take Dee there to wait. No classes were going on right then, but Arrina hoped Dee had found something to occupy her. Arrina also hoped she'd be satisfied with a two-minute introduction to the department and college. Arrina didn't have time for anything else, but she also didn't want the woman to quit—she couldn't add one more problem to her list.

Arrina rounded a corner and almost ran straight into Dee. 'Oh, goodness, I'm—'

'Shhh,' Dee said. She even put a finger to her lips to reinforce this frankly ridiculous message.

Arrina's mind immediately leapt to the list of other candidates for the chemistry teacher position. The ones she'd interviewed so far had been pretty ropey, though none had shushed her in her own college.

Dee beckoned Arrina over to the door she was pressed up against, and Arrina looked around. This was usually the time when Sampson Morgan, the college's head of security, would make an appearance. He always seemed to know when he was needed. But right then, he was nowhere to be seen.

Arrina thought of dashing away and tracking Sampson down, even though he surely despised her for what had happened to his nephew Wallace. Dee pressed her head against a door and held a finger to her lips. There was nothing particularly dangerous about that, so perhaps she didn't need Sampson straight away. But the action was certainly odd. And oddness in a building full of young people could quickly become quite worrying.

But then Arrina realised what Dee was doing. She was listening at the door of the chemistry lab, which should have been entirely empty but in fact had a loud conversation going on inside it.

'He said it would be in a brown bottle,' one voice said.

'This is sort of brown,' replied another.

'It's just dusty. I think we need a—'

'It looks like there's nothing here,' a new voice interrupted. 'We should just go.' Arrina recognised this voice. It took her a moment to place it, but then an image of dark-blonde curly hair surged through her mind, and she realised the voice belonged to Patience. The girl had hung signs at the Careers Fair that Saturday, trained with Peregrine Anderson's business that morning, and now she was sneaking around in the college that afternoon. Arrina was about to push through the door and ask the girl what on earth she was doing when Dee held up a hand to stop her.

'They're looking for something,' Dee said in a whisper. 'We ought to find out what it is. If there's one teenager looking for something, there's likely to be more.'

Arrina cocked her head in surprise. She was used to new teachers being nervous and following her lead. This one seemed to have her own ideas.

'Mother of four, remember?' Dee said with a wink. 'All teenagers. Most of what I learn about my kids these days, I get from listening at doors.'

'What's it called again?' asked someone in a loud voice from inside the lab. 'I thought you wrote it down.'

'I reckon we're best going now and coming back when we know for sure,' Patience said.

'Don't stress. You know there's no one coming. They're all busy *trying*.' Laughter came from the other side of the door. A cruel, teasing laughter that Arrina rarely heard in her college. Arrina ground her teeth to keep from charging into the lab and shouting.

But she knew Dee was right. They needed to find out what these teenagers were after so that they could make sure nobody else came looking for it. Every week, the news carried details of some new synthetic drug that killed people or sent them crazy. Arrina hated to think of chemicals from her college being used to manufacture anything like that, but it was possible. A little eavesdropping here could stop that happening.

'We're only supposed to be *looking* on this visit, anyway,' Patience said, ignoring the laughter.

'Do you really think we're going back empty-handed?' said one of the other people. 'Perry would throw a fit.'

Perry. Of course Peregrine Anderson was connected to these young thieves. Arrina still didn't entirely know what the boy was up to, but she was sure it wasn't good.

Dee shot Arrina a worried look. Arrina wanted to reassure her that the college wasn't normally like this, but she didn't trust her voice to come out quietly. Everyone was lying to her—Maggie, Perry, and even her own students. Arrina couldn't control herself in the face of this.

Just then, the door to the lab opened. Arrina and Dee leapt back in surprise. Three shocked teenage faces stared out at them. The two boys looked familiar, but Arrina didn't think they were college students. They nudged each other and gave Arrina wide grins before racing away, dragging Patience with them.

The girl's wild halo of curls bounced behind her down the hallway. 'We didn't take anything,' she said. 'Honest. I'm sorry.'

Then the boys muttered something that Arrina didn't hear, and Patience gave Arrina a nervous, toothy grin of her own.

Before Arrina could chase after the teenagers, they were gone—disappearing down the corridor that led to the back of the college. Out there, the car park gave them an easy route for escape. It also led directly to Maggie Lee's farm.

'Well,' said Dee, 'that was certainly a dramatic how-do-you-do.'

'Yes...' Arrina said, still staring after the students who'd run away.

Dee straightened the bag on her shoulder and looked ready to shake Arrina's hand and leave. 'I suppose I should—'

'No, don't go,' Arrina interrupted. 'It isn't always like this. It *definitely* isn't always like this. There's a...' But she didn't have a good explanation for what was happening.

'Oh, I'm not going. I just thought I should take a look around the lab.' Dee pushed open the door that Patience and her friends had raced out of. 'I can check the inventory in here for you. It didn't look like they took anything, but it's best to be sure.'

'Right,' Arrina said, too surprised to even thank her.

'It'll give me a good chance to get to know the place better as well.'

Arrina almost asked whether Dee was serious about her plan to stay. But she didn't want to put ideas in the woman's head. She certainly looked committed as she walked into the lab and then studied a clipboard on the wall.

At least Arrina had done one good thing that week—hiring Dee. And it was thanks to Julie that she'd considered the middle-aged woman with the huge gaps in her CV. Julie's internship programme for people who had fallen out of the world of work had given Arrina a push in the right direction.

As Arrina watched Dee work her way along the shelves of the chemistry lab, checking items against the list, Arrina wished she had a list of her own—some way to work through the confusion of what was going on.

Teenagers were breaking into the lab to steal chemistry supplies for Perry Anderson. Perry was working with Maggie, who was *supposed* to be helping at Do-Re-Mi. The café's Wi-Fi had been used to steal millions from a government agency—the same agency that Kingsley Peters worked in. Kingsley had investigated Julie and Phil's farm and seemed to have blackmailed Phil, who had taken on extra work that brought him to the very corner of the field where Kingsley's dead body was found.

Arrina needed a *list*, but all she had were looping connections that swirled around one another like crop circles. She was *sure* that if she made sense of everything that was happening in Heathervale currently, she'd find Kingsley's killer. But there were too many different worlds. Peregrine Anderson didn't belong in the same group as Julie and Phil. Perry was more likely to attend a cocktail party held by the snobbish Yateses than spend time with a dairy farmer and his baker wife. Kingsley seemed to have known both worlds, but he wouldn't be able to give her any answers.

Maggie was the only other link between them—she was a family friend of Julie's and a business associate of Perry's. Arrina left Dee to her list-checking and then drove around to Maggie's farm to find out what was going on. Arrina had been planning to question her about not helping Julie in the café that week, but now it seemed she needed to speak to Maggie about many more things. Perhaps she had information that would lead to Kingsley's killer.

But there was no sign of her anywhere—not in the farmhouse and not in the fields.

So Arrina headed to the last place she'd seen Maggie—Perry Anderson's house. Arrina needed to get some answers, and this time, Maggie wouldn't get rid of her so easily.

31

The sun was slouching towards the horizon as Arrina drove across the village. Pale, thin rays glinted on the frost all around as one of the shortest days of the year neared its end. Arrina lowered her sun visor and squinted. On any other day, she would find the sparkling world beautiful. But right then, it felt sharp and dangerous.

She pulled up outside Fernella Anderson's house and stared at its long picture windows. The house had stood there for hundreds of years. It was the sort of place that always looked ready for a ball, and Arrina half expected a Brontë sister to step out and wave a gloved hand of welcome.

But nobody emerged from the house to meet her. In fact, the place seemed entirely empty from where she was sitting. Arrina knew, though, that a hive of industry was in the annex at the back. Somewhere out there would be Perry Anderson and Maggie Lee, neither of whom Arrina trusted, even though she couldn't understand what was going on clearly enough to know why.

As Arrina opened her door, a blast of cold air cut through the cosy warmth in her car. She shivered and reached into her handbag. The heart wood in there would bring her the comfort she sorely needed. But it wasn't there. She'd given it to Mr Wen to pass along to Julie. Arrina's hand squeezed tight in its absence. She hoped the carved wooden talisman was bringing her friend some comfort, though as Arrina walked towards the tall and imposing front door, she wished she had a little such reassurance herself.

Before knocking, she reached into her bag once more and took out her phone. She pulled up the number stored as DO NOT CALL. Tony had been the one to suggest that Arrina investigate this murder—or, at least, he'd strongly implied it. Did that also mean he'd be there to help her when things got serious? Arrina wasn't sure. She had once known everything that Tony thought. Or, at least, she'd felt she did. But their break-up the year before had come utterly out of the blue. And the closeness they'd seemed to regain that summer had slipped away like a dream in the harsh light of day.

Arrina had Ian's number as well—she could call him. She'd once been close with the large, friendly man. But the high-ranking officer had surprised her outside her own cottage and then in the corner of the Yateses' farm. She could think of no good reason why he'd been in the field so early in the morning. She could think of a few bad ones, though, and those kept her from calling him then.

The signal bars on her screen told her she didn't have a choice anyway—or rather, the *lack* of signal bars did. There wasn't even the faintest flicker of connection.

Arrina put her phone away. She was just visiting the Anderson house to chat with an ex-chemistry teacher. Arrina was sure the woman wasn't up to anything good. But it was hard to see her as a cold-blooded killer. Arrina was just there to get her help unravelling the mystery of Kingsley Peters' death. She banged the large black knocker against the door. Then she waited.

The door was opened within moments, and the wide frame was filled by the even wider Fernella Anderson.

'I *told* Peregrine you'd be back,' Fernella sang out gaily.

Arrina stepped away from the woman as smoothly as she could. She'd been so focused on speaking to Maggie that she hadn't even considered that someone else would answer the door instead. 'Yes,' she said after recovering from her surprise. 'I'm back. Is—'

'*Of course*—I told him—*of course* you'd be eager to firm up the details of his new position as soon as possible.'

'Well—' Arrina stepped back a little further from the woman's powerful voice.

'And don't worry, I've made it very clear to him that he can't be leaving meetings even when important calls come in. Unless it's a call from Mummy, that is.' Fernella laughed, and her plump cheeks blushed as they jiggled. 'When he's working at your college, I'm sure he'll be a paragon of professionalism. And the sooner we get the details confirmed, the sooner he can get started.'

'I am very keen to get this sorted out today,' Arrina said. She didn't specify *what* exactly it was that she wanted to get sorted, so she didn't feel that she was entirely lying to the doting mother before her. However, if Fernella asked her directly, Arrina would have to be honest—the devil would be lacing up his ice skates before she let Peregrine Anderson work at her college.

'Of course, of course. My Peregrine's also very eager to get this firmed up. You know, he's very dedicated to this community, especially the young people. The two of you are such a natural fit in that way, I'm sure you'll have an excellent working relationship.'

'I'm sure. Is he in?' Arrina would say anything right then to get through the house to the annex. She eyed the corridor behind Fernella, hoping that somebody would appear there to distract the adoring woman. Arrina wondered if she could just dodge around her, but the hallway was high and narrow. She would have no way to get past the former opera singer short of squeezing through her sturdy legs.

'You know, he's made *such* a success of himself,' Fernella continued. 'I really am very proud of him, and I'm sure his father would be also.' Fernella looked upwards and clutched a hand to her significant chest. 'Now that he's hired that old chemistry teacher of yours as a consultant, it seems the sky's the limit.'

'Maggie is his consultant?' Arrina didn't quite know what this meant. She'd first thought Maggie was Perry's assistant, then it had seemed she was in charge and merely using Perry's money and connections with the local teenage workforce. But that didn't match with what Fernella was saying.

'Well, of course, he's handing all the business side of things. That's his real forte. But she's apparently proved very useful with the chemicals. Lots of Perry's suppliers like to talk with someone who can roll out a hexa-fluoro-this or a pheno-whatsit-that. She's simply a marvel at all of those complicated names.'

Arrina didn't know much about chemistry, but she did know those complex-sounding words weren't in the sort of natural pesticides that Maggie had claimed to be focusing on. And the attempted theft of supplies from the college's chemistry lab supported the idea that some dangerous substances were involved in whatever it was Perry and Maggie were doing. Arrina had initially been concerned about teenagers being encouraged to drop out of the college and become salespeople. But now she wondered if Maggie's work was more harmful than Maggie herself had suggested.

Arrina couldn't say any of this to Fernella, or the door would quickly be slammed in her face. 'It's all Greek to me, unfortunately. Maggie must be such a help to Perry.' Arrina tilted her head to the side, hoping Fernella would usher her inside to speak to the young pair about their work, but she didn't take the bait.

'It's the same with this app he's creating. All of this code and the database and... Well, I'm not entirely sure. I just let the young folks get on with it. But it all sounds terribly important. They're really going to help the farmers of the area. And then, of course, the rest of Britain. Knowing my Peregrine, he'll have his eye on the whole world next.'

'An app?' Arrina couldn't fathom what an app had to do with chemicals.

'It's all apps these days, isn't it? You hear so many reports about them collecting data from people and selling it to the highest bidder. Not my Peregrine, of course. He's helping farmers cut out the middlemen between themselves and suppliers. It's a huge cost saving. Really, it's something the government ought to be doing. But they don't care enough about rural folk, do they?'

Arrina smiled and nodded. Pieces of the puzzle were slotting together in her brain, and they didn't make a pretty picture. Agricultural chemicals were lethal in the wrong hands. Arrina was old enough to remember the DDT crisis, which had almost wiped out several bird of prey species. If

Perry was helping farmers cut out steps in the supply chain of the chemicals they used, that couldn't mean anything good.

'Innovation is the key,' Fernella continued. Arrina ignored the woman as she went on and on about her genius son.

Arrina couldn't listen because she was busy thinking about something she'd seen in Kingsley's book of newspaper clippings. It was a recent case in which a farmer had been sent to prison for using banned pesticides on his land. The article went on to say that chemicals like this came over from other countries in a dangerous and illegal underground trade.

That couldn't be what Perry and Maggie were doing, could it? Arrina remembered the arrogant boy who'd dropped his college application on her desk two weeks late and incomplete. Yes, she had to admit, trading in illegal chemicals did seem like something he might do.

Then Arrina thought of Maggie Lee. The young woman had seemed so nice, and Julie's whole family was fond of her. Arrina had been surprised enough to learn that Maggie was involved in poaching students from the college. It seemed impossible to imagine she'd be involved in a company that sold chemicals so dangerous they were banned.

And how did that tie in with Kingsley's death? Had he been investigating Perry and Maggie? Could he have threatened to blackmail them and...

'It's here!' Fernella trilled, pushing past Arrina and almost knocking her over. Then Fernella dashed back into the house and filled the hallway with another sonorous blast. 'It's here, Peregrine! It's here!'

Arrina's mind was still spinning with all the unexpected discoveries she was trying to bring together. Now she was being turned around by the suddenly spry Fernella Anderson, who hopped and skipped down the long driveway to meet an enormous vehicle coming up it.

Arrina couldn't believe her eyes, but she blinked several times, and the vision was still there. On the back of a flatbed truck was a bright red Lamborghini. Fernella reached up to stroke it gently before barking out strict unloading instructions for the delivery people and hurrying back up the winding driveway.

'Isn't it marvellous?' she sang as she trotted back towards Arrina. Then another announcement in the direction of the house: 'Peregrine, sweetie, your new car is here.'

Of all the things she'd heard that day, this was the most shocking. Peregrine Anderson couldn't have been more than seventeen. At his age, Arrina had been allowed to occasionally borrow a cousin's smoke-spewing Ford Escort. A Lamborghini seemed like overkill for such a new driver.

Arrina forced a smile to her face. 'That's an awfully nice gift.' Then when Fernella blinked expectantly, she added, 'Perry's very lucky to have a mother like you.'

'This is Peregrine's new *company* car.' Fernella clapped her hands in glee.

'That's very... generous of you.'

Fernella shook her head vigorously, setting her cheeks jiggling. 'This isn't from me. I know there are many around here whose families fund their little ventures, but we Andersons are made of sterner stuff. Peregrine has raised the capital himself from investors.'

Arrina's blood cooled to the temperature of the frosty air around her. She turned to glance again at the bright red car. With the sun setting behind it, the vehicle looked as though it was on fire.

That car must have cost a fortune. And Arrina knew where a fortune had come from just recently—the Environment Agency accounts linked to Kingsley Peters.

Could Perry have killed the man and stolen his money? The idea seemed unthinkable, but Arrina considered everything she knew and came up with a theory—Kingsley had tried to blackmail Perry over his illegal agro-chemical company, but the tech-savvy boy had turned the tables on him and gained access to the Environment Agency's accounts. That explained things far better than the police's idea. They thought that Phil had taken the money, but he couldn't have done it without Kingsley's help. Perry could, though, with the technological skills his mother had just raved about. Perry could have taken the money in the morning then killed the man to cover his tracks.

Arrina didn't want to think of young Perry as a cold-blooded killer, but then she looked over at the car he'd bought just days after Kingsley's death. The timing was too perfect, and Arrina couldn't really believe anyone would *invest* in Perry's business. There was only one way he'd get hold of so much money.

It must be him. Perry Anderson had taken the Environment Agency money and killed Kingsley Peters.

'Mummy,' said a loud voice from inside the house, 'did you say something?'

Arrina could feel the stiff mask of her shocked face. She couldn't let Perry see it. He wouldn't let her get away. If Peregrine Anderson could kill a man on Saturday and spend his stolen money on Tuesday, there was no telling what else he might do. Arrina didn't want to stay and find out.

A thunder of feet on stairs sounded from inside the house.

'I... I've just remembered...' Arrina said, backing away. 'I've got an appointment at... the college. I'll come back another day.' She pulled out her phone and glanced at it. Then she prodded the screen to mime checking her calendar or swiping at a reminder. She glanced at the signal bars—still nothing. She had to get away to call the police.

'Mummy?' asked the dangerous boy again, his voice closer this time.

Arrina dashed over to her car and got in. She turned the key frantically, trying to *think* of scooping egg yolks even while she yanked like she was opening a stuck lid. Her car coughed and growled, but the engine came to life. She could have kissed the steering wheel, but she didn't have time. She had to get away.

The driveway was still blocked by the bright red Lamborghini and the lorry that had just delivered it. She wasn't going to let that stop her. Not for one second.

Arrina pressed her foot to the floor and swerved across the edge of the driveway. Her wheels soon thundered on the lawn's hard, frozen earth. She didn't look back to see Fernella's reaction. She swerved around first the Lamborghini, then the large truck, which almost blocked the exit of the long driveway. She didn't think about what would happen if she couldn't get past it. She had to get away. She raced through the small gap between the truck and a line of trees.

She reached the road and instantly slammed on her brakes, screeching to a stop just inches away from a collision with a rainbow-coloured VW Camper. Arrina panted for breath while the driver beeped at her. She glanced backwards and jammed her car into reverse. The house was a long way down the drive, but Arrina still felt her skin prickle as she eased back the way she'd come.

Or at least, she tried to. She pressed down on the accelerator, but she didn't move. Her wheels spun, her engine revved, and the car didn't shift one inch.

The VW kept beeping, and Arrina glanced back at the house, praying that Perry wouldn't hear and investigate. But far at the other end of the driveway, Perry and his mother both fawned over the shiny new Lamborghini.

The Camper in front of her continued to honk. Arrina tried to reverse again, but her wheels were stuck in a furrow of churned earth. Arrina got out and dashed over to the other driver to explain what was happening and beg them to be quiet. But when she reached the window and saw who was inside, her words failed her entirely.

32

The rainbow-coloured van should have been a clear giveaway. Arrina had never seen such a bright vehicle before, but she *had* seen someone in a rainbow-coloured outfit just yesterday. And that very same person was in front of her now. It was Ophelia, the woman who ran the Longnor Village Store and knew all about different, delicious varieties of tea. More importantly, Ophelia was also the sister of Kingsley Peters's widow.

The woman looked just as surprised at the encounter as Arrina. And for Ophelia, the surprise clearly wasn't a good one.

'I knew you were no good!' the woman shouted through her window. 'I just knew it.'

Arrina stepped back in shock. The woman's face was contorted in anger, and there were dark circles around her eyes. 'I'm... I don't—'

'I've spent the entire day tracking Kingsley's last movements, but it turns out, I could have asked around after the local hussy and come straight here.'

Arrina looked back towards the main house. Her confused mind tried to connect the word *hussy* with Fernella Anderson. Then she realised what Ophelia meant. 'Me? No, I told you, it was nothing like that. My name's Arrina Fenn. I run a local sixth form college, and—'

'I don't want to hear it. My sister had *years* of lies from Kingsley, and I'm not going to take them from you as well.' She gunned her engine loudly.

Ophelia's van was stuck at an awkward angle, with her front end turned towards the driveway, stopped just inches from Arrina's bumper. Meanwhile, the back end brushed against the high hedgerow at the far side of the road. She ground her gears as she tried to turn around and get away.

Arrina dashed over to her car and stood beside it, watching the back-and-forth shuffle of the van as Ophelia tried to turn it in the tight space. Arrina checked her phone again. Still no signal. Still no way to report what she'd realised about Perry.

And in fact, she was starting to have suspicions about Ophelia as well. Because it couldn't be a coincidence, could it, that she was there exactly when Perry's new car was being delivered? She'd claimed to be tracking Kingsley's movements, but Arrina had her doubts.

The blonde woman had been *very* happy the day before. The sort of happy a person might be if they'd just added several zeros to their bank balance. And now she was here at Perry's house, right as he was getting his first big treat with the windfall he'd stolen from Kingsley.

Her anger at Arrina seemed extreme. Perhaps a little *too* strong to be real.

Arrina couldn't even begin to guess how Ophelia had come to be mixed up in Perry's awful dealings, and she didn't have time to think about it then. She was stuck here between Perry's house and Ophelia's van, with no way to escape and no phone signal to use to call for help. She ran through a list of the people who lived nearby in this isolated part of Heathervale, hoping she knew the way through the woods to one of their houses.

The only name she came up with was Gillian DeViers, who Arrina was nearly certain lived straight ahead and to the left as the crow flew. Gillian's house was not exactly her idea of salvation. But right then, she'd take anything.

A loud thud broke through Arrina's thoughts. Ophelia's van was now tilted at an angle, with one back wheel dangling in a ditch. The blonde woman leapt out and raced over to it.

Ophelia pulled out her phone as she stared daggers at the stuck wheel. 'Now look what you've made me do!' She jabbed at her phone and let out an angry yelp when nothing happened.

Arrina glanced back at the house behind her. Far down the driveway, Fernella pointed at something on the Lamborghini, and the delivery people were leaning in to see. Perry was busy taking selfies with the vehicle. She still had a few minutes to get away.

'Look what... Look at...' Ophelia stammered. And then the angry blonde woman dropped down in a heap on the ice-cold road and started crying.

Arrina glanced past her at the high hedge boundary. On the other side of that were woods that promised escape. In the last light of day, she could stumble through them to Gillian's house and use a landline to call the police.

But Arrina didn't move.

This didn't seem right. If Ophelia really *was* part of Perry's plan, it didn't make sense for her to be weeping now.

Arrina could understand why the woman might point the finger at her to confuse Arrina while she made her escape. That made sense, and it had certainly been working. Arrina had been about to run away through the woods. After which, she'd assumed, Ophelia would drop her mask of anger and trot over to Perry to see his flashy new car.

But Ophelia was shivering on the ground in the shadow of her van and making no move to go anywhere.

Arrina crouched down near the woman but said nothing. She'd spent years dealing with emotional flare-ups from teenagers. She'd learned long ago that people in this state were like wild animals. The best way to handle them was to slowly get closer, giving them a chance to get used to the new presence in their space, and then wait.

In the distance, Arrina heard an ear-splitting engine rev that could only be Perry's Lamborghini.

She thought again about running away—escaping and calling the police—but she couldn't leave Ophelia here in the icy road. The delivery lorry was still blocking the long driveway, so Perry's car wasn't going anywhere. She still had time.

'Everyone's going to blame Callie,' Ophelia said between sniffling sobs. Arrina's cold, jumbled thoughts took a moment to recall who Callie was. She was Ophelia's sister and Kingsley's widow. 'I know you won't care about that. But *I* do.'

'I care,' Arrina said softly. But she didn't push the subject.

'The police have already started asking what she's doing in Venezuela.'

Arrina had realised the implication of the place earlier, when she'd thought Kingsley himself had taken the money. 'There's no extradition treaty.'

Ophelia nodded. 'Criminals can live there forever, and the police can't touch them. A *criminal*, that's what they're calling my sister.'

'But she didn't...?' Arrina spoke softly, trailing off to keep Ophelia talking. Talking would get her closer to standing, which would get them both away into the woods, where they could be safe from Perry. Arrina still didn't entirely trust the emotional blonde woman, but Perry seemed the far greater threat right then.

'She didn't know anything about this.' Ophelia shuffled on the ground. The last rays of sunlight didn't reach her in the shadow of her van, and the hard evening frost was setting in. 'She only knew about the... the other money that Kingsley took. She opened his post by mistake a few months ago, and she found strange amounts going in and out and tens of thousands of pounds worth of debt.'

'He was in debt?' Kingsley had taken bribes from local farmers—lots of them, if the Drabbles were correct—so it made no sense that he was in debt.

'He confessed everything. He'd got a gambling problem, and to cover it up, he'd pocketed the fines from some of his cases.'

'It wasn't from fines. He blackmailed innocent people into paying him off so he wouldn't bring charges against them.'

Ophelia wiped the tears from her face. 'Nothing would surprise me about that man. He told Callie that he'd got his gambling under control and his new promotion brought in enough money to cover what he owed. He was going to clean up his act and make things right.'

Arrina thought about Phil and Julie, whose lives had been turned upside down since Kingsley first visited their farm just a couple of months earlier. She hadn't seen any sign at all of Kingsley making things right. Not at all.

Ophelia shivered. 'The holiday in Venezuela was supposed to fix things between the two of them.'

'But Kingsley didn't go with her.'

'No. At the last minute, he said he had to do something on Saturday, and he rebooked his flights. When I saw you yesterday, I thought that you were the reason he stayed, but—'

'I promise, nothing was going on between us. I'd never even met him before Saturday morning.'

Ophelia knelt in front of Arrina and peered at her through the gloom. The look of anger was gone from her face, though it had been replaced by one of suspicion, which wasn't much better.

'He was at my college that morning,' Arrina said. 'We had a Careers Fair, and he was running a stall. I thought he was using it as an alibi to steal the money himself, but—'

'Was he there at 9.27 that morning?'

A cold breeze crept across Arrina's neck and tousled her short hair. She was about to tell Ophelia that she wasn't entirely sure. He'd been at the fair for its start at half past nine, so it was a pretty good guess he'd been there three minutes earlier. Then she remembered her interaction with Kingsley from that day.

'He *was* there at 9.27,' Arrina said. 'He asked for my number. He said he wanted it in case there was any follow-up from the fair. He remarked that he'd got my number at 9.27 exactly.'

'That's when the money was taken,' Ophelia said.

Cold air tingled on Arrina's scalp. Kingsley *had* been using the college as his alibi, which meant that he was involved in the theft of the money. Did that mean, then, that her theory about Perry was wrong entirely?

'The police called my sister and accused her of being in on it. They even suggested I helped her, but I was at my shop all day Saturday. When they called, Callie was about to get on a plane to come back here, but now...' She shook her head.

Arrina reached out and squeezed Ophelia's shoulder. The woman was trying to prove her sister's innocence, just like Arrina was trying to help Phil and Wallace. If only they'd teamed up earlier, perhaps they'd have solved this case and avoided getting stranded in the middle of nowhere, piecing clues together in the dark.

Ophelia looked up at the house. 'My sister guessed the password for Kingsley's online calendar. He came here five times over the past few months. He marked it as a livestock check, but it doesn't look like a farm.'

An ear-splitting alarm went off nearby, making both women jump. They finally stood up from behind the Camper and saw that Perry was leaping out of his Lamborghini and pointing at it accusingly. His mother and the delivery people scrambled to find out what he'd mistakenly pressed.

'That's who lives here,' Arrina said. 'Peregrine Anderson. I'm fairly certain he's the one who took the money. I thought he was doing it as payback for being blackmailed, but there are too many things that don't make sense. If Kingsley needed an alibi for Saturday morning, then he must have been involved with taking the money or at least known it was happening. And he planned a holiday to Venezuela, which also suggests he was going to take the money and run. But I don't know why he and Perry would have worked together.'

Ophelia didn't say anything. Arrina peered at her in the last light of the day. 'You don't look convinced.'

'I don't know,' Ophelia said. 'It's just... my sister was sure he was meeting a woman. That's why I thought it was you. Callie could have misunderstood. Or just jumped to that idea because, with Kingsley, it was usually a woman. But she said there was something which made her think Kingsley was visiting a woman here—and not for a farm visit.'

As if she'd been waiting in the wings, Maggie Lee stepped out of the shadows. Arrina's heart froze. Maggie had a key to Perry's office. She spent a lot of time there, and she'd been keeping lots of secrets. Could *she* have been the woman Kingsley Peters was visiting?

33

Maggie Lee's face was hidden by shadows. The sun had now entirely disappeared, and the only light came from the lamps at the front of the Anderson house.

For several long seconds, nobody spoke. The Lamborghini's alarm blared from the other end of the driveway. Then it stopped, and the whole world held its breath.

'If Aunty Julie was here right now,' Maggie said, 'she'd make a joke. Something about bubble, bubble, toil and trouble.' The young woman tugged at the hem of her skirt. 'Because we look like the three witches meeting on a heath.'

'Julie's not in the mood for joking these days.' Arrina's voice was low and firm.

'I...' Maggie glanced over her shoulder at the Anderson house. The two delivery people now had the bonnet of the Lamborghini up, and they were peering into it while Fernella and Perry pointed at the engine. 'I'm sorry I've not been able to help much. I wanted to keep Do-Re-Mi open for her. I really did, but things are... they're getting quite serious here.'

Ophelia stepped towards Maggie. 'Getting serious? That's one way of putting it. Are you the one? My sister's not going to take the fall for what you've done.' She turned to Arrina. 'This is her, isn't it?'

Arrina gazed at Maggie. The young woman had only come into her life a few months earlier, first as a teacher at the college and later as a friend. At least, Arrina had *thought* they were friends. Now, she didn't know *what* Maggie was.

A businesswoman poaching students from Arrina's college? A consultant for a company selling illegal chemicals? A double-crossing embezzler and murderer? Maybe all those things combined.

Maggie's face was visible now as she turned to look between Arrina and Ophelia. The panicked expression made Arrina want to believe Maggie was just as nice as she'd always seemed—just a sweet girl who'd got mixed up in something she didn't really understand. But guilt lay beneath the panic on her face. Maggie Lee was hiding something.

'I'm not here about the café,' Arrina said. 'I want to know what's going on. What have you been doing here?'

'I wanted to tell you earlier, but I couldn't make him suspicious, and I couldn't leave today because I think everything's about to go down with the delivery, and I couldn't call anyone because there's no signal here, and... It's so much worse than I thought.'

It seemed that all three women were having different conversations—Arrina's about murder, Ophelia's about money, and Maggie's about... Arrina didn't exactly know. 'What's worse than you thought?'

'The chemicals. I thought you knew—that's what Perry's been working on, and I've been pretending to help so I could find out more details. I thought he was just trading stolen pesticides, which is bad, but it's common enough, and I was just going to get some information and report it, but then I realised that Perry was planning something worse.'

'Something worse?' Ophelia's dark-ringed eyes glared at Maggie. 'Framing my sister for stealing millions of pounds is a *lot* worse. If you know anything about it, you have to go to the police.'

'What? I didn't... I don't know what you're talking about.'

Arrina wanted to believe Maggie, but this situation involved so much that she still didn't understand.

Ophelia pulled up a picture of her sister on her phone. 'Callie can't come home because of you. Her whole life has just been taken away from her, and she's done nothing to deserve it. The police are accusing *her* of taking the money that you and her crooked husband stole.'

A loud slam from the other end of the driveway drew all three women's attention. The bonnet of the Lamborghini was down, and the delivery people were wiping off their hands and waving goodbye to Fernella and Peregrine Anderson. The delivery people would head back to their truck in a matter of moments. They'd soon discover the blockage in the road formed by Arrina's car and Ophelia's Camper. And if that happened, Perry could be drawn down there and see the three women who were piecing everything together.

Arrina still wasn't sure whether she could trust Maggie Lee. But the young woman's focus on chemicals and her confusion in the face of Ophelia's accusations made Arrina want to believe she was innocent.

Arrina grabbed the two women by their sleeves and pulled them over the road and through a gap in the hedge. She led her companions into the dark woodland on the other side of it.

She needed to find out what was going on. And she needed to do it before Peregrine Anderson figured out that anyone was onto him.

Dry leaves crunched underfoot, moonlight sharpened the world's frosted edges, and the three women stared at one another with open suspicion.

'Maggie,' Arrina said, 'you need to explain exactly what you've been doing with Perry.' She looked back towards the high hedge that hid them from the road. They were safe there for the next few minutes but not much longer than that. 'And you need to do it quickly.'

34

'It's like I said,' Maggie whispered, following Arrina's nervous gaze to the hedge that stood between them and the Anderson house. 'I've been trying to find out what Perry's doing. I heard he had a new company selling pesticides and fertilisers. He set it up at the same time I started my own business, so I thought maybe we could work together.'

'Selling illegal chemicals?' Arrina remembered Maggie's nervous eyes recently. Both earlier in the annex and before then in Do-Re-Mi that Sunday. She hadn't been able to meet Arrina's gaze at all.

'No.' Maggie ran her hands over her head and tugged at her ponytail. 'I didn't know that's what he was doing at first. I see you and Aunty Julie helping people so much, and I wanted to do the same. I thought I could help him learn more about safety and regulations, but...'

'He didn't want to know?'

Maggie shook her head. Her shadowy ponytail swished behind her. 'He asked me lots of questions about banned chemicals, and I thought he wanted to make sure he was... Well, I think now I was being naïve. He wanted to get information about illegal pesticides so he could ship them into the country and sell them. I realised that last week, and I've been trying to find out when his first shipment's coming in so I can stop it.'

'What has this got to do with Kingsley?' Ophelia asked.

'Nothing, I don't think. I'd never even heard his name until Saturday, when...'

'When Phil was arrested for killing him,' Arrina finished.

'I don't believe you.' Ophelia's feet shuffled loudly in the undergrowth. 'Trading illegal chemicals is just the sort of thing Kingsley would be involved with.'

'I've never seen him at the office.' Moonlight glinted in Maggie's eyes, which were wide with apparent desperation to be believed. 'Maybe he met up with Perry somewhere else.'

'He's been to this address five times in the past few months. The visits are in his calendar.'

'I'm not always there.' Maggie's voice was that of a little girl. She was only twenty-four, Arrina reminded herself. Young enough to get mixed up in someone else's deception without realising it.

'Why didn't you tell me what Perry was doing?' Arrina asked her.

'I didn't want to upset you.'

At first Arrina didn't understand what she meant. Then she thought about all the college students who'd quit to work with Perry. She *was* upset about that, and she could see why Maggie hadn't wanted to break the bad news. 'It's OK. I—'

'Were you with Perry on Saturday?' Ophelia interrupted. 'Saturday morning at 9.27 exactly.'

Maggie didn't say anything. A flush of doubt passed through Arrina. She deeply wanted to trust Maggie, but the young woman's silences and secrets were making it hard.

'I was with him,' Maggie said in barely more than a whisper. In that instant, Arrina wondered if Maggie was going to admit to some sort of affair with the teenager. But what

Maggie confessed made even less sense. 'We were at the college, setting up for the Careers Fair.'

Arrina frowned. A breeze sent dry leaves skittering around her feet. She felt as though she could be swept away too. The world was making so little sense right then. 'Perry wasn't there. I have a list of everyone who was in the hall before we opened the fair that morning, and Perry isn't on it.'

'He wasn't in the hall.' Maggie raised her voice only slightly. 'I set my table up in there. Then I snuck out and went to help Perry.'

'Out where?'

Maggie gave a nervous whine, the sort of sound students made when Arrina called them into her office to explain long-overdue pieces of coursework and lies about the dogs that had eaten them. 'He had a table outside your office. It wasn't my idea, I promise. None of it was. But he had a table there to sign students up to his business, and I had to help him so that he'd trust me and I could find out about the shipment this week, and I...'

Maggie's garbled stream of words broke down into soft sobs, which tugged at Arrina's sympathy even as she reeled from Maggie's revelations. Perry had been at the college that Saturday, right under her nose. He had been there with a table of his own. He'd been signing up students to his business.

'9.27,' Ophelia repeated. 'You're sure you were with him then?'

Maggie's dark silhouette nodded.

'Was he on a computer? Could he have been transferring the money while you were with him?'

Maggie's response was muffled by the hands over her face, but Arrina understood it well enough.

'There's no signal at the college. That whole part of the village barely has any reception at all.' Anyway, Arrina knew, the transfer had been traced to the Wi-Fi at Do-Re-Mi. If Perry had been setting up for his own personal Careers Fair right then, he couldn't have *also* been in the centre of the village, transferring millions of pounds out of the Environment Agency's bank accounts. There must have been *another* accomplice. The culprit didn't seem to be Maggie, but Arrina didn't have a clue who it could be. She knew what the police would say, though—it had to be Phil.

Maggie said something else, but this time Arrina didn't understand it. Maggie to wipe her face and get herself under control before trying again. 'At 9.27, Perry and I were putting stickers on the paintings on your walls. I'm so sorry. I didn't want to do it. I tried to tell him—'

'*He* put the stickers there?' Arrina remembered them clearly—bright red cartoon mouths, spoiling every sweet face that Olly had painted in the scenes of village life.

'We both did. I'm sorry for—'

'Why?' Arrina couldn't focus on Maggie's apology right then. She was freshly incensed about the vandalism of the college's murals. Somehow, the act was that much worse now she knew that Perry was the one responsible. 'Why did he stick those hideous smiles all over my walls?'

'They're not smiles. They're *grins*. Perry's grins. Like Peregrine. He's so proud of that joke. He calls the people who work for him Perry's Grinners. They've all got packs of those stickers. They put them everywhere. You can see them all over the village.'

Arrina couldn't remember seeing any. Then she recalled the few she'd spotted on the sign in the corner of the Yates land—the same place where Kingsley had been murdered. She didn't think she'd seen any others. But then, she hadn't really been looking for them either. She *had* seen some strange smiles on the faces of teenagers recently. Several of the students had flashed big smiles at the Careers Fair, and Arrina had just thought that meant they were happy, but now she wasn't so sure. She thought about the three young people she'd caught breaking into the chemistry lab earlier that day. They'd all given wide smiles that, she realised then, would be better described as grins.

Arrina couldn't believe it. Perry had been right there under her nose on the day of the Careers Fair. In all the dashing to and fro that day, Arrina hadn't returned to her office after half seven that morning. Perry must have been counting on that. Because she'd been working so hard, she'd missed him sitting outside her office all day, poaching the very students she was trying to help.

Anger heated Arrina until she no longer felt the cold of the woodland in which she stood. She had half a mind to storm up to the Anderson house and demand an apology from Perry for his arrogant behaviour.

But she knew he'd done much worse than just stealing students away from the college. He'd also been involved in Kingsley's embezzling scheme and his murder. She was sure of it, though the revelation that he hadn't been the one to transfer the money that Saturday confused things.

Someone else was in on the crimes, but Arrina didn't know who. She needed to find out who had been in Do-Re-Mi that Saturday morning. At the thought of the café, her stomach rumbled. She'd had yet another day of snatched, sugary snacks. She would have given anything right then for one of Julie's doorstop sandwiches and a bowl of pumpkin soup.

But the only thing she had of Julie's was the tin of parkin in her car. She'd only eaten a couple of pieces earlier, and plenty more were still left. She was tempted to sneak back through the gap in the tall hedge to retrieve them.

But she could hear a loud beeping from the narrow road there. It was the delivery people in their truck, honking to call back the drivers who had mysteriously abandoned their vehicles and blocked them in.

Even Julie's parkin wasn't worth coming out of her hiding place for. If it had been Julie's ganache-and-dashes, that might have been another matter…

The thought of the tartlets sent a spark across her brain. Arrina didn't have a clue why. She thought of them again, and the spark flared brightly again. She tried to follow it. But it faded quickly. Something about Julie's dark chocolate tartlets and Arrina's current situation was causing a connection to try to form in her brain. She couldn't work it out, but it suddenly felt very important.

'Maggie,' she hissed, 'tell me about Julie's tartlets.'

'What?'

'What?' echoed Ophelia.

'I know this sounds crazy, but tell me about Julie's ganache-and-dash tartlets.'

'I... I don't know what you mean.'

'I don't know either, but you know her recipes, and I just need you to talk about this one for a minute while I try to get hold of a thought that's lost somewhere in my brain.'

'I don't know the recipe. Aunty Julie says it's too complicated. That's why she only makes the things occasionally. I've never even eaten one.'

Maggie stopped there, but the spark leapt across Arrina's mind again, and she gestured for the young woman to keep talking.

'Ummm. I know she made a batch of the tartlets early on Saturday morning. She said there were some in Do-Re-Mi, but when I went in at the end of the day, they'd run out. Apparently, they didn't even last until ten, and—'

'Am I interrupting something?' Fernella Anderson stepped through the gap in the hedge, her looming silhouette as unmistakable as her loud, melodious voice.

The spark in Arrina's brain fizzled out. Then she couldn't think of anything at all. She saw Maggie's eyes widen and catch the moonlight. Ophelia stood as still as a statue. Her blonde hair looked ghostly as it waved in the gentle breeze.

'Phone signal,' Arrina blurted out. 'We've had a little car trouble, and luckily, we ran into Maggie. She said that if we just wandered around a bit, we'd be able to get some signal so we could call a mechanic out.'

Ophelia still had her phone in her hand from showing Maggie the photo of Callie. She brought the screen to life and waved the phone around. 'Still nothing.'

Fernella gave a tinkling laugh. 'You should have come up to the house. We'd have sorted you out straight away.'

'We didn't want to inconvenience you,' Arrina said in a small, weak voice. Perry was back at the house. Arrina didn't want to get any closer to him. At least, not without the police for backup. 'In fact, I think we can probably sort the cars out ourselves. We'll go and do that now and get out of your way.'

A shaft of moonlight fell on Fernella's face, and Arrina saw a look she'd never seen there before. All trace of friendly charm had disappeared. The bright roundness was gone from her cheeks. Instead, her face was carved in marble planes—heavy and immovable.

Arrina wondered how long the woman had been standing on the other side of the hedge before she'd made her presence known. How much had she heard of their conversation about Perry?

Fernella caught Arrina's eye. 'It's no trouble at all. Let's all go up to the house now and get this sorted out.'

'Really. We—'

A loud mechanical sound rang through the air. An unmistakeable heavy click, which Arrina took a moment to identify. She'd never heard the sound before moving to the countryside. It was the sound of farmers keeping foxes from their chickens. It was the sound of pheasant season. It was the sound of a shotgun snapping shut—its cartridges loaded and its trigger ready to pull.

'I wasn't asking.' Fernella's voice was low and forceful. There was no light music beneath her words, only the threat of someone who always got what they wanted.

Moonlight glinted on the barrel of the gun. Fernella didn't have to say another word to get the three women moving.

35

Arrina walked at the back of the huddling group. Maggie and Ophelia went ahead, and Arrina kept herself between them and the barrel of the gun.

She was sure Fernella wouldn't be foolish enough to shoot while the delivery people were still around, if she'd do it at all. Arrina didn't even understand what the woman was doing with a shotgun—they weren't uncommon in the countryside, but they were usually owned by taciturn men in tweed. As Arrina glanced back over her shoulder, the large woman in velvet looked as though she were back in her opera days and heading for a dramatic finale.

Once they were through the gap in the hedge, Arrina stumbled. Her feet tangled together in surprise—the large delivery truck was gone. Now there was just Ophelia's rainbow-painted Camper and Arrina's own silver-blue Jaguar. In the dark evening, anyone else driving down the road would be sure to crash into the vehicles, but that wasn't very likely—this road only led to a tumbledown stable that had been empty for years.

Arrina couldn't understand where the delivery truck could have gone. That had been her last hope for rescue, and she searched vainly in the spot where it had been. Then a flash of headlights in the distance explained the absence. The bright lights illuminated the front of the Anderson house as the large vehicle backed down a side exit. Perry's Lamborghini had pulled onto the lawn to make room for it to pass.

With all the vehicles parked haphazardly around the place, the Anderson house looked like the site of some terrible disaster, which, Arrina supposed, it was.

As she trudged up the long driveway to the house, Arrina cursed herself for not worrying about Fernella earlier. Of course the woman would know everything that Perry had done, and she'd be working hard to protect him from the consequences. Perry didn't blow his nose without asking her permission. If he'd killed Kingsley Peters, surely he'd run straight to his mother to confess it. And she'd helped him cover it up. Just as she fixed every mess for her precious son.

Perry was waiting at the front door. His eyes widened slightly at the sight of the shotgun in his mother's hands. But he said nothing, and when she ordered him to make a pot of tea, he nodded and scurried away.

Fernella told Arrina, Maggie and Ophelia to go inside the house as well. Then she directed them to the formal front sitting room, which Arrina had glanced into earlier. Further down this main hallway was the back door that led to the annex. In there, Arrina was sure, were eager teenagers who would stumble upon them within minutes.

Fernella followed Arrina's eyeline. 'Lock the back door, won't you, Peregrine.'

'Yes, mother,' the boy replied instantly from the kitchen.

Arrina took one last look down the hallway and went through to the sitting room. Fernella sat down on the stiff red sofa and leaned the shotgun beside her. She gestured at the array of uncomfortable-looking chairs on the other side of the coffee table, folded her hands neatly in her lap, and waited.

Arrina ran through her options. The most dramatic of these was to leap through the picture window at the front of the house and commando-roll across the front lawn. Others included snatching the gun from Fernella and possibly getting shot in the process, running out of the room and calling the police from the landline, and sitting there and waiting for the tea that Perry was making.

She took the last option, since that was least likely to get her killed, and also, it included tea.

A grandfather clock in the corner grew louder with every tick. Arrina glanced between Maggie and Ophelia, but neither of them showed any sign of knowing how to get out of this. When Perry came in with a wobbling tea tray and clattering cups, the whole room breathed a sigh of relief.

Perry knelt on the floor beside the coffee table and laid out the tea service. He was still wearing his sharp suit, but, sitting next to his mother, he looked like a little boy.

Soon, five cups were poured and handed around. Arrina felt measurably calmer with a cup of tea in her hands. A sliver of normality finally appeared in this otherwise crazy day.

'I'm afraid we've no cakes or biscuits in,' Fernella said. 'I did bring several items home from Sunday's fundraiser, but with so many teenagers around, it's impossible to keep things like that in. I'm sure that won't impede our ability to come to some sort of arrangement here though.'

Once again, the spark ran through Arrina's mind—the same one she'd had in the woods—the one that tried to connect Julie's tartlets with the situation she was in. The spark was stronger this time, and she traced its path all the way from the baked treats to the fundraiser that Sunday.

A box of ganache-and-dash tartlets had been there. Arrina had eaten one herself. But that wasn't it. The spark drove on through her brain, guiding her past the tartlets themselves and on to Fernella, who'd stood at the table that day and said... and said...

That was it! Fernella had said she'd seen the tartlets in Do-Re-Mi.

Maggie had just told Arrina that they were sold out by ten am that Saturday morning. If Fernella had seen the tartlets in the café, she'd been in before ten. The money had been taken from the Environment Agency on the Do-Re-Mi Wi-Fi at 9.27 that morning.

'You're in it together,' Arrina said, too shocked to keep the realisation to herself. She locked eyes with Fernella and got all the confirmation she needed in the woman's expression. '*You* took the money from the Environment Agency.'

Fernella pursed her lips as though finding it crass to discuss money before finishing their first cup of tea. 'As I said, I'm sure we can come to an arrangement about all of this.'

Arrina stared at the woman in disbelief. 'You took it. And then you fed me that line about Perry raising capital from investors. But it was you all along. You stole the money.'

Perry was still kneeling on the floor beside his mother. He cocked his head to the side like a confused puppy. 'What does she mean? I have investors, don't I, Mummy?'

'Of course you do.' She turned back to Arrina. 'Don't go upsetting my poor Peregrine like that. Kingsley Peters was very serious about investing his money in my son's successful company. The man was here several times to discuss the matter himself.'

Again, Perry cocked his head in confusion. Clearly Kingsley hadn't been there to meet with Perry. The furrow in the boy's brow showed him coming to the same realisation as Arrina. Fernella had done all of this herself.

'It was that shrew of a wife of his,' Fernella continued.

'Leave Callie out of this,' Ophelia said. 'Whatever you and Kingsley were up to, she knew nothing about it.'

'Believe me, I know. His wife was nagging him to settle down and lead a dull little existence and to not even think about the possibility of getting rich. And I know all about you as well. Kingsley hated you. He couldn't wait to get his wife away from your bitter influence.'

'Kingsley Peters was a liar. If you believed whatever he told you about why he couldn't give you money, you're a fool.'

'*He* was the fool. The man had access to millions, and he didn't know how to get hold of it. He thought coming around here and threatening my son's company with a fine was the way to get rich. But I only had to spend five minutes with him to work out how to access the goldmine he was sitting on. It was an easy hack with someone on the inside.'

'But—' Arrina started. Then she sat back and looked at Fernella. The woman smiled slyly and sipped her tea.

Arrina cursed herself again for having fallen for Fernella's deception. The woman had acted old and out of touch, talking about apps as some confusing modern technology she was *letting the kids get on with*. But Fernella was in her mid-fifties at most. She wasn't exactly a dinosaur. And Zena Brown—whose VR pig unit had caused such a commotion at the Careers Fair—taught a popular adults' computing class that had got the older generation fired up about technology.

Fernella had plenty of time on her hands to find out whatever she wanted about cryptocurrencies and hacking. And apparently, she'd found out an awful lot indeed.

'Mummy, I—'

'Be quiet,' Fernella snapped at her son. He looked as though he'd been slapped. 'You're just as stupid as your father. I've done everything in my power to make you successful, just as I did with him. And look what I've got in return.'

A flicker of movement in the doorway of the sitting room caught Arrina's eye. She stayed as still as possible, only glancing around to see if anyone else had noticed. Ophelia focused on her tea. Maggie was staring in disbelief at Fernella and Perry, neither of whom could see the doorway clearly from where they were sitting.

Arrina could see it, though, and she also knew what the flicker of movement out there meant. She only glimpsed it briefly, but the wild curly hair was unmistakeable as it streamed behind someone heading towards the back door. Arrina took a sip of her tea to hide the hopeful twitch of her lips. Patience was out there—she must have been in the house to use the bathroom. The girl's name echoed around her mind, as it had done so often in recent months. *Patience, Patience, Patience*.

Peregrine had locked the back door. If Patience unlocked it now, then more of Perry's workers would flow in and out of the house in search of snacks or to use the bathroom. Arrina hated to think of them getting close to gun-wielding Fernella, but Arrina wouldn't let the woman hurt anybody, and she hoped one of them would get in touch with the police.

Within moments, though, Patience was back outside the sitting room. Perry must have taken the key when he locked the door. Patience poked her head around the frame, looking nervous at the idea of interrupting the adults in the room.

Arrina shook her head and tried to catch the girl's eye. Again, Arrina glanced around to check that nobody else had spotted the movement in the hallway. Then she turned her gaze back to Patience and signalled her with wide eyes to run away and call the police. At least, she tried to convey that. But the girl's furrowed brow showed she didn't get the message.

'I work hard, Mummy,' Peregrine said. 'I've got dozens of employees, and—'

'And you haven't a clue where the funds to pay them come from.'

'My investors—'

'How did I raise such a fool?' Fernella banged her hand down on the coffee table. 'I've tried my best, doing everything I could. But you're a man, just like your father... There *are* no investors. It's been my hard work that's got you here.'

Fernella's hard work was stealing millions from the Environment Agency and... Arrina shuddered as she thought of the full extent of it. The woman must have agreed to split the stolen millions with Kingsley but then double-crossed him and...

In the doorway, Patience raised a fist to knock on the door. Arrina couldn't let her be seen.

'Hard work,' Arrina said loudly, shocking Patience into dropping her hand. 'Does that include murder?'

Patience darted back into the hallway. Arrina prayed that the young girl would find a phone and call the police.

Fernella reached for the barrel of her shotgun, and Arrina knew the police would reach the isolated house too late.

'Nobody likes a clever woman,' Fernella said, her grip closing around the deadly weapon. 'That's what my mother always told me. I've spent my life hiding just how clever I am—always pretending a man was making the decisions—first my husband and then my son. Each as useless as the other, but I did what I could.' The fire in the woman's eyes shot through Arrina. It told her everything she'd thought about Fernella was true. Everything and more. The mention of her money-wasting husband—who had conveniently died before he could lose everything—told Arrina just how much Fernella had done. 'I've done everything to hide my cleverness. But you—you just can't help yourself.'

Ophelia's teacup clattered to the floor and broke into jagged pieces. Arrina gestured for her and Maggie to get behind her chair, and she stood between the other women and Fernella.

'I tried to make this easy for everybody,' Fernella continued. 'Nice and polite, just as I was raised. I was prepared to give everyone a healthy cut of the money, but I can see now that you won't be able to keep your clever little mouth shut.'

Perry huddled on the floor at Fernella's feet. She nudged him out of the way with her toe and walked around to face Arrina, pointing the barrel of the gun directly at her.

Arrina stared into the end of the barrel. The black void threatened to swallow her. She couldn't look away.

36

A creak from the hallway caught everyone's attention. Fernella's head whipped round. Arrina clenched her hands into fists to keep herself from reaching out to grab the gun. That wouldn't end well, and she knew it. There was another creak, and Arrina pictured Patience cowering and afraid.

'Go and see who's out there,' Fernella barked. Arrina thought the command was meant for her, but Peregrine was evidently used to following his mother's orders. He scrambled to his feet and darted into the hall.

Arrina didn't dare breathe. She knew who it was—poor Patience, who had a habit of always being in the wrong place. Now, it looked like she would get in real trouble because of it. Thoughts whirled round Arrina's head, and she tried to find *any* way at all of helping the girl when Perry brought her into the room.

But he didn't bring her in. Every person in the sitting room had their eyes fixed on the doorway, and nobody walked through it. There were several more creaking sounds, which could only be footsteps on old floorboards, but nobody walked into view.

'Peregrine,' Fernella called. When the boy didn't respond, Fernella took a step towards the hallway herself but apparently thought better of it. 'Maggie. You go and see what's going on. If you're not back here in one minute, I'll shoot the other two.'

Arrina watched Fernella as she said this. There was no flicker of doubt on her face. Fernella had all the conviction of an opera diva in her final, fatal scene.

Tears streamed down Maggie's face as she walked towards the door. She glanced back at Arrina. Her eyes were pleading, and Arrina's chest ached with the guilt that she couldn't make this all go away.

In the sitting room, Arrina, Ophelia, and Fernella stood with their eyes fixed on the doorway. Arrina had no idea what was happening out there. She tried to picture Patience somehow restraining Perry while Maggie worked out what to do with the pair of them.

'Thirty seconds,' Fernella called out. She stared along the barrel of the shotgun at Arrina, and the expression on her face said she was sticking firmly to her one-minute deadline.

'Mummy,' Perry called from the hall. 'They say you have to put down the gun.'

'Nonsense. I'm the one in control here. Nobody is going to tell me what to do.'

Slowly, Peregrine Anderson inched through the doorway. 'I'm back now, Mummy. They say you have to put the gun down.' Perry was still wearing his sharp suit, but his hunched shoulders and quivering lower lip made him look like a toddler playing dress-up.

Fernella opened her mouth to reply, but then she saw who followed Perry in, and closed it without saying anything. It was Ian, the large detective inspector who Arrina had seen only that morning, though it felt like years. For a heart-stopping second, she thought that Ian was working with Fernella. But he was holding Perry's handcuffed wrists in one hand and a police radio in the other.

'Backup is ten minutes away,' Ian said. 'If they have to fight their way in here, people will get hurt. You have the choice to end it now.'

Fernella shifted her glance among her handcuffed son, the stern police officer, and Arrina. Fernella's fingers tightened on the barrel, and Arrina forced herself to stand firmly between the gun and Ophelia.

'I did everything right,' Fernella said. 'Everything just as I was told.' The gun wavered but didn't stray from its target. Arrina did not breathe.

Then Fernella threw the gun to the floor. The weapon clattered against the edge of the coffee table, and Arrina and Ophelia leapt across the room. Arrina thought of Julie, happy at home with Phil. At least something good would come out of this awful night. Arrina tensed her falling body for the bang of the gun and the searing pain of hot metal tearing through her body. But they didn't come. The weapon didn't go off.

'It isn't loaded,' Fernella said as she slumped down onto the sofa. 'It isn't even real. It's a theatre prop.' She drained her cup, smoothed a hand over the velvet of her dress, and gazed fondly around her sitting room for what she must have known was the last time she would see it.

Soon, a flurry of flashing lights and sirens spilled into the peaceful rural air. Fernella protested about being handcuffed and ordered the police officers to be careful of her Cartier bracelet. Perry objected, too, saying he hadn't done anything wrong and was going to sue the police for every penny they had.

Then they were gone, leaving Arrina, Maggie, Ophelia, and Patience to try to explain to Ian what had gone on that evening.

Once they'd told their sides of the events, including Patience's *Mission Impossible*–style sneaking through the house to call the police, Arrina asked Ian how on earth he'd got there so quickly. There couldn't have been more than two minutes between Patience's phone call and his sudden appearance in the hallway. From the police station to the Anderson house though, the trip should have taken much longer.

His face flushed bright red, and Arrina couldn't imagine what he was going to say.

'I was... ummmm... sort of following you,' he said, staring down at his shiny black shoes and revealing the full extent of the bald spot on top of his head.

Arrina wasn't entirely sure who he was talking about, but then he raised his eyes and met her gaze. 'Me?'

'Not exactly. Not in a creepy way.'

'It sounds pretty creepy,' Patience piped up from the corner of the room.

Ian interlaced his fingers and wrapped his arms around his large stomach. 'Well, it was more of an accident, really.' He shifted from foot to foot. 'I was driving over to see Gillian DeViers, as I do every week to give her an update on local police matters.'

Back when Arrina and Ian used to socialise together, he'd often complained about these weekly debriefs, which

Gillian, in her role as chair of the Parish Council, insisted upon. Now, he limited himself to a slightly sour look as he mentioned them.

Ian unlaced his hands and stuffed them into his pockets. 'I spotted you driving this way as well, and I beeped my horn to say hi, but you didn't seem to hear. I thought maybe... well... maybe you were onto something in the Kingsley Peters case.'

'What?' This was the last thing Arrina had been expecting.

'I remembered this summer...' His hands came out of his pockets, and he clasped them together behind his back. Arrina had never seen him look so uncomfortable. 'The detective work you did this summer was very... very impressive.'

Arrina glanced over at Maggie, who had also been wrapped up in that case. The two of them shared a look of understanding.

'I thought,' Ian continued, 'that you might have found something this time as well.'

Arrina's first instinct was to respond sharply and ask why he hadn't been out doing his own investigating. But harsh words wouldn't get the answers she wanted. 'Were you following me this morning as well? Was that why you were up in the corner of the Yates field?'

Ian's face flushed an even brighter red. He glanced round at the other women in the room. 'I came to your cottage last night to ask if you had any ideas, but... I didn't know how to... how to ask without...' He sighed heavily. 'I thought you might be onto something, so I had one of the new recruits watch your house and call me when you left this morning.'

'That *is* creepy,' Patience said.

A smile twitched on Arrina's lips. Brutal honesty was what she liked best about working with teens. They saw the world entirely in black and white and weren't afraid to call things as they saw them.

Ian's eyes fell to his shoes again, but he forced them up and looked Arrina directly in the face. 'I'm sorry. I shouldn't have done that. There are a lot of things about this investigation I regret. I...' He took a deep breath. 'I've sent a car off already to bring Phil and Wallace home. They'll both be getting formal apologies from me, and I'll issue one to you as well.'

Arrina looked at the faces of the other women. Their expressions were a mixture of exhaustion and relief. These women were far more important than an apology from the police right then. She turned from Ian and focused on making sure the three of them were all OK.

Maggie had got herself wrapped up in a murder while trying to stop Perry's illegal chemical importation schemes, but she showed no sign of giving up on her original plan. She pulled her ponytail tighter and reached in her pocket for a small notebook. She flicked through it and underlined a few things. Then she handed it over to Ian to add to his pile of evidence against Perry.

Patience twirled her dark-blonde curls tightly around her fingers and didn't catch anyone's eye. She looked like she'd collapse into floods of tears if someone hugged her. Arrina knew the girl was close to her mother, so as soon as she got home, she'd be doted on and quickly put the nightmare evening behind her.

Ophelia gazed at the picture of her sister on her phone, no doubt eager to have her home again. Arrina would be sure to visit Longnor when the woman was back and check that the two sisters were OK. There was also that impressive display of teas in the Village Shop that Arrina might just pop in and look at as well. Her own tea stocks were running low, and she was down to only a dozen or so varieties, which wasn't nearly enough. She had no idea what tea she'd drink when she got home. Nothing in her cupboard was suitable for relaxing after having a shotgun pointed at her and then watching the police haul off a murderous former opera singer.

Before she could do that, though, she needed to get Patience and any of Perry's other employees home. She sent Patience to go and round up the teenage workers, who were now suddenly without jobs. Arrina would drive them home and fill them in on the many virtues of Heathervale College. She looked forward to seeing several of them signing up for classes the following morning.

By this time next week, Arrina hoped, things in Heathervale would mostly be back to normal. Phil and Wallace would be home, Do-Re-Mi would be open, and the young people of the village would be attending her college.

The week after that, life would be *better* than normal, because that week would bring the Lantern Parade. She was certain that Gillian would reinstate the parade now that the murder was solved and Phil and Wallace were free. The parade was one of the biggest tourist draws of the year, and Gillian loved to show off how much she did for local business. Plus, Arrina suspected, the tweed-trussed woman loved the excitement of the celebration just as much as everyone else did.

Arrina smiled at the thought of the parade. Christmas was her very favourite time of year, and now that Kingsley's murder was solved and her friends would soon be home and happy again, Arrina could really enjoy it. She could almost smell the sweet spices of Julie's Christmas biscuits in the air as she thought of the holiday season.

After getting Arrina's car out of its rut and thanking her yet again for her help with the case, Ian waved her off. 'Be careful as you drive back,' he said. 'They're forecasting snow for this evening.'

Arrina smiled again, imagining a perfect, pristine blanket of white over the village. 'I can't wait.'

37

Two weeks later

Arrina's car was refusing to join her in the Christmas spirit. The vehicle growled and grumbled as she turned the key, and it utterly refused to start. Arrina hummed 'Jingle Bells' to give the car a little inspiration, but once again it coughed, spluttered and died.

She clenched her hands into fists, ready to threaten the scrap heap, but then she remembered Julie's trick—scoop the key like an egg yolk. When Julie had first suggested this, Arrina had reminded her friend that she wasn't a frequent egg-yolk scooper. '*Imagine* you're scooping them,' Julie had said drily. Arrina smiled at the memory. For a worrying few days, she thought she'd never see that teasing, joking Julie again. But now Phil was home, and she was back to her old self.

'OK,' Arrina said to her car, 'I'm going to imagine I'm scooping egg yolks as I turn this key, and...' The engine roared into life. Arrina whooped in excitement, too happy about where she was going to be annoyed at her temperamental car for even another minute.

Then she cranked up the volume on her favourite Mahalia Jackson Christmas album and sang along loudly as she drove to the centre of Heathervale. She didn't turn the music off when she reached the village hall. There was no need to play down her love of Christmas despite the many people milling around. *Everyone* loved the holiday right then. It was the evening of the Lantern Parade.

Arrina grabbed a large, decorated wreath from her boot and dashed off towards the High Street. She made a Christmas wreath every year for Julie to put up on the evening of the Lantern Parade. The rest of the village was decked out in red, gold, and green, but Julie always claimed a month before Christmas was too early for decorations. Arrina's wreath was the only nod to the holiday her café would have for the next couple of weeks.

The wreath was a gorgeous one, if Arrina did say so herself. It was similar to the one she had on her own front door, though Julie's had a little less tinsel, and Arrina had limited herself to twelve glittery baubles rather than the thirty she'd crammed onto her own.

She received many compliments as she hurried past people who were waiting on the village green. Many of them offered to get her a mulled wine or hot chocolate from the nearby Horse and Hound, but she made her excuses and rushed on.

Arrina loved the snippets of village life there on the green, and she very much wished she could stay longer to enjoy them. Zena Brown was explaining her new digitally controlled thermos flask to old Mrs Pangle, while her brother, William, tried to turn the conversation to pigs. Mrs Pangle smiled and nodded, and Arrina suspected she'd turned her hearing aids off long ago. Ryan Thompson, a former student of hers, was reminiscing with his parents about his own Lantern Parade days. Several current students waved and wished her 'Merry Christmas.'

The village green was an excellent place to watch the parade from, and most of the locals chose to stand there for the evening. Other streets around the village were lined with people from miles around, eager to catch a glimpse of the beautiful tradition. Arrina was slightly disappointed to remember that the parade wasn't *quite* as traditional as she'd once believed. She wished Gillian DeViers had never revealed that fact to her. But enough Christmas spirit was in the air for Arrina to push away thoughts of it entirely.

Arrina pressed on through the crowds, protecting her wreath as best she could, and saying hello to everyone she passed. She only had a few minutes until the High Street would be closed to pedestrians. Victor Stones—the chair of the college's Board of Governors—was in charge of keeping people out once the parade started. Arrina didn't think that even their recent bonding over the Julie and Phil situation would override the man's natural officiousness. She had to get there quickly.

Thoughts of the treats that awaited her at Do-Re-Mi filled Arrina's mind as she continued on through the crowds. In spite of Julie's protests against early celebration of the season, she usually made an array of delicious goodies to enjoy with Arrina while the parade passed by. Arrina had her fingers crossed for Christmas biscuits and mince pies, though Julie always liked to experiment with new flavour combinations for each holiday. Arrina was trying to decide whether Julie's suggestion of cinnamon-chilli Santa shortbread had been serious when she bumped straight into Patience, who was rushing down the street.

'You're here!' Patience squealed, covering over Arrina's protests that she had to be hurrying on. 'I'm so glad to see you. It's great. It's really great that you're here.'

'It's good to see you too.' Arrina meant it. She had missed the girl's boundless energy. Arrina had expected Patience to return to the college once Perry's business shut down. But instead, the girl had sent a long email saying that college wasn't really for her and she was going to explore some other options.

'I want to introduce you to my mum. She knows all about you, and she's really excited to meet you.' Patience disappeared into the crowd before Arrina could respond. She followed the girl's wild halo of hair through the packed bodies. When Patience stopped and turned around, there were suddenly two of her. In a moment, Arrina realised that the girl's mother was standing there, looking like a carbon copy, with only a few fine lines around her eyes and hints of silver in her beautiful crown of curls to mark any difference.

'I'm Grace.' She pumped Arrina's hand eagerly. 'I've been so excited to meet you.'

'That's what I just said.' Patience wrapped her arms around her mum, and the two of them beamed.

'I'll be seeing a lot more of you soon,' Grace added. 'I've been awarded the internship at Do-Re-Mi, and Patience here tells me you're in there quite regularly.'

'That's great to hear,' Arrina said. 'You'll learn a lot from Julie. She not only makes the best biscuits for miles around, but she knows everything worth knowing about running a small business. Do you have any thoughts about what you'll do after you finish the internship?'

Grace hugged her daughter tightly. She was clearly excited about the changes on the way now she'd got the internship. 'Yes. I've been through a rough few years, when

I stopped going out or doing much of anything. The only thing I stayed passionate about during that time was hair. If I leave this mop to do what it likes, I look like I've been pulled backwards through a hedge.'

'Me too!' chimed in Patience. 'Mum saves me from looking like a scraggly scarecrow.'

'I'm going to set up a salon right here in Heathervale. There's a space coming up for rent in the new year, so I'm going to take that on.'

'And I'm going to help. I've realised that I really love working in a small business. It didn't go great last time, but I loved what Perry was trying to do.'

Arrina expected the mention of Perry to bring a frown to Patience's face. After all, the last time she'd seen him, his mother had been pointing a gun at Arrina, and the boy himself had been arrested and charged over his plans to sell illegal chemicals. But instead, Patience blushed and smiled widely. Arrina understood why when she saw Peregrine Anderson walking towards them. He was juggling three cups of hot chocolate and returning Patience's broad smile and puppy-dog gaze.

Then he caught sight of Arrina and froze.

After a few seconds, Perry handed two of the hot chocolates to Patience and Grace. Then he held the third one out to Arrina, took a deep breath, and glanced over at Patience. The girl nodded at him, and he said, 'I sincerely apologise for all the harm I caused you and your college. I have been sentenced to extensive community service for the crimes I committed and planned to commit. I am taking this very seriously and aim to make up for my wrongdoings in every way possible. If there is anything I can do to earn your personal trust and forgiveness, I would greatly appreciate the chance to do so.'

He took another deep breath. The boy had clearly rehearsed the speech many times, and Arrina appreciated the effort he'd put into it. His mother had been sentenced to a long stretch in prison, and many in the village had been surprised to hear Perry had got off with community service alone. But he was clearly repentant, and the judge must have seen this and let Perry go free to have a second chance at life.

Behind the boy, Patience and Grace hugged each other again and gazed fondly at him. Arrina had a feeling that with these two loving presences in his life, Perry would stay on the straight and narrow with ease.

'There's only one thing I can think of,' Arrina said.

Perry looked worried. He'd already scraped off the hundreds of cartoon smiles that were stuck all around the village, picked up litter from the High Street, and single-handedly decorated the village hall for Christmas. He must have expected Arrina to give him a task ten times as hard, judging by his expression.

'I'd like you to come to the college first thing on Monday morning and sign up for some classes. I know you're being kept busy with your community service, but with a little flexibility, I'm sure you can continue your education as well. You worked hard to set up your business, and you're working even harder now to clear up the fall-out from your mistakes. I think we'll make a great student of you yet.'

'I... Thank you. Thank you so much.' Perry had tears in his eyes, and Patience wrapped her arms around the boy and hugged him fiercely from behind.

'I was speaking to Maggie Lee about you recently,' Arrina continued. 'She was impressed by how quickly you picked up the chemistry she told you about. I'm sure she'd be happy to help you catch up with any material you've missed.'

'Really?'

'Why don't you ask her? She's heading this way.' Arrina smiled fondly and waved at Maggie but didn't stop to talk to the woman. She had to press on to get to the High Street before it closed to pedestrians. She didn't even stop when she saw Nancy Morgan wave at her from the other side of the crowd. Nancy smiled and pointed over at her brother Wallace, and Arrina was happy to see that the young man stood with his arm around Imogen Yates. A sparkly ring glittered on Imogen's left hand, and Arrina knew it wouldn't be long before they were heading down the aisle. The happy couple were eager to start their lives together out in the open, and soon they'd be a happy trio, finally joining the Yates and Morgan families together after decades of bad blood.

Finally, Arrina reached the end of the High Street. The road was empty of both people and cars, and Victor Stones was standing at the edge of the crowd. He was ushering everyone further away from the parade route and twitching his moustache furiously at those who refused to follow his directions.

Arrina was about to hurry past him and into Do-Re-Mi when she saw Tony Mellor. The man's dark eyes locked onto hers. Then they darted to the beautiful blonde at his side.

Arrina recognised her as the local medical examiner, Lissie. Arrina wondered whether this woman was the reason Tony had kept his distance since that summer. She braced herself for a stab of pain at the thought. But the pain didn't come.

The entire village of Heathervale was happily huddled together in their best winter woollens, sipping hot drinks and humming along with the carol that was starting in the distance. It was 'Silent Night,' one of Arrina's favourites. She couldn't feel anything but joy right then.

She would catch up with Tony soon and try to smooth over the awkwardness between them. Perhaps one day, he'd even tell her why he broke up with her so suddenly the year before. But that could wait. The faint glow of red and green lights in the distance could mean only one thing—the parade was starting.

Arrina sped down the High Street, expecting Victor Stones to shout after her or perhaps even chase her down. She was pleasantly surprised to find her path to Do-Re-Mi uninterrupted. She quickly hung her wreath on the waiting hook on the café's front door and ran inside.

Arrina hugged Julie and Phil tightly, and then the three of them tucked into Julie's wide range of Christmas-themed treats. Mince pies and Christmas biscuits were piled high on a table, just as Arrina had hoped. There were also meringue snowmen, gingerbread Santas, and a glittery red-velvet cake that tasted even better than it looked.

Faint notes of carols drifted across the village as the parade wound slowly around it. Arrina kept half an ear on the snippets of songs that reached the café, waiting for the one that signalled the parade had reached the High Street.

When the last notes of 'Good King Wenceslas' rang through the air, Arrina's head snapped around to check the street. It was still empty out there, but it wouldn't be for long. She dashed over to the full-length window at the front of the café and pressed up against it. Far off to the left, she could just make out a flicker of candlelight.

'They're coming!' Arrina shouted. She glanced back at Julie and Phil, who were gazing into each other's eyes like newlyweds. She ran over and grabbed them both by the sleeve. 'This is very sweet, really, but you'll have to save it till later. You're going to miss the parade.'

'There's no arguing with her, is there?' Phil asked Julie.

'You know only a fool would get between Arrina and Christmas.'

'And yet,' Arrina said, tugging at their arms, 'you're still not moving.' She dragged them to the window, which had the perfect view of the parade. That year, their view would be even better than normal. The large bouquet of heather across the road was the reason behind this. It was wound all round with fairy lights and marked a stop on the route of the Lantern Parade.

The singing outside grew louder, and Arrina started to hum along.

'You're going to sing, aren't you?' Julie asked, taking a couple of steps away.

'It's *Christmas*,' Arrina said, which surely explained everything. She pressed even closer to the glass and saw the front of the parade walk slowly into view.

At first, she could just make out the bobbing green and red globes of the lanterns. Then as they got closer, she could make out the faces of the children who carried them. Each and every person under sixteen in Heathervale was entitled to collect a lantern at the start of the evening from the village hall. They also carried baskets they'd spent weeks preparing. As the children walked past the bakery, the greengrocer's, and the gift shop, Arrina caught glimpses of the baskets each child had made.

'Look at them!' Arrina said. 'They're even better than last year.'

'Mmmm,' Julie responded.

'There's so much tinsel and glitter,' Arrina continued, unperturbed by her best friend's lack of enthusiasm. 'Oh! I can spot some really creative ones. That one's a snowman head, and over there I can see one that looks just like Santa's sleigh.'

Arrina nudged Phil, who stood beside her, until he followed her pointing finger and made vague noises of excitement.

'And now they're reaching the door,' Arrina said. 'This is my favourite part.'

'Every part is your favourite part,' Julie said.

Arrina joined in with the last few lines of the carol the children were singing: *'Born to give them second birth. Hark the herald angels sing. Glory to the newborn king.'*

Then she, too, fell silent, matching the crowd of children and the leader of their parade. The leader held up an ornate golden sceptre and rapped on the door of Flora's florist shop. This girl was, as tradition dictated, the oldest member of the parade.

In a loud, strong voice, the young girl uttered the ceremonial call:

'Stir up, stir up! All goodly habitants stir up! Plenteously bring forth the fruit of good works.'

Then the door flew open, and Flora and her cluster of eager volunteers dashed out. They wound among the children of the parade, who now held out the decorative baskets they had made. The adults carried handfuls of brown paper sachets, and they dropped one into each of the baskets.

'I wonder what's being given out at this stop,' Arrina said, standing on her tiptoes and trying to see if there were any clues in the shapes of the packets the adults carried.

'Flora's been giving Gillian free bouquets for months,' Julie said. 'She's been angling for something good.' The florist and her volunteers looked very happy as they handed out their brown paper packets, so it looked as if Flora's campaign had worked.

'It's random, isn't it?' Phil asked.

'In this village,' Arrina said, 'nothing is.'

Phil made a disgruntled sound but said nothing. Arrina wondered how long it would take for the sting of the arrest to wear off. Arrina and Julie had tried to keep people's reactions from him, but he'd clearly got an idea of what the village had been saying about him during the time he was away.

Arrina thought it must be harder still to get over how deliberate Fernella Anderson had been when she framed him. That was worse, even, than Kingsley's awful blackmailing plot, which had almost driven Phil to ruin.

Fernella had been at an event with a member of the Yates family the evening before the Careers Fair, where she learned that Phil would be working in the corner of their field until noon. Fernella had arranged to meet Kingsley there later in order to finalise the splitting of the money she'd taken. Kingsley had demanded more than his share, which Fernella had expected. She'd pulled out her prop shotgun, but he hadn't believed it, so she'd picked up a length of twine dropped during Phil's work on the land that morning and killed Kingsley with it. The woman had watched Phil be arrested and seen everyone in the village turn against him and still said nothing.

Over the last couple of weeks, Phil had proclaimed loudly and often that he was fine. But Arrina had seen his face cloud over as he'd walked through the village, looking around at people he worried had doubted him. She only hoped that the warm glow of Christmas festivities would ease some of his pain.

'Arrina's right,' Julie said, with a forced brightness that said she mirrored what Phil was thinking. 'The Lantern Parade packages have a very clear pecking order. It goes: nuts, candied orange peel, raisins, cloves, ginger, cinnamon, and nutmeg.'

'And nuts are the best?' Phil checked.

'No,' Julie said. 'They're the worst. They're what Gillian DeViers gives to whoever she's most annoyed at that year. The volunteers have to lug a heavy sack of them over to their shop and count out an exactly equal share into the sachets. When Pearl Kendal dinged Gillian's car a few years back, she got nuts in the next year's allocation, and Pearl never spoke to Gillian again.'

'So nutmeg's the best,' Phil said.

'I always thought it went ginger, nutmeg, then cinnamon,' Arrina said.

'Either way,' Julie said, 'the spices are at the top because they're light and easy to spoon into the bags.'

'And they smell fantastic,' Arrina added. 'I only wish the college was on the parade route. I'd definitely volunteer to be a stop.'

'I don't think you would,' Phil said.

'Of course I would. Look at those kids out there having such a lovely time and getting into the spirit of the season.'

'*I* don't think you'd volunteer either,' Julie said. 'Not taking into account who decides what each stop gets.'

'Oh,' Arrina said, 'right.'

'Gillian DeViers would give you nuts every year till kingdom come,' Julie said.

'Or worse,' Arrina said. 'I heard a rumour she's adding holly to the route next year. The last stop of the parade will hand out sprigs to go into the top of each child's basket.' Arrina had thought the idea was nice when she'd first heard of it, but now she wondered if it wasn't just Gillian's way of punishing people who'd got on her bad side.

As she turned to see what Julie and Phil felt about the suggestion, her thoughts of Scrooge-like Gillian melted away. Phil's arms were wrapped tightly around Julie, and her head was nestled against his chest. Together, they gazed out at the group of children waving their thanks to Flora and then setting off again on their parade.

The parade leader raised her golden sceptre in the air and waved it to beat in a rhythm for the next carol, 'Ding Dong Merrily on High.'

The High Street was the last stretch of the Lantern Parade, and soon the children would head home to their families. There, they'd unpack their baskets of goodies and add them to bowls containing flour, sugar, eggs, and suet. Then the whole family would take turns stirring the bowl as they made their Christmas pudding. When the big day came a month later, the whole village would steam their delicious, spiced concoctions, and every street would become infused with the same blissful smell.

Arrina hummed along with the children as the parade slowly headed on down the street.

'We can go out and join them if you like,' Julie said. She leaned away from her husband and gestured towards the trailing crowd of onlookers who followed the parade as it now headed towards the village hall. Once it reached there, glasses of warm mulled wine and fresh mince pies would be handed around, and the carols would continue until the call of the Christmas pudding bowls finally carried people away.

'Yes,' said Phil, after a nudge from his wife. 'Let's head out and join the celebrations.'

Arrina looked out at the group of locals, all snuggled together in their hats, scarves, and coats, and all sharing the same tingling excitement about the upcoming Christmas as Arrina. Then she looked back at her friends.

Julie and Phil had decorated Do-Re-Mi with every Christmas decoration they could scrape together—each bauble, scrap of tinsel, and dangling star they owned had been hung around the café, and even the local woodland had been scoured for every available fir bough and holly sprig.

And they were happy. Julie and Phil wore smiles that brought as much cheer to Arrina's heart as Christmas.

'No,' Arrina said as she stepped closer to Julie and Phil and wrapped her arms around her good friends. 'I've got everything I need right here.'

Author's Note

Dear Reader,

Thank you for joining me on this journey into Heathervale and all the mysteries it contains. If you've enjoyed Arrina's adventures, head over to my website (MatildaSwift.com) to **sign up to the mailing list** and learn about the upcoming books in this series. Please also **rate and review** this book wherever you can. Reviews help other readers find the book, which is essential for the series to succeed.

Read the free prequel to this series, *Rotten to the Marrow*, on my website (MatildaSwift.com). Set five years before the events of *Dying over Spilled Milk*, this free novella covers Arrina's move to the village of Heathervale and her very bumpy start there.

Read on to the end of this book for a **sneak peek** of that **prequel**, which explains how Tinsel first entered Arrina's life, and the mystery he was tied up with. As always, the book includes plenty of murders, mysteries and mugs of tea.

See you again soon, Matilda Swift

Acknowledgements

As with Arrina, friendship is central in my life. I am lucky to have a whole host of incredible friends, many of whom I've known for decades. These bright, funny people provide wonderful support for a writer and save me from spending all my time with the characters I create.

This book is dedicated to Rachel Evans, who I met at eighteen and who I've followed around the world ever since. I can't wait to see where the next years of our friendship take me!

As always, I am thankful to my father, who is everything.

About the Author

Matilda Swift lives in the Peak District, in a village that's less eventful but just as beautiful as Heathervale.

She's originally from nearby Manchester, and after travelling the world from Madagascar to Malaysia as well as living in Hong Kong for several years, she's back amongst the hills and rain in the place she loves best.

Follow her on Instagram (@matildaswiftauthor) for more updates on writing, baking, hiking, and all the fun of life in an English village.

MatildaSwift.com

The Heathervale Mysteries

Have you read the other books in this series? Sign up to Matilda Swift's newsletter on her website (MatildaSwift.com) so you never miss a new release. Read on for the details of the other books in the series.

Rotten to the Marrow (Book #0) – free prequel novella
Cakes, kittens and... killers? The English countryside isn't all it seems!

The rural English village of Heathervale has everything Arrina Fenn wants—a cosy cottage, a cake-filled café, and a cute silver kitten to curl up with.

Unfortunately, a quarrel in the middle of the village and a run-in with the local police make Arrina's first day a rocky one. When she stumbles upon a dead body the next morning, all fingers point in the newcomer's direction.

The local police detective—short, scatter-brained and soon to retire—can't solve the case. With her perfect job starting soon, hard-working Arrina Fenn must find the real killer before she loses her home, her position and the cosy life she dreams of in this idyllic English village.

The Slay of the Land (Book #1)
Tractors, tea and trouble in an English country village...
Hard-nosed Arrina Fenn can deal with the local gossips, petty vandals and even runaway tractors in Heathervale village. They're easy to overcome with a cup of tea in one hand and a delicious cake from her best friend's café in the other. But

when a dead body crops up in the middle of the busy college she runs—getting it shut down and her shut out of the investigation—life doesn't taste quite so sweet.

Determined to solve the murder before both she and the college are exiled from the village, Arrina swaps her smart suits for hiking boots and sets out to uncover just what's going on.

Fresh out of Cluck (Book #3)
Murder most fowl comes to an English country village...
Head teacher Arrina Fenn has big plans for the new year. Heathervale's elegant New Year's Eve party is the perfect place to raise a glass and make resolutions for success.

But when she stumbles on a dead body before midnight, Arrina learns not to count her chickens before they hatch.

With no suspects in sight, whispers and rumours threaten to tear the village apart. Can Arrina crack the case before the chickens come home to roost?

The Heathervale Mysteries Box Set 1: Books 1-3

Wreathed in Mystery (Book #4)
Have yourself a merry little mystery...
Heathervale's Christmas traditions are well underway in the five short stories of this collection. Arrina is hanging a wreath, the Morgans are decorating their woods, and Julie is

concocting creative new bakes in Do-Re-Mi. But in this rural English village, even the holidays aren't safe from mysteries, and nothing is going to plan.

In these festive stories, the residents of Heathervale point fingers and follow clues (still taking time to eat mince pies and drink mulled wine) while they race to solve mysteries and save the special day.

As an extra treat, each story is paired with a recipe, so you can bring a Heathervale Christmas right to your kitchen.

Sneak Peek: The Heathervale Mysteries Book 0: Rotten to the Marrow

Arrina Fenn was new to the village of Heathervale, and nobody would let her forget it. As she drove down the rural main road in search of a place to park, she caught sight of several people pointing and staring. Her car was a classic Jaguar, an XJ6 with unusual mistral blue paintwork. She often turned heads when she drove it. However, Arrina was convinced that people weren't looking at the *car* that day.

It was a warm June morning, and as she drove along the busy and simply named High Street, Arrina rolled down her windows. The air carried scents of cut grass, turned earth and freshly baked bread. Underneath those, there were also several murmurs of *Arrina Fenn*.

Friends back in Manchester had warned her that village life would be a change, that every detail of her existence would be noted and discussed. She'd laughed this off as big-city paranoia. But now she wasn't so sure.

Arrina wished that she'd worn something different that morning, especially if everyone she passed was going to stare at her. But she hadn't had much choice. Her tight black jeans and fluffy, emerald-green jumper had been rescued from the charity pile at the last minute and stuffed in with bowls and plates as she packed. Now they were her only clothes not covered in dust from the move or packed away beneath piles of boxes.

She tried to put a positive spin on it: the green jumper *did* bring out the hints of red in her hair. Unfortunately, its thick, fleecy wool also brought a bright red flush to her cheeks on that warm June morning.

Arrina sat up straight in her seat, kept a smile plastered to her face, and held her hands at ten and two on the wheel.

Finally, she found an empty parking spot just outside a tiny building at the end of the street. A sign outside said Heathervale Supermarket in ornate gothic lettering. The front windows were thickly plastered with notices. Arrina saw flyers reading Morris Dancing Lessons, The Jams and Preserves Society, and Ferret for Sale before pushing through the squeaky front door.

From the street, the shop had looked no bigger than the place she'd bought her morning papers from back in Manchester. But inside, Arrina was pleasantly surprised to find a brightly lit room with tall rows of neatly arranged produce.

A tinkling bell announced her entrance, and Arrina braced herself for the attention of everyone in the shop. But of the dozen people there, only two looked up. One was a teenage boy with thick, carrot-coloured hair, who smiled and nodded and then returned to contemplating chocolate bars. The other was the old woman behind the till, whose dancing green eyes were outshone by a lime-coloured cardigan stretched over her tall, plump frame.

'Oh, my giddy aunt,' said the woman loudly. She dashed out from the high wooden counter and over to Arrina. 'Look at us! Twins!'

'Twins,' Arrina echoed brightly with a smile and a nod, while trying to work out what on earth the woman could possibly mean.

The old lady clapped excitedly and then plucked at Arrina's emerald-coloured jumper, holding up her own green, woollen sleeve beside it.

'Jumper twins,' Arrina said. 'Great minds think alike.'

'Did you make this yourself?' the old woman asked. The jumper was in fact shop-bought, but before Arrina could say this, the woman continued. 'Ethel and Maureen always say young folk nowadays don't know one end of a needle from the other, but this is very good! Very good, indeed. I'll be seeing them in a couple of hours when the coach comes to collect us for our trip. I'll have to tell them all about you.'

Arrina had no idea who Ethel and Maureen were, or, for that matter, who this enthusiastic shopkeeper was. But she was pleased that the woman called her young, especially because she was closer to thirty-five than she cared to admit.

'I'm sorry,' Arrina said. 'I'm not sure—'

'Will you be teaching knitting at that new school of yours?' the old woman asked, with her fingers still poking and prodding at Arrina's jumper and inspecting its stitches and seams.

'At my school?' Arrina asked.

'You're Miss Fenn, aren't you? The head of the new school up by the Hayes place. I'm Pearl, by the way.'

Arrina took a deep breath and reminded herself that this was a *very* small village. She needed to get used to everybody knowing her business, although her first instinct was to smile politely and back away.

'Pleased to meet you,' Arrina said. 'It's actually a sixth form college, which is *like* a school but just for 16-to-18-year olds.' She spoke loudly, hoping to engage the interest of the ginger teenager a few feet away, but he was engrossed in the choice between a Yorkie and a Snickers. Arrina knew teenagers well enough to be sure that he wouldn't hear anything until he'd made that difficult decision.

'I'd not thought about a knitting class before,' Arrina continued. 'It sounds like a wonderful idea—I'm sure it would be a popular extra-curricular. Do you think Ethel and Maureen would want to help?'

'Oh, no,' said Pearl, with a shake of her head that set her wrinkled cheeks jiggling. 'You'll not want to ask them. A right pair of nattering Norahs, they are. They'd have your kids bored stiff with their jabbering on—always gossiping are those two. Of course, Ethel can't help it, bless her. Not with that husband of hers—deaf as a post, he is. Farm machinery, Ethel would have you believe was the cause of it, but mark my words, it's got more to do with decades down at the race-track with his ear pressed up to the Tannoy, praying for a win.'

As the old woman talked, a small queue formed at the till. The red-headed teenager caught Arrina's eye and gave her a conspiratorial smile. He waited until Pearl paused to take a breath and then cleared his throat loudly.

'Oh, look what you've made me do,' Pearl said with a cackle and a strong nudge of her elbow into Arrina's ribs. 'I've got all distracted talking to you. Now, these good people are liable to riot.' She gestured to the patient queue of people at the till. 'I'll have to watch myself around you, Miss Fenn, I can tell.'

Then with another loud laugh, the plump woman returned to the counter, where she gossiped and chatted with the customers about her upcoming trip away.

Arrina enjoyed the background noise of Pearl's conversation while she walked around the supermarket and picked up the essentials she needed for her new kitchen. She found everything she wanted, despite the minute size of the place.

Only when Arrina came to the tea shelf was she disappointed. There were a few boxes of PG Tips and some bags of Tetley's but nothing like the selection that Arrina was used to. She was glad she'd stocked up on all her favourites before moving to Heathervale. Earlier that morning, she'd started her first full day in the village with a pot of Russian Caravan tea. Its smokiness still lingered on her tongue as she headed towards the counter to pay.

Just then, a bald man pushed through the door, holding a Labrador tightly to heel. The bell overhead jangled loudly. 'Who on earth has taken Ursula's space?' the man asked, glaring at everyone in the supermarket.

The man wore a bright red fleece zipped up to the chin; his cheeks glowed even pinker than Arrina's in the warmth of the day.

Arrina stood by the rows of yoghurts and milk cartons in the fridge and looked around at the other people nearby. Nobody answered the irate-looking man.

'It's a silver-blue car,' the man said. 'A G-reg with a Christmas CD on the passenger seat and—'

'That's mine,' Arrina said, stepping forwards before the man could describe anything else he'd seen inside her car. She'd driven it over from Manchester the day before and was not entirely sure what she'd left strewn across her seats. She didn't need the entire supermarket to hear about it.

'You have to move it,' said the bald man.

Arrina looked around at the other customers again. Nobody met her eye.

'I checked the sign,' Arrina said, forcing her voice to sound friendlier than she felt right then. 'I've got two hours on a weekday morning, and I've only been here about twenty—'

'You have to move your car,' the man repeated. He tapped his watch. 'It's Ursula Martin's spot, and she's due here any minute.' The man's panting Labrador pulled at its lead.

The spot Arrina had parked in did not belong to anybody. She was certain. The village of Heathervale was recorded in the Domesday Book of 1086. Nothing was mentioned back then about the reservation of parking spaces on the High Street, and there was no sign that things had changed in the village since.

But Arrina didn't say this.

'Right,' she said, her skin prickling with awareness of the many eyes on her. 'I'm sure I can find another spot. I'll just pay up here and move further down the street.'

She took her basket to the counter, where Pearl tugged at her lime green cardigan as she rang up Arrina's items in hurried silence.

'Parking on the High Street is reserved for local people,' said the man in the tomato-coloured fleece.

Arrina composed her face into the politest expression she could manage and then turned around to face him. 'I am local, actually,' Arrina said. 'I moved here yesterday. I'm up at the old Talbot place.' She reached out a hand. 'Arrina Fenn. Pleased to meet you.'

The man's eyebrows shot up to where his hairline must once have been. Clearly, she'd said the wrong thing.

'Young lady,' the dog-walker said, pulling his impatient Labrador to heel again, 'living in Heathervale one day does not a local make.'

Then the man yanked open the front door again and waited until Arrina passed through it and got into her car. For once, the ancient Jaguar cooperated and started on only her second turn of the key. Arrina kept her eyes fixed straight ahead and drove off down the High Street.

As she passed the greengrocers, the bakery, and the gift shop that she'd been looking forward to visiting, she felt her heart sink. Fitting in to the village was not going to be quite as easy as she'd hoped it would be—not with people like the bald fleece-wearer around.

But Arrina would not be put off that easily.

As she drove back to her cottage, she reminded herself of the many good reasons she'd had for moving to Heathervale. Her new job was interesting, the pace of life was relaxing, and the views in the surrounding countryside took her breath away. And perhaps most importantly, Arrina had first visited the village at Christmas. She had walked through knee-deep snow, drunk mulled wine by the pub's open fire, and joined in with candle-lit carols on the village green.

Christmas was Arrina's favourite time of year, and Christmas in Heathervale was the most wonderful she'd ever known.

Now she just had to figure out how to live there for the rest of the year.

***

Grab your free copy of The Heathervale Mysteries Book #0, Rotten to the Marrow, *at MatildaSwift.com.*

Printed in Great Britain
by Amazon